A Weekend To Remember

Roy Clark

Published by New Generation Publishing in 2021

Copyright © Roy Clark 2021

First Edition

ISBN 978-1-80031-191-6

www.newgeneration-publishing.com

New Generation Publishing

Chapter One (Friday)

Kenny Bradley smiled to himself. "Yes! Come on!" He said to his cat Pickles, who didn't appear to be remotely interested.

When Kenny smiled he was usually happy. But if you actually saw him in the act of smiling you might doubt that as he sort of grimaced, more like a man with trapped wind, rather than smile in the generally accepted sense of how most people do it.

But whether it looked like a smile or not, Kenny was genuinely pleased and he even did a little jig of delight as he walked up the path towards his front door.

He had just waved off his Wife Maureen, (or Mo as he called her), and two of her friends, Barbara (very bossy) and Sally (extremely scatty), as they left in a Taxi to join a larger group of their friends for their annual 'weekend away with the girls' as Mo called it. This year they were off to Edinburgh.

Kenny had been carrying a burden of worry around with him for the last few weeks ever since he'd found a letter from the Hospital addressed to Mo which was in a drawer in their spare bedroom. He'd only found it when he was looking for something he'd mislaid and thought straightaway that she must have hidden it there. The letter was requesting Mo to contact them about an appointment and as she hadn't mentioned anything to him Kenny feared all was not well.

He'd also seen Mo wince in pain once or twice recently when she hadn't realised he was looking at her and the absence of any discussion, coupled with the general way they had been around each other for some time, had all served to fuel his apprehension. But because of their lack of communication recently he hadn't been able to summon up the nerve to ask her about it.

However, Mo's enthusiasm for her upcoming trip away and the fact that it would also leave him with some time on his own, had given him some much needed light relief.

Now that the day had arrived he felt as if the weight of worry had been lifted, for the time being at least.

So he was now keen to put into action phase one of his plan for some type of excursion, or 'adventure' as he'd imagined it, for himself and his assortment of mates and acquaintances, most of whom had been similarly left without their respective partners that weekend as they had also gone on the same trip as Mo.

The only immediate barrier to achieving his objective was the small matter of actually deciding what this so called adventure was going to be.

From his first mention of 'what shall we do when the girls go away' and all subsequent suggestions that Kenny had tried to discuss with his motley crew of mates, he had so far encountered only mild interest and scant enthusiasm on the planning front.

This went against the grain for him as he was a born organiser, come list maker, come itinerary arranger. Or at least that's how he saw it. To some he was sometimes just perceived as 'a pain in the arse.'

He picked up the phone and called his first intended cohort.

Robert Oliver Gordon. 'Robert' to his Mother and 'Rob' to his wife Sally and a few other family members. But for many years since his schooldays, from a corrupted interpretation of his initials, ('B for Bob' instead of 'R for Rob'), mostly known as 'Bog' to pretty much everyone else who knew him.

Although this could often turn into derivatives, such as 'Bogmeister,' 'Boggster,' 'Bogalardo' or occasionally even more unkindly to 'Bog Brush' during severe banter with his so called friends. This largely being due to the added element of his mop of thick and unruly tousled hair, which with a little imagination did sometimes resemble a toilet brush.

When the phone rang Rob was lying on his sofa engaged in one of his favourite activities, doing absolutely nothing.

He considered the sound of the phone for several seconds, before lazily reaching for the receiver which he'd left under a small pile of papers on his coffee table.

'Hello,' he said, as he stifled a yawn which made his voice come out about an octave higher than usual.

'Bloody hell, Bog!' Said Kenny.' Have you finally had that sex change?'

'Bollocks, Lard arse!' came the more recognisable reply.

'Oooh! Someone's tired.' Kenny continued. 'Touched a nerve, did I?'

'I'll touch one of your nerves when I see you, fatty.' Rob replied.

'I am not fat!' Kenny said indignantly. 'How many more times?'

'Nah. You just do a good impression of a blimp.' Said Rob, warming now to the easy task of turning the tables on his friend.

'Anyway,' he continued. 'What can I do for you, Twiggy?'

'Oh, you're so funny.' Kenny said indignantly. 'I was calling to sort things. What are we doing, then?'

'I dunno.' Rob said half heartedly. 'Can't we just go for a beer and maybe a curry later?'

'Oh, come on Bog!' Kenny said with more than a trace of disappointment. 'We normally do something like that pretty much every Friday anyway. Where's the enthusiasm? If the women are doing something original, then we should at least be making an effort.'

Rob smiled to himself. 'What? Do you want to go shopping and then get trollied in some poncey wine bar, then? 'Cos that's all that lot will be doing up in Jockland. Tarts on tour!'

3

As Mo was the main organiser and instigator of the girls trips away, Kenny was quite defensive. 'Well at least they're doing something a bit different, aren't they?'

Rob heard his pain, so let him off lightly. 'Alright, keep your wig on Shirley. I've got a few things to do this morning, but I'll make one or two calls in a bit to get the word out and see you in 'The Feather's' about two ish for a livener. Then if need be we can confirm things from there to meet with Bertie and some of the others about three for a few holes of Golf. OK?'

'Alright. But I can make the calls if you like?' Kenny huffed.

'No, I'll do it.' Rob assured him. 'Just chill out for a change. It's a day off. Remember?'

'Alright then. See you in a bit.' Said Kenny, sounding a bit deflated.

Rob laid back and smiled. 'He's such a dick sometimes,' he thought aloud about his mate. 'I bet he'll be running around now cleaning his golf clubs and stressing about what to wear.'

He picked up the phone again to call one of their mates to make the arrangements for later.

A few minutes later he concluded a call to Alan Bassett, (usually referred to by his friends as 'Bertie'), with; 'Nice one Bertie! I think we're all set then. It should be a laugh. If you don't mind rounding up those we mentioned, we'll see you at the course about three. But I'll phone you from the pub just after two to confirm we're still on.'

As Rob predicted, Kenny was indeed engaged at that moment in using a cloth to wipe the faces of his already spotlessly clean golf clubs and was busily thinking of what they might do next after playing a few holes of golf.

'I wonder if I should wear my new polo shirt?' He mused.

Chapter Two

Just before two o'clock Kenny walked into the bar of 'The Feathers.' The pub was actually called 'The Prince of Wales Feathers' but was pretty much universally just known by the shorter name. Although Kenny's wife Mo often referred to it as 'your second home' due to the frequency that he and his mates occupied it.

There were a few Friday lunchtime punters still in the bar reading newspapers and studying racing form and also a smattering of people in the restaurant area who had taken advantage of the 'Senior Citizen Specials' that the pub advertised to draw in a bit of extra trade during the week.

Kenny waved to a couple of people around the bar.

Nancy the barmaid smiled at Kenny as he approached. 'Alright Nance?' He said.

'Yeah. Not too bad thanks Ken.' She replied. 'Usual?'

'No, I'm driving. I'll just have a pint of Lager Shandy please.'

'What are you doing in here at this time of day?' Nancy asked.

'I'm on long weekend Nance. Off till Tuesday.' He replied. 'How's things between you and your dopey boyfriend?'

'Oh, you know. Same old, same old. We broke up again last weekend. He came round to pick up some clothes that he'd left at mine and I'd put them in a bag which I'd sprayed with my perfume. So that did the trick and we're back on again now! He said when he smelt my perfume on his things that he really missed me.'

Kenny said, 'knowing your Simon, it's just as likely that he likes the perfume because he uses it himself!'

Nancy laughed. 'Yeah, that's true.'

Kenny took a sip of his pint.

A few minutes later the vision that was Rob 'Bog' Gordon appeared in the doorway of the bar. Rob's hair had a life of its own at the best of times, but today looked even more of a bad hair day for him than usual.

'Jesus. You look rough Bog. Did Sally kick you out into the garden to sleep last night or have you finally got that part time job in a field scaring birds?' Kenny said.

'Funny guy.' Rob replied. 'Anyway. What's with you Tango man. Why are you all dressed up?'

'What's the Tango man shit all about?' Came Kenny's immediately defensive reply.

'Well, you're all orange and being a bit porky, you look like Tango man off those adverts that used to be on.' Rob sneered.

'Listen, you terminal knobber, I've been for a couple of tanning sessions because we're going on holiday in a few weeks and I don't want to look like a milk bottle on the first day. So I'm just having a few sun bed sessions beforehand.' Kenny whined.

Rob sensed blood, so he continued. 'Yeah, but how did you squeeze into one of those tanning booths? Did they have to let you have a double?'

Kenny gestured with his middle finger.

Rob looked at him again and suppressing a laugh said; 'And your shirt is orange too!'

Kenny rolled his eyes and responded; 'For your information, this is a designer polo shirt and the colour is rust, not orange. You Worzel Gummidge lookalike twat! Now do you want a pint, or do you want to wear one?'

Banter over, the two of them had a drink and Rob made a call to Alan Bassett to confirm step one of their weekend adventure, which they agreed to settle on as nine holes of golf at the local course a few miles up the road.

Quite a few of their friends were self employed tradesmen who tried hard to make Friday a day for an early finish. But Kenny and Rob were both Maintenance Electricians at a local distribution plant for a major retailer and often pulled the same shift rota, as they had that weekend.

Enough of their mates had agreed to meet them at the course to make up a few four balls. Although Rob had spoken earlier to another of their friends Kevin Morris and asked him to meet them in the pub as he lived close by.

'We'll hang on for Speedo, Ken.' He said. 'I spoke to him earlier and he said he'd definitely be here.'

'And here indeed is Kevlar!' Said Kenny, gesturing towards the door.

In came Kevin Morris, 'Speedy Gonzalez' or 'Speedo' as he was often somewhat cruelly referred to by his alleged mates due to him being a bit slow to grasp the point, be in the same conversation as everybody else, or sometimes even on the same planet.

Kevin was also extremely gullible and had yet to develop the instinct for knowing when he was being subjected to a wind up, despite this having happened on numerous occasions.

'Speedo! Speedo!' chanted Kenny and Rob, as he entered the bar.

'I was just trying to call you.' said Kevin/Speedo. 'But I couldn't get a signal on my new phone after I left home.'

'I'm not surprised pal.' Kenny replied. 'You're holding your house phone.'

'Yes I know that. I'm not stupid.' Speedo said indignantly. 'But I'm using it for all my calls now because it's got a fifty mile range according to the box it came in.'

He nodded to them both sagely as he said this, as if to confirm his wisdom.

'So I thought I'd save on my mobile phone bill by using the land line phone for all my calls instead now.' He continued.

The two of them thought about this for a few seconds and then Rob said, 'Hang on a minute. A fifty mile range? No cordless land line phone has a fifty mile range.'

Speedo fished a piece of paper from his pocket. 'I knew you two wouldn't believe me, so I brought the instructions. See?....' He said triumphantly, pointing to a paragraph on the first page; '50 miles.'

Rob and Kenny perused the instruction sheet held before them and then nodded to each other confirming their joint thought. Then Rob offered, 'That says 50 metres. You complete plonker! Look. It says 50m. That's metres, not miles. Dufus!'

'Oh.' Said Speedo deflatedly. 'I did think it might be too good to be true.'

The look between Kenny and Rob said all that was needed.

'Anyway,' he continued; 'Like I said, I couldn't get a signal anyway.'

Kenny looked perplexed. 'But we just told...'

'Leave it Ken.' Rob interrupted. 'I don't think I could stand it.'

The three of them left shortly afterwards and made the short drive down to their local golf course to meet their friends.

Chapter Three

On arrival they witnessed the sight of several men of varying shapes and sizes changing in the car park from overalls and jeans into a vestige of golf attire.

'Boggie, Lardy and Speedy!' Came the joint chorus from several of their so-called mates as the three of them emerged from Kenny's car.

'Nice to see you all as well, ladies.' Kenny retorted.

The guys pulled on golf shoes and retrieved bags from the boots of cars and the back of vans until they were all more or less ready. Then they all as one stopped to look in some amazement at Rob as he emerged from behind Kenny's car wearing a very strange looking hat.

'Is it a Raccoon? Is it a Weasel? Or is it a Ferret? No, it's worse than that. It's a bog brush with a bog brush on its head,' shouted Alan Bassett, one of the assembled throng, drawing a round of laughs and guffaws from the gathered specimens of sartorial elegance that made up the motley crew.

'Bollocks, Bertie bloody Bassett!' Came the predictable reply from Rob. 'This is my lucky golfing hat.'

'It wasn't very lucky for the poor Ferret they killed to make it, was it?' Alan (A.K.A 'Bertie') replied.

Rob's gesture required no supporting comment.

They organised themselves into groups comprising three lots of four. Rob nudged Kenny and said, 'stick with me darling. I'll look after you and give you a few tips.'

'Thanks.' Kenny said ironically. 'Just as long as they're not fashion tips though.'

Rob was a good golfer and in truth Kenny was always a bit relieved in these situations to play with his mate as he was a bit self conscious about his game. Although he would never admit to it.

'I'll tag along with you chaps if you like?' Bertie said, winking at Rob as he did so.

'Always a pleasure Bertie.' Rob replied ironically.

The banter continued as each of the guys got under way, hitting their drives mostly in the intended direction of the first fairway.

Kenny, Rob, Speedo and Bertie made up the last group of four and when it eventually came to their turn to play Rob was quick with words of advice.

'Easy Tiger!' He said to Bertie who was preparing to hit his tee shot at the first hole, 'You don't want to be hitting your driver here. You know how tight this hole is. Just go with a four or five iron and knock it down the middle. Then you'll have an easier iron shot to the green.'

Somewhat surprisingly, Bertie took heed of his friend's advice and changed clubs.

'Yeah, I suppose so.' He said. I've hardly ever hit the fairway here. Who am I trying to kid?'

'Blimey.' Kenny said. 'This is a first! Wise words from the Boggster AND someone actually taking notice!'

He shut up fairly quickly though as Bertie's ball landed safely on the fairway.

'Shot!' They all echoed.

Speedo was up next and he similarly took the same route and found the fairway safely, albeit from a scruffier shot and a fortunate bounce.

'Shot Speedo!' Bertie and Rob chimed together in surprised astonishment as their friend was not the world's best golfer.

'You jammy git Gonzalez!' Said Kenny ungenerously. 'No pressure on me then.'

'Come on Kenny Bradley!' chirped Rob. 'You can do it my son!'

'What are you on Bog?' Kenny enquired. 'You are annoyingly cheerful.'

'Just high on life pal.' Rob responded. 'And there's a lot worse places to be on a Friday afternoon than being on a golf course with your so called mates. Work for one place.'

'Fair enough.' Kenny conceded.

Kenny could feel the nerves. 'Come on fat boy,' he whispered to himself under his breath as he stood over his ball. 'Don't mess it up.'

He was just about to begin his back swing when Speedo said encouragingly, 'Don't mess it up Ken.'

'Thanks!' Came his less than friendly reply as he fixed Speedo with a stare and a snarl.

But fate was on Kenny's side and he connected sweetly with the ball and sent his shot straight and true, bouncing down the fairway past both balls from the previous shots.

'Shot!' Chorused his friends.

Although inwardly relieved he picked up his tee peg, turned to his mates and smiled cockily saying, 'Never in doubt!'

He swaggered to his bag and smoothly returned his club inside with all the aplomb of a professional.

'I'd like to see you do that again.' Said Bertie mockingly.

'You will in a minute old son. When I hit my next shot.' Kenny retorted.

'Oh my gawd! What have I done?' Said Rob. 'I've released a monster. The inner Kenny. The lesser spotted golfing sloth!'

The others laughed. Kenny just made a predictable gesture.

Rob strode up to take his turn.

'Come on then Bogmeister.' Said Bertie Bassett encouragingly. 'Show us all how it's done.'

Rob had taken his driver out of his bag.

'I thought you said we should hit an iron for safety.' Kenny whined.

'That's for you girls.' Rob confidently replied, shaping over his shot. 'But for us professionals....' he said, as he drew his club back and hit his shot...

'Oh bollocks! Fore left!' Rob shouted as his ball curved dramatically off line to the left towards a group of golfers on a neighbouring fairway.

His friends helpfully laughed as one voice at his misfortune. But Bertie composed himself quickest to volunteer, 'Jesus! That's miles left Bog. Nearly on the railway line!'

Rob's ball had soared over the heads of the group on the neighbouring fairway, heading further to the left and eventually disappeared into a large patch of heavy rough grass and undergrowth in the nether regions of the course.

'That's about as far off line as I've ever seen anybody be!' Sniggered Kenny.

'I've never been over there before.' Said Rob.

'I doubt anyone has ever been over there before.' Said Bertie.

'Perhaps you should have taken an iron too.' Opined Speedo.

'Well at least you will have a nice walk this afternoon, Bog.' Said Kenny.

'Better than working!' He continued.

'Thanks mate.' Rob said weakly. 'Will you help me look for it please, Ken?'

'Why don't you just hit another ball?' Kenny said. 'We're only playing for fun, so it doesn't exactly matter. Does it?'

'No. I like that ball.' Rob replied. 'It's one of my lucky balls.'

'Yeah I can see that Bog!' Kenny retorted ironically.

'Nice one Boggie.' Bertie whispered to him with a wink as he picked up his bag.

The four of them strode off. Bertie and Speedo making for their balls and Ken and Rob heading off at a tangent to the far reaches of the course to search for Rob's ball.

'This is pointless Bog,' said Kenny as they traversed through deep grass and undergrowth. 'We'll never find it over here and you'll have no sort of a shot out of this shit even if we do.'

'No. It'll be alright.' Rob said hopefully. 'I had a line on where it bounced and at least I'll only have a short pitch to the green from here.'

'Which particular green though?' Kenny offered.

Rob strode purposefully towards a clump of bushes near an old metal sit-on mower and heavy roller that had been left to rust next to an equally ancient and rusty metal Green keepers hut.

'I'm pretty sure it bounced about he....., owwfff..fuck!' Rob's voice cut off as he tripped, stumbled then fell, disappearing into the dense undergrowth.

Kenny nearly fell over himself from laughing at his mate's misfortune.

'Are you alright, mate?' He eventually managed.

Rob got up looking surprised and slightly the worse for wear. 'What the fuck was that?' He said somewhat uncertainly. 'I just tripped over something.'

He walked carefully back a pace or two to where he'd fallen.

'Bloody hell. It's a bag. A flippin' sports bag.' He said, still looking and sounding surprised and perplexed; 'Who would leave a bloody sports bag half buried on a golf course?'

'Are you sure?' Kenny said walking towards him.

'What are you two tarts up to?' Called Bertie from across the course.

'Bog fell over.' Shouted Kenny. 'We'll see you on the green.'

'Hurry up then.' Bertie called, walking back towards Speedo.

'What are they doing?' Said Speedo.

'Pissing about as usual.' Bertie replied. 'Ken said Bog fell over in the rough.'

'Is he alright?' Speedo enquired.

'Can't have done any damage if he fell on his head.' Said Bertie. 'Yeah, I think he's ok. I told them to get a move on though. All will be revealed later my son.'

'Eh?' Speedo replied.

'Just watch this space.' Bertie said smiling.

Kenny walked over to Rob. 'What are you doing, knobhead?'

'Look!' Rob said slowly, showing him the bag he'd retrieved from the pile of earth and scrub that he'd fallen over and which he'd now opened, 'It's cash! Loads of bloody cash!'

'Jesus!' Said Kenny. As Rob held up a wad of notes from the sports bag that looked full of similar bundles.

'There must be thousands here.' Rob said uncertainly.

'More like hundreds of thousands.' Replied Kenny peering in the bag. 'Where was it exactly?'

'Buried in this pile of scrub.' Rob gestured to the uneven pile of vegetation that he'd fallen over, while still looking around him with a puzzled expression.

'What are we going to do, Ken?' He said.

'We have to tell someone I suppose. The Police?' Kenny replied.

'We could just leave it here.' Rob said. 'Or we could take some of it. Or all of it! What do you think?'

'Bloody hell Bog. It must've been left by someone dodgy. And they're bound to be back for it. We have to hand it in... don't we?' Kenny said uncertainly.

'It's a lot of money though, Ken. But whatever we do, we'd better do it quickly, mate.' Rob said. 'We're lagging behind a bit.'

'We can't drag this bag round with us.' Said Kenny. 'Will it fit in your golf bag, Bog?'

'Only if you put some of the cash in your bag, mate.' He replied.

'Come on then,' said Kenny. 'We can sort it out later. But, Jesus it is an awful lot of money.'

'Let's not say anything to the others about it for now though, eh?' Rob said. 'It'll only make it a bit awkward, don't you think?'

'Yeah, fair enough.' Kenny replied. 'We'll keep it to ourselves for now.'

Chapter Four

The two of them hurriedly stuffed the bag and its contents into their golf bags and after giving up the search for Rob's ball, eventually made their way back to catch up with Bertie and Speedo on the green.

'Come on you tarts.' Said Bertie. 'Could you go any slower?'

'Sorry Bertie.' They echoed.

'Bog had a bit of trouble giving up on his ball.' Kenny said.

'It was a bit like saying goodbye to an old friend.' He continued.

Rob gave Bertie a quizzical look and nodded his head as Bertie mouthed to him, 'all ok?'

The guys continued their game without too much further incident, save a few bad shots followed by the inevitable mickey taking and the equally inevitable bad language.

But for the next couple of hours, as they hacked their way around nine holes of extremely forgettable golf, Kenny's mind was in overdrive. He kept replaying the ramifications of what had suddenly happened. In his and his mate's golf bags was quite literally a fortune.

The legend of Rob's first tee shot had spread to the other guys by the end of the round and they were all waiting to watch the final shots of the last group at the final hole.

'Was it down to the lucky hat then, Bog?' Called Dean 'Dino' Willis, as Rob made his way to the green. 'I notice you're not wearing it anymore.'

'Eh? Oh bloody hell!' Rob exclaimed as he put his hand to his head. 'It must've fallen off when I fell over in the rough earlier. Bollocks!'

He was greeted with a gale of unsympathetic laughter and a few more choice comments.

After the last group had putted out they all made arrangements to meet for a few beers in The Feathers later and then started to head off from the car park.

Bertie smiled knowingly at Rob. 'See you later then Bog. Look after Tango man!'

'Thanks for that, Bertie Bassett.' Said Kenny. 'You were well named today by the way. Your game was in ALL SORTS of a state!' He laughed at his own joke.

Those remaining groaned.

'Hang about Ken.' Rob said quietly, pulling him to one side. 'I want to have a quick look to see if my hat is at the spot where I fell over. I must've lost it there.'

Before Kenny could answer Rob had turned towards Speedo who was climbing into the back of Kenny's car.

'You don't mind waiting a few minutes while I go to look for my hat do you Kev?' He called.

'No I don't care.' Speedo replied. 'But it's funny how I'm Kev when you want me to agree with you and Speedo, or worse the rest of the time.' He said, more to himself than anyone else.

'Bloody Hell, Bog!' Kenny said gruffly through gritted teeth. 'It's in the middle of nowhere for one thing. The hat's worth about tuppence for another and'....he lowered his voice and whispered;....If you're that bothered, take a note out of your golf bag and buy yourself a new one!'

Oh come on, Ken!' Rob pleaded. 'Sally bought me that hat. It's got sentimental value. I'll just have a quick look.'

'Oh alright then.' Kenny relented. 'More like mental than sentimental though.'

They drove along the road adjoining the old railway line until Rob got Kenny to pull over onto a grass verge,

'This is about in line with where I fell over.' He said. 'Look. That's the old mower and roller and there's the hut over there.' He pointed across the course to a spot in the distance.

'Yeah. And there's the frigging railway line in between, you knob!' Kenny replied.

'You two don't have to come.' Rob said defensively. 'I'll only be a few minutes.' He winked at Kenny and smiled as he got out of the car, saying, 'I think I can remember the spot where I fell.'

Kenny suddenly felt a wave of brotherly love for his mate and found himself saying; 'Oh bollocks! Wait up Bog.'

He turned to Speedo in the back. 'Stay here Speedy Gonzales.' He said smiling and raising his eyebrows. 'I s'pose I could probably do with the exercise anyway.'

He climbed out of the car and called out again to Rob. 'Wait up you tart. I'm coming with you.'

They climbed over the low stone wall next to the railway line and crossed the track which served as a local route for goods and the occasional passenger train.

Kenny blurted out, 'I've thought of nothing else for the last couple of hours, mate. But perhaps we should keep at least some of that money. What d'you reckon?'

Rob played a straight bat. 'Well like we said earlier, mate. It is an awful lot of money.'

As they walked across to the rough grass and undergrowth that they'd been in earlier, Kenny said; 'I feel really strange, mate. Do you know what I mean?'

Rob knew what he meant, but now felt a bit guilty. So he reverted to the defence of piss taking, replying; 'Well you are more than a bit strange, pal!'

'Nah. You know what I mean?' Kenny said. 'We've found shed loads of cash, Rob. It could be life changing, mate?'

Kenny's far from usual use of his name rather than his nickname provoked more of an uncomfortable feeling within Rob. He felt a growing sense of guilt and embarrassment.

'Look Ken,' he began, 'I thought you'd be set on handing it in and it was....'

'I know,' Ken interrupted. 'But the way things are right now, mate, that money could do a lot of good. Like I said, I've been thinking about it for the last couple of hours.'

'What do you mean, Ken?' Said Rob. 'Things are alright, aren't they?'

'Mo's not well, mate.' Kenny said softly. 'She doesn't even know that I know. But I found a letter from the hospital and I'm sure she's not well.' Kenny looked at his mate with watery eyes and suddenly Rob felt awful.

'Oh Jesus, Ken.' He said. 'I had no idea, mate. Look, I'm so sorry. I really had no idea. Oh shit!'

Kenny smiled. 'It's alright, mate. I didn't want to say anything. But I've known for a little while and I know she's been trying to keep it from me. I don't think she's told anyone, apart from the Doctors.'

'But you've both seemed so...so....normal.' Rob said. 'I had no idea, Ken.' He repeated.

'I've tried to pretend it wasn't happening.' Kenny said. 'It's probably why I've been making so much of this weekend thing lately. I think I just wanted something to put in the way of it. And with Mo not saying anything and the girls' trip coming up too, it...., well I s'pose it was just easier to pretend everything was normal. But I've just been kidding myself, mate. Till now.'

Rob felt as bad as he'd ever felt.

'Mate, I had no idea.' He said again. 'Look, Ken. The money...It's all a wind up. I'm so sorry. If I...if we'd have known... It was all meant to be a laugh. You know?... As part of the weekend thing you've been going on about...Me and Bertie....Well,... Bertie mainly.' He spluttered;...'We...'

'What?' Kenny stared at him as he interrupted. 'What the fuck are you saying?'

'Look, Ken. It was all meant to be a joke. Bertie's cousin works at a film company and he said he could get some fake cash from him, 'cos they've just done a film about a robbery and they had this fake money. We thought we could have a bit of a laugh. You know?'

'You absolute shitbags!' Kenny said glaring red faced at him.

Rob looked suitably shame-faced. 'Ken...Mate...It's the sort of thing we've done to each other for years. You know that! It was meant to be a laugh. Come on mate, you know that if I....if we'd had any idea, we'd never have done it. Ken, I'm so sorry.'

'Fuck you, arsehole.' Kenny said.

Rob pleaded with his friend. 'Ken....I couldn't feel worse. Mate, please try to see it from the other side. We've planned a trip away tomorrow. It was all meant to be a joke. We'd have let on later tonight. You know...setting light to £20 notes. That sort of thing. Please, mate!'

And the trouble was that for all his anger and disappointment, now that it was all out in the open, Kenny could see exactly how and why this had happened. He didn't want to forgive his mate for snatching away this new found opportunity. But he knew that, had things been different and had he been party to winding up one of the others, he would've willingly gone along with it.

Chapter Five

'Arsehole.' Said Ken. Less severely than before.

'I am really sorry, mate.' Rob said contritely. 'You know I'd have never let this happen, if I'd known?'

'Alright, alright, you dick! Don't keep on. It's done now.' Kenny said. 'But I'm buggered if I'm going to look for your poxy hat now!'

Rob smiled at his mate thinly.

'What d' you mean about planning a trip, by the way?' Kenny said. 'You? Planning things?'

'Me and Bertie Bassett thought we'd take the heat off you for a change.' Rob replied, relieved to be talking about something else.

He continued, 'You're always the one having to organise the rest of us. So we had a word with Gracie Fields' mate from that coach company we used last year when we all went to Newmarket and he's done us a deal on a 30 seater. We were going to tell you tonight in the pub.'

'Bloody hell.' Said Kenny. 'You devious buggers! After all my whinging at you and trying to get any of you to make any sort of decision, you had something planned all along.'

'Mind you. It's about flippin' time someone else did the organising for a change.' He continued.

'What do you mean?' Rob countered. 'You love all that shit! All the sorting out itineraries for trips and stuff. You love it.' He repeated.

'Whatever.' Kenny muttered. 'Well at least we're doing something. Where are we going anyway?'

'Cleethorpes.' Rob replied defensively, knowing his mate's dislike of local resorts. 'We can't go too far, 'cos we don't want to spend all day in the coach. We thought, you know, a couple of hours getting there, then get on it at Lunchtime. Then maybe have a mooch about in the afternoon. Play footie on the beach. Then have a few more sherbets. Then come home.'

'Cleethorpes? Very exotic!' Kenny replied sarcastically.

'Scoff all you like, Ken.' Said Rob. 'But once you've had a couple and got pissed up, it won't matter to you where you are anyway.'

'Oh, ha, ha, ha!' Kenny whined, knowing at the same time that he had disgraced himself more than a few times before with his mates when it came to boozy occasions.

'Tell you one thing though.' Said Rob, pointing. 'Bloody Bertie was supposed to leave the money by that old sit on mower over there. The way we planned it was for him to leave it there earlier and then I would try to hit my ball in that general direction as part of the wind up. That's why I was so surprised to fall over the bag in the rough. It totally caught me unawares.'

'Serves you bloody right, you plonker!' Kenny replied. 'Lucky you didn't break your scrawny neck and even luckier for you that I didn't break it for you when I found out.'

'Yeah, alright tough guy.' Said Rob.

'Anyway,' Kenny went on; 'Just goes to show you can't trust Bertie bloody Bassett to get anything right. Doesn't it?'

'I dunno, Ken.' Rob countered. 'If it'd been Speedo, then fair enough. But Bertie's usually pretty reliable.'

'Well, obviously not on this occasion. 'Kenny snapped. 'Who else knew about your little scam, anyway? I suppose they all bloody did?'

'Only me and Bertie knew about the money, mate. Honest.' Rob replied.

He continued; 'Dino was with us just after we'd booked the coach last week and he helped us get the others involved and also to tell them to keep quiet about it to you. But we didn't let him, or anyone else know, because it would've been bound to have come out beforehand otherwise. All we told him was that we were going to do some kind of a wind up involving you, but to keep it to himself till we'd sorted it.'

Kenny's amazed expression required no accompanying words. But he repeated his earlier comment anyway; 'You devious buggers.'

He scratched his head and continued; 'How on earth did you manage to get Speedo to keep quiet though?'

Rob laughed. 'We're not that good, mate! We figured it was best to leave Kev where he usually is, blissfully unaware in his own little world!'

Rob went on; 'Like I said, Bertie's cousin works for some film company and he'd mentioned to him about some fake notes that they'd used on a recent film they'd made about a robbery and Bertie asked if he could have the money, as they were only going to get rid of it anyway. Mind you, he said it would be about a hundred grand in fake notes. It looked a lot more than that though, didn't it?'

Kenny nodded and replied; 'Not that I've ever seen that much money before, but, yes it did look a lot more than that.'

Rob had walked over to the rough ground where he'd fallen earlier.

'Bollocks! My hat's not here.' He said. 'I must've lost it somewhere else on the course after all.'

'Oh, boo hoo! What a bloody shame!' Ken sneered. 'I'm so sorry for your loss. Serves you bloody right! Ha, ha, ha!'

'That's just plain nasty.' Rob said. 'I thought I'd lost it before and only found it in the garage the other day. But at least it's cheered you up again, lardy.'

'Don't push it, knobhead.' Kenny sneered. 'I'm still coming to terms with being potless again.'

Rob ignored him and walked towards the old hut and the mower a few yards away.

'Where are you going now, you tart?' Called Kenny. 'Come on, Bog! Forget about your bloody hat and let's get moving. I'm in the mood for a drink now.

'It's just....' Rob started. 'Yeah! Ken!' He called to his mate excitedly. 'Come here, quick!'

'Look!' He said, pointing as Kenny joined him.

'What am I supposed to be looking at?' He replied, sounding more than a bit fed up.

'The package that Bertie left for me!' Rob said, incredulously. 'It's here by the mower.'

'If this is still part of your bloody wind up I swear I'll stick one on you, Bog!' Said Kenny, in an exasperated voice.

'No really, mate. Honestly. Look! By the front blades.' Rob said, pointing.

Kenny's eyes widened as he looked at where his mate was pointing.

There on the ground hidden behind the front blades of the mower was a blue plastic package.

Chapter Six

They approached it as carefully as they might have done had it been an unexploded bomb.

Rob bent down and retrieved the package from the ground and took off the elastic bands that secured it.

Once again he said to his mate; 'look!'

And this time when they looked they saw what Rob had expected to find the first time.

'See?' Rob said after they had examined the contents. 'Fifty pound notes in ten grand bundles! Ten, ten grand bundles! A hundred grand, Ken! Do you know what that means?'

'Fuck me!' Said Ken. 'I can't take this all in! This is like one of those dodgy late night films I end up watching when I wake up on the settee after coming home from the pub. This means....' he looked at Rob; 'This means we've got a fortune in our golf bags after all.'

Rob looked dumbstruck.

Kenny continued; 'Level with me, Bog. This really isn't still part of your dopey wind up, is it?'

Rob looked at him as if he was speaking a foreign language.

'BOG!' Ken shouted at his mate, totally forgetting where they were.

'Nuh, no.' Rob stuttered. 'No wind up, mate. Fuck me!'

They both looked nervously around, but there was nobody in sight except a couple of groups of golfers several hundred yards away, obliviously going about their golfing business.

'Let's get out of here, Bog. I suddenly feel very nervous.' Said Kenny.

'I can't quite take this in, Ken.' Rob said uncertainly as they made their way back towards the railway line.

'Do you think...no. No. NO!' Rob spluttered.

'What? Do I think what, you dick? What are you talking about?' Ken was exasperated again.

'I can't believe Bertie could pull off a double wind up.' Rob muttered.

'Hang on a bloody minute.' Kenny said. 'Are you saying now that you think Bertie has set you up as well as me?'

'I can't see how else this could've happened.' Rob replied.

'Look.' Kenny reasoned. 'This is now all so convoluted we're in danger of disappearing up our own arseholes in a minute! Nah! I can't see it. There's no way! There'd better be no bloody way, or we'll have to kill him!'

'I can't think straight anymore, Ken.' Said Rob.

'Well, I'll have a go.' Kenny replied.

He continued; 'Right. You and Bertie had a drink and he came up with the scam. Is that right?'

'Yeah.' Said Rob. 'We started off by saying that a few of us were going to be minus the wives this weekend and how, despite you going on at us, we should arrange something, like you'd been saying.'

'Oh thanks.' Interrupted Kenny, sarcastically.

Rob ignored him and continued;

'So we spoke about arranging a coach. I went over to Gracie and mentioned his mate from the coach company and he said he'd get onto him about prices. We guessed on numbers and I told Gracie it would need to be hush, hush as far as you were concerned because we were planning something. We'd said originally about winding up Speedo. But that's been done to death however many times. Then Bertie mentioned about his cousin and the fake money and we just went from there and we thought that if we got you going it would tie in well with the weekend.'

Kenny sneered at him.

Rob laughed. 'Well you kept saying you wanted an adventure!'

He was about to continue, but Ken interjected.

'So you're saying now that you think Bertie has invented this whole scam where he's got you to think you were winding me up and then he's put out two piles of cash to wind us both up?'

'Yeah. That's what I was thinking.' Rob replied. 'I think?' He said less certainly.

'Well I'll tell you what I think.' Kenny said. 'That's total bollocks! There's no way he'd have put money in a different place to where he told you he was going to put it, in the hope you'd find it by some miracle.'

He continued. 'It doesn't stack up, Bog.'

'Then, how the hell do we end up with two stashes of cash within yards of each other?' Said Rob.

'Dunno, mate.' Kenny replied. 'But we'll find out in a bit when we speak to Bertie bloody Bassett.'

They made their way back to the car where they found Speedo asleep.

'He is asleep, mate, isn't he?' Asked Rob. 'I mean he 'ain't been killed by some Mafia hitman or something, has he?'

'Not unless dead people snore.' Said Kenny. 'But I know what you mean. This all seems surreal. I'm not convinced you're not still winding me up either.'

'I can understand that, mate and I'm really sorry for starting this whole thing.' Rob pleaded. He looked at Kenny. Then his expression changed.

'Wait a minute! You and Bertie aren't winding me up, are you? Because it's just the sort of thing you'd do.'

'I don't bloody believe you. You tart!' Kenny exclaimed.

'I've just told you about Mo, for Christ's sake. Do you think I'd make up something like that? You knobber!'

'No. I'm sorry, mate. Really I am. My head's all over the place. It's just so much to take in. What are we going to say to Bertie though? Do we tip him off about the money or what?

Kenny thought about it for a moment before they got into his car.

'What if we just play along with it for a while? I don't want anything to come out about Mo and if you let on that you told me about it being fake money, then Bertie will just be all over you to find out why. What d'you reckon?'

'Yeah. That makes sense.' Rob agreed. 'But we'll need to be careful what we say.'

Chapter Seven

It would be a massive understatement to say that Ashley Richardson was a desperate man. But, as deep as the hole was that he'd dug himself into, he would never have wanted to have to agree with that assessment of his current situation.

Although he was acutely aware of the precarious position he had got himself into, as far as he was concerned he was sorting it out and he continued to display all of the bravado and arrogant disregard for day to day reality that marked his character.

He lived close to the edge. He thrived on close to the edge. And it would be fair to say that unless he was close to that edge, Ashley (Ash), as he was always more than keen to tell people of his preference for his name, found life to be mundane.

Ash Richardson was a Policeman and had been in the force for nearly ten years. The last seven as a Detective Constable. He knew that any career ambitions he may once have aspired to had long since departed, as his unconventional working methods and above all his own personality had seen him overlooked by his seniors for others who he considered to be inferior.

These days all he looked for in any given situation in either his working, or personal life, was what possible advantage he could gain and he largely couldn't care less who he trod on, or upset in getting what he wanted. He truly was the centre of his own universe.

His popularity with his colleagues could be measured by an experience a few years before when he was out for a drink with workmates to celebrate his birthday.

He had been 'approached' by a young lady in the bar, who had made it clear to him that she had been hired by his friends for his enjoyment. She had then enticed him out to the car park where she performed a particular act for his gratification and when they returned twenty minutes later, he grinned smugly to his colleagues. A few minutes later he went to the gents, where to his dismay he was joined by his lady friend at the urinal and realised that 'she' was in fact a 'he', much to the amusement of everyone but him when he returned to the bar.

His attitude at work was very much about taking whatever he could get.

Obviously, he'd never let on to anyone that he was partial to backhanders, bribes and any other incentives he might be offered and he had largely been allowed to get away with things due to a combination of his ability to play people off against each other, allied to the fact that he was even more devious and cunning than most of the criminals he was supposed to be up against.

But even he was now beginning to panic inwardly as he sought to find a way to dig himself out of the mess he was in and his self assured mask was ever so slightly beginning to slip.

This more than spilled over into his personal life and he had regularly been in scrapes that had exasperated his first wife to the point where she had kicked him out and subsequently divorced him.

But now he was doing much the same with his current partner who, having initially been attracted by his brash, flash and arrogant character, was now becoming more and more disenchanted with his non appearances, lame excuses and irrational behaviour.

In the last eighteen months Ash had become an acquaintance of a man called Ronnie Senior. He had met him in connection with a job he'd been working on and it became apparent that Senior and his cronies had pretty much taken control of all of the main illegal activities in their local area. He had formed a working relationship with

Senior whereby they traded information that served their mutual interests.

Ash had been tipped off about the activities of Senior's rivals, which had enabled several good arrests and convictions to be made, for which Ash had gained some credit and Senior had as a result cleared the field of his main competitors.

But this had also allowed Senior to go largely unchecked in his own nefarious dealings and had made sure things had gone smoothly for him, with little or no police interference.

Ash had taken this to the point of receiving money and personal services from Senior's operations that, if they came to light would not only finish his career, but would also see him go away for a long time in prison.

The impact of his own recent actions was becoming an issue at home as his behaviour became more irrational and unpredictable. In addition to the huge gambling debts he had run up, he'd also been drinking more heavily and had often come home in the early hours, or occasionally not at all. As a result things had started to spiral out of control.

Ronnie Senior had also begun to make additional demands on him as Ash became more deeply involved in his affairs.

This had initially appealed to him, as the chances he took gave him the thrill he'd always enjoyed when he did things that he knew he shouldn't be doing. But as the demands on his time became more excessive, Ash began to resent being told what to do.

He knew that Senior was a man to fear though. So Ash planned to wait for the ideal opportunity to turn on him and also if possible, find a way to make himself a lot of money, as well as get out of the situation he had gotten himself into.

Recently he had seen large amounts of cash at Senior's house which had been brought in by people Senior used as money launderers.

Senior had several businesses which were fronts for his illegal activities and the people who ran these operations had been bringing more and more cash to him.

Ash had felt sure that something was being planned with other criminals and suspected that Senior wanted to buy or force his way into larger criminal operations as his greed for money and power grew.

He hoped that what happened next would involve him being in the right place at the right time, in order to bring about a double cross. He had thought of little else lately, as he knew he would have to be seen to be free of any blame by either Senior, or his gang.

Ash's chance to bring this about came when, a few days before, he and his colleagues had been advised they would be drafted in to help with an impending Regional Crime Squad operation on their patch.

During the briefing they were given the heads up that a major drugs deal was being busted and they would be needed as extra officers on the ground to search for, seize and collate evidence and information.

After the initial meeting Ash pushed his Sergeant for a bit more information as to who was being targeted and had managed to find out that it was Ronnie Senior.

This news both pleased and worried him at the same time.

On the plus side, if Senior's operation was busted and he and his gang went to prison, then Ash would be out from under in regard to his own dealings with him. But the other side of this was the importance that he remained blameless in Senior's eyes, or it could prove to be disastrous for him if what he'd been up to then got out.

He had decided to sit on the information and wait till he knew more. Then, when it was too late to make any real difference, he planned to contact Senior to tip him off and cover all bases. He hoped then that he wouldn't be implicated by Senior, who he figured would have far too much on his plate to even consider blaming him.

Although he was well aware that his involvement with Senior would certainly be of interest to his senior officers, Ash knew that it wouldn't be of enough merit for Senior to use as a bargaining chip, if he tried to negotiate a lower sentence for what was likely to be coming his way.

But he still needed to tread carefully as he couldn't afford any comeback from Senior or his associates.

Chapter Eight

Ash had kept a low profile for the last couple of days. But on the previous afternoon, he and other local officers had been called into an official briefing headed up by a Detective Chief Inspector from the Regional Crime Squad.

The operation was scheduled for early the next morning. Crime squad officers were going to raid two adjoining units that Senior had on an industrial estate, as they had information that two lorry loads of flowers were being delivered around 5.30am which contained bags of Heroin and Cocaine. Their information was that Senior was reportedly paying £1 Million for the drugs.

Ash and other local officers were being detailed to Senior's house to search for any other incriminating evidence there.

As Ash left the briefing he decided that he'd leave it till early the next morning before phoning Senior. He spent the evening at home, which had been a rare occurrence lately. But, he thought to himself, if all went well the next day, perhaps he could start mending fences at home and keep out of scrapes. At least for a while.

On Friday morning, Ash woke early with the alarm. When he was ready to leave he used a non contract mobile to phone Ronnie Senior and got through to his voicemail. He left his usual message merely saying, 'phone me as soon as you get this.' However, he added two words. 'It's urgent!'

He spoke gruffly to make his voice sound as nondescript as possible just in case the message was retrieved later by the investigating officers.

He knew Senior wouldn't recognise the number. But whenever he'd contacted him before using a 'burner phone,' he'd been called back within a few minutes. That was the arrangement they had in order to avoid any trace of the phones Ash used.

Ash had phoned as he left the house. He was due in by 5.30, but had only got a few hundred yards up the road when the phone rang.

'You called me just now?' Senior's voice was instantly recognisable.

'It's me, Ron, Ash.' He replied. 'You've got some trouble coming.'

'What sort of trouble?' Said Senior.

Ash tried to sound concerned as if he was doing Senior a favour. 'I've only just had a call from my guv'nor, calling me in to work right away. He said the crime squad are doing a raid any minute on your units and he wants me and some other officers over at your house to look for evidence. If I'd Known before, mate, I.....'

'Fucking bastards.' Senior interrupted him. 'Bollocks!'

'They gave us no heads up, Ron. If I'd have known earlier, I would have contacted you straightaway.'

Senior's voice grew louder. 'What the fuck am I paying you for if this is the notice you give me, you twat? You told me you knew everything that went on at that nick, dickwad!'

Ash could hear the panic in Ron's voice, which somehow made it easier for him to stay in control.

'But the crime squad doesn't work out of our nick, Ron. You've obviously become big time. I phoned as soon as I knew anything, mate. Whatever they're after, try and get rid of it and quick. Is there anything at the house you don't want found?'

'Yeah, plenty! I'm not at home. I'm at the units now. There's a delivery due soon. Bollocks!'

Senior sounded worried and frightened like so many smaller time villains that Ash had seen in similar situations when the heat was on them. He actually felt a bit sorry for him.

Senior continued; 'I've got a million quid in a couple of sports bags upstairs at my gaff. I wanted to be sure this delivery was kosher before I had the money brought here.'

Ash stopped any further notions of feeling sorry for Senior and tried to ignore thoughts of all of that money at his house and attempted to play a straight bat.

'Listen, Ron. I'll phone Sue now to let her know what's happening and tell her I've spoken to you. Just concentrate on trying to cover your tracks as best you can. You won't be able to get back to the house, as there's already uniformed officers at the end of your road and the Crime Squad Officers will be in place nearby to your units waiting for the delivery lorries.'

'Too fucking late to cover my tracks, Ashie.' Senior said resignedly. 'I've got two lorry loads of Dutch smack, covered with tulips, arriving here any minute. I'm fucked son.'

'Can't you contact the drivers and get them to abort?'

Ash knew that wouldn't be likely and that the crime squad officers already had enough information on the operation to arrest and charge Senior anyway, but he was showing false enthusiasm to try and throw Senior off from attaching any blame to him.

'The drivers left Holland hours ago. They don't work for me and I don't have their numbers. Jesus! What a fucking mess!'

Ash kept up the pretence. 'What about the people you're dealing with? Can't you get in touch with them, to see if they can call their drivers off?'

Senior was resigned to his fate. 'I've arranged this through an intermediary. It would take ages to get in touch with them and get a message through. This was all supposed to be bomb proof. Too good to be true! What a fuck up! Someone must've grassed to the police.'

Ash wanted to deflect any potential suspicions away from him and tried to sound concerned.

'Well if that's the case, it can only have been at the other end, Ron. Just destroy what you can before the crime squad turn up. Try to muddy the waters as much as possible. I'll phone Sue now and then try to stall at the nick to give her more time to at least hide some of the money.'

'Alright, Ashie. Thanks.' Senior sounded defeated as he hung up.

Ash then phoned Sue Senior.

'Hello.' Said the familiar voice as she answered.

'Susie. Hi. It's Ash.'

'Hello, babe.' Said the sleepy voice. 'This is a ni..' Sue started to reply.

Ash interrupted. 'Sorry, darling. This is urgent. '

He kept the call short but tried to sound concerned for Ron. He told her the same story he'd told her husband and then went on to say that she would need to stay there until he and other officers arrived, as there were already uniformed officers in place at the end of her road to stop anyone coming in or out. He said they would be over soon with a search warrant and added that he'd do whatever he could and would keep her informed with any news he could find out about Ron, but told her obviously not to let on that she knew him when he turned up at the house.

Sue hadn't panicked at the news. She'd been through this situation before and Ash felt he could trust her not to let him down, as he knew that she'd got one or two secrets of her own that she wouldn't want Ron to know about. Although one of those directly involved Ash, after he'd run her home as a favour to Ron when she was a bit the worse for a few drinks late one night a few months ago. And that little episode and what they'd got up to afterwards had had a few repeat performances since then.

She hadn't said anything about the money when he told her about the impending raid and he half considered not mentioning it. But, as he knew it would certainly come to light eventually, he told her that Ron had said there were 2 sports bags containing a lot of cash upstairs in the house.

'Jesus Christ! What am I supposed to do with that? We've only got a small floor safe. Did he say where it is?' Sue sounded suitably concerned.

Even as he spoke to her about the money Ash was visualising getting his hands on at least some of it. But until he was there, he obviously had no idea if he could make that happen.

'Ron only said it was upstairs, love. So, in one of the bedrooms I'd imagine.'

But from Sue's mention of a floor safe, he then had a moment of recall from a previous visit to the house and continued;

'Don't you have one set up as an office?'

Sue briefly checked and then confirmed that she'd located two bags full of money in the room Ash remembered as an office.

'What the hell am I supposed to do with all of this?' She exclaimed.

'Just put as much of it in the safe as you can explain when you're questioned about it, because they will want to see what you have in there as well. Leave the rest of the money in the bags and cover them under some washing or something and if I can, I'll try and get at least some of it out to my car. But that won't be easy.'

'Ok. I'll put some in the safe and say it's from my beauty business and one or two other family things.' Sue said, sounding a little calmer.

'I'll cover the bags with duvet covers. But Ron has been a knob over all of this. I knew he was out of his depth and now he's going to pay for it. There's no way I'm getting myself in bother and neither should you, babe. Don't be taking any more risks for him. He don't deserve it.'

'Alright, Suze.' He said. 'We'll play it by ear when I get to yours, but you can deny all knowledge of what's going on. Ronnie wouldn't want you getting mixed up in it anyway, or he'd have told you about the money. They'll want to know about any money we find, but you can at least try to deny that any money in the safe has anything to do with any other cash found in the bags. Ok?'

'Yeah. Alright, love.' Sue sounded more her normal self now. 'But we'll just look after ourselves, eh?' She said. 'Ron had this coming. When this is all over perhaps we can have ourselves another little party, eh?'

'You always know how to make a positive out of a negative.' Ash replied, half smiling.

'Look forward to taking you up on that! Just make sure that nothing we find implicates you, or leaves you open to any dodgy questions, Sue.'

'I won't.' She said. 'I'll play dumb. Won't be hard for me! That's before you say it. Flash Ash!'

He hated her calling him that, but bit his tongue and said his goodbyes.

He smiled at how things had gone and again visualised a pile of cash that he hoped to get his hands on at least some of.

Chapter Nine

When Ash arrived at the Police Station he and several colleagues briefly went over their instructions with one of their own Sergeants Danny Perkins and Detective Sergeant Mike Phelan from the Regional Crime Squad.

Then shortly afterwards they headed over to Ronnie Senior's house to carry out their part of the operation.

They had been told to search for anything that might potentially be incriminating evidence. Things like laptops, mobile phones, tablets, notebooks, ledgers, weapons, or just any item they thought might have some significance.

Interestingly though, cash had not been mentioned.

They had obtained a warrant confirming their right to search the house. But before leaving the station they'd already heard several messages passed via the force radio from the industrial estate where Senior's units were located, that all local targets had been arrested, in addition to 2 Dutch lorry drivers.

They had also had this confirmed by Phelan after he'd spoken to his guv'nor, who told him that everything had gone to plan and Senior and his various associates were being taken to force headquarters for questioning.

Ash was glad that the interviews wouldn't be held at his station as it put Ron out of his remit and absolved him of any real responsibility towards him. He hoped that Ron would have enough to worry about and it would be a case of out of sight, out of mind, as far as he was concerned.

Ash left the station and drove alone, rather than be tasked with driving over with any other officers. He wanted to see the lie of the land at the house and keep his options open as to how possible it would be for him to get his hands on any of the money. The thought of what a million pounds might look like was very much in the forefront of his mind.

When he and the other officers arrived at the house in convoy, Sue Senior answered the door.

Ash smiled inwardly at Sue's performance. She was surprised, indignant, disbelieving and a complete innocent all at the same time. As always she could not resist the opportunity to play up to a group of men and was showing her usual generosity in the amount of cleavage she displayed.

They showed her the warrant and went in and then split into two groups.

Ash's Sergeant and Phelan from the crime squad spoke to Sue, while other officers searched the rooms downstairs. But Ash went upstairs, followed by two other officers, Steve Lewington and Graham Ellis.

From his earlier conversation with Sue, Ash knew where the money would be. When he reached the top of the stairs he said over his shoulder, 'we might as well take a room each. I'll start on this side of the stairs and you guys might as well start at the other end and we'll work towards each other. It's better than tripping over each other in the same room. But shout if you need any help. Ok?'

'Yeah alright, that makes sense.' Said Lewington. He and Ellis went along the landing in the opposite direction.

The room Ash was most interested in was the second of the three rooms on the side of the stairs he had chosen to take. He remembered the layout of the house from previous visits and remembered the middle room as being where the office was and also where the floor safe was situated.

He had to make his search appear realistic and he initially went into the first of the rooms. By its appearance it looked as if this was mainly used as a dressing room and he also remembered it as such.

He made a quick search through drawers and cupboards. But apart from household items, clothes, etc there was nothing there that would be classed as potential evidence in this operation. There was a laminated floor in the room. He looked under a sofa bed and in various cupboards, but found nothing of interest.

Then he went into the next room where he expected the money to be. There was a small wicker basket with several mobile phones inside on top of a drawer unit. But they all looked as if they were no longer in use and they were certainly not of recent design.

In the corner of the room was a pile of bedding, as he'd expected to find from his earlier conversation with Sue. He opened the curtains to let in some of the early morning light and noticed the handle of a sports bag which wasn't quite covered by the duvet cover on top of it

Ash pulled the pile of bedclothes apart and saw that there were two sports bags underneath the duvet covers. On closer inspection both appeared to contain a lot of banknotes, although one seemed to have more inside than the other and he figured that Sue must have transferred some of the contents of the smaller bag to the floor safe as they'd discussed earlier.

His heart was pounding and he felt an overwhelming temptation being so close to all that money. He thought about taking one of the bundles of notes. There must be about ten grand there alone he thought as he took one small pile of crisp £50 notes neatly wrapped in a yellow elastic band and held it up in front of him.

But a combination of greed, desperation and naked desire swept over him all at once. He reasoned in the part of his mind still capable of rational thought, that ten grand was a drop in the bucket to the debt he'd run up with various money lenders and it would take a lot more than that to even come close to balancing the books.

He'd taken over £25,000 alone out of an investment account that his Grandfather had put in Ash's name for his children before he died. Although he rarely felt guilt or remorse for any of his actions, that particular act had weighed heavily on his mind, as he'd loved his Granddad like no other person and held him up as a role model. He remembered the throng of people at his funeral and the amount of respect shown and kind words said to Ash's Dad that day about his father.

But his Granddad had also been a high achiever, who was rumoured to have been absolutely ruthless in business. So Ash reasoned he would understand that his Grandson was doing what he had to do to try and make his mark and would still be proud of him.

So he looked again at the money and any sense of duty and honesty was easily swept aside by his other self. That side of him was screaming at him, 'you'll never a get another chance like this again. This is your time. Do it! Go on! DO IT!'

He quickly decided that trying to get both bags downstairs and out to his car without anyone noticing would be close to impossible. So while he had time he transferred as much of the cash to one bag as he could. The money all seemed to be a combination of twenty and fifty pound notes and given what he already knew, Ash realised he was staring at several hundred thousand pounds.

He zipped up the bag and lifted it. It was heavy enough to make the job of taking it downstairs in a hurry no easy task. But the pound signs in front of his eyes would not allow him to lighten the load now. So he put the bag behind the curtains and placed the duvet covers in a pile in front to conceal it.

'I'll be back.' He said quietly in a mock Arnold Schwarzenegger/Terminator voice.

He picked up the other sports bag containing the remaining cash. There was still a great deal in it, but it was noticeably lighter than the other bag. Ash's mind was made up now though.

He knew from a previous visit that the floor safe was over by the computer. But he figured he could mention that after he'd hopefully got the bag full of money out to his car because that was all he could focus on now. That money represented his freedom. It would make him free of debt and worry and set him up to live the life he figured he had always deserved to live.

He went over to the computer table in the corner and shifted it several feet away from the wall which exposed the area containing the floor safe. It was covered by a small rug which he moved to one side. Then he gathered up two laptop computers from the office and the basket of old mobile phones and rested them on top of the sports bag. He then disconnected the computer tower and removed that as well. He took the computer tower outside to the landing and then went back into the bedroom and picked up the other items and brought them back out to the landing before closing the door behind him.

There was only the bathroom left on his side of the landing. So he left everything outside the room he'd just left and went through the motions of searching the bathroom where he found nothing of note.

He then went across to where his colleagues were searching the other upstairs rooms. They had found another laptop, two phones, a tablet and another notebook.

Ash helped to complete the search of the other rooms and then retrieved the items he'd put on the landing and followed his colleagues downstairs.

Another officer was in the Lounge cataloguing everything they wanted to retain in a record book and putting each of the items in various sizes of evidence bags. Each bag was labelled to correspond with the evidence log.

One of his colleagues began to assist with the evidence recording and the other went into the conservatory where the other officers were. Ash noticed his Sergeant and Phelan the Detective from the Regional Crime Squad in there with Sue Senior, who appeared to be furiously challenging them over each item that was being taken away.

'No! Those files are from my nail and beauty business. You don't bloody need them!' He heard Sue's unmistakeable tones echoing from the other room.

Ash looked around and gauged that at that moment everyone seemed to be occupied. So, with some trepidation he quickly returned upstairs. He checked to make sure no one was in the other rooms and then retrieved the sports bag from behind the curtain in the office.

He started downstairs with it. The sound of talking was all around, but it was as if temporarily no one was looking his way. His heart was hammering as he opened the front door and went outside. He checked that no one was in the immediate vicinity and went over to his car which he'd parked just outside the driveway in the road outside. His footsteps on the gravelled drive seemed louder than ever and the driveway seemed twice as long as it had on the way in.

As he opened the boot of his car and put the bag inside he heard two people come out of the house opposite. They hadn't seen him yet, but he had no time to cover the bag. So, slightly panicked, he closed the boot and returned quickly back towards the house.

He felt a wave of nausea hit him. His brain was in overdrive. What if he was asked to put something in his boot? He either had to cover the bag, or better still get the hell out of there.

Chapter Ten

The uniformed officers detailed at the entrance to the road had been stood down after he and his colleagues arrived at the house and Ash hoped that he would also soon get the ok to return to the station. He knew he wouldn't be able to slip away yet though, as he would be missed. But, with the bag full of money now in the boot of his car, he couldn't focus on anything else other than how to get away as soon as possible.

He managed to slip back into the house without being noticed, but his heart was hammering in his chest and he was finding it increasingly hard to concentrate.

Acting as if he was still continuing the search for evidence, he made towards the room downstairs that he knew Senior used as a bolt hole-cum study. As he reached the door a voice from behind him called out;

'We've already been in there, Ash.' He turned, half startled, to see one of his colleagues Detective Constable John Fry.

'You alright?' Said Fry. 'You looked a bit shocked then.'

'What? Oh yeah. Miles away, John.' Ash replied, trying to regain his composure.

'I think we're all done upstairs apart from a floor safe in one of the bedrooms.' He continued.

'Oh. That'll please Madam in there!' Fry smiled. 'She's already gone ballistic at   the Skipper and that guy Phelan at least three times.'

'Yeah, I thought I heard all the fuss from upstairs.' Ash lied.

He hung around for a while and then saw Danny Perkins in the Lounge talking on his mobile.

As soon as Perkins had ended the call Ash went over to him and told him about the safe upstairs.

Perkins smiled wryly and rolled his eyes. He did not look his usual composed self and the smile soon disappeared.

'We've been rowing with the lovely Mrs Senior in there,' he said pointing to the Conservatory...'about every fucking item in this house. And to be honest Ash I'm more than a bit pissed off that we've been landed with all the fucking donkey work while the RCS boys get all the fucking glory as per fucking usual.'

'So,' he continued... 'as we've just about searched everywhere now I'm going to let Detective Sergeant Phelan over there deal with her about searching that safe and get us out of here asap, so that we can then get on with doing some of our own fucking jobs!'

Ash knew that Perkins had been turned down for a job in the Regional Crime Squad a while back and rumour had it that he'd pretty much been told he needn't bother re-applying. The bitterness he felt had obviously not been helped by this assignment.

He seized his moment. Trying to sound as normal as possible he said, 'I know what you mean Skipper. It does seem like we've been used as lackeys. Do you still need me here? As you said, there doesn't seem to be anywhere else that needs searching does there? And I've got enough to be getting on with back at base.'

Perkins' rant had calmed him down and he was surprisingly amenable. 'I think we've more than done our bit for the crime squad.' He said. 'They'll get any credit that's going anyway. So, like I said, I'll let Phelan get his ear hole chewed by Senior's missus before I go back with him and John Fry. We'll sort anything iffy we find in that safe. You get off Ash. But I'll need you to do a full report of your part in the search of the house back at the nick before we get on with any of our own work. Ok?'

'Alright Skip.' Said a relieved Ash. 'I'll head back now then.'

'Did you give anyone a lift over here?' asked Perkins.

'No. It was all a bit up in the air first thing.' Ash lied. 'No one could make their minds up, so I came on my own. I think Lewington and the others all came together in one car.'

'Alright then.' Perkins said as he walked towards the Conservatory. 'See you back at the factory.'

'Ok Skip.' Said a relieved Ash.

He couldn't wait to get away from the house and didn't try to see Sue before he left. He knew she could handle herself. He would try and phone her later, but he also wanted to avoid any potential questions from her about the money for now.

Ash also avoided speaking to any of his colleagues about being given the nod to leave in case they asked for a lift back. He left the house and quickly got into his car and drove off. He was debating what to do with the money for now as he knew he wouldn't have time to drive home with the bag.

He didn't want to leave it in his boot in case that led to trouble. He also considered using a locker at the Railway Station in town. But the thought of carrying the heavy sports bag through a busy public area with the added issue of any CCTV cameras did not make that a viable option.

He needed time to think, so chose a road back that eventually led into town by a more meandering route through several local villages and ran along the side of the local golf course. He figured the more rural surroundings would afford more opportunities to hide the bag.

Although still anxious about his next move Ash started to feel less stressed as he approached the stretch of road that ran parallel to the course. He remembered this was where he'd had lessons years before that had been paid for by his Grandfather. But he'd only occasionally been back to play here since.

He thought to himself; 'I'd like to play a bit more golf again. Perhaps I can now?' He smiled.

At that moment his work mobile rang.

He looked at his phone. It was Danny Perkins.

'Bollocks!' Ash said aloud.

He hit the receive button.

'Ash? It's Danny. Sorry, but I need you to come back. We haven't got room in the other motors now for what we need to bring away as John Fry has had to drive that arsehole Phelan back immediately which has left us high and dry. Evidently he was needed at HQ urgently. Anyway, we'll need you to assist here. How far away are you?'

Just for a split second Ash wondered if they were on to him and he felt his stomach turn to ice.

'Umm.. I'm a little way down the road back into town and there's a bit of traffic.' He lied. 'I'll find somewhere to turn around when I can and I'll see you shortly. Ok?'

'Ok. Thanks.' Danny hung up.

'Fuck! Fuck! Fuck!' Ash panicked. 'Where can I leave the bloody bag?' he said aloud to himself.

He pulled into the lay-by opposite the railway line that bordered the golf course to think for a minute.

'Come on Ash!' He said. 'Think!'

Chapter Eleven

Ash knew that he'd only got a few minutes, but his brain wasn't engaged as he stared out of the window. He suddenly snapped out of his inertia and began to consider his options.

He couldn't chance taking the bag back to Senior's house so he had to hide it. The lay-by wasn't secluded enough and there were no nearby ditches. He looked across at the golf course and the only landmark within his eye line was an old green keepers hut in the distance on the far edge of the course which was surrounded by heavy undergrowth.

He retrieved the sports bag from the boot. It weighed more than thirty pounds so it wasn't something that he was keen to lug around too far.

He checked that no cars were in sight before crossing the road and climbing over the stone wall near the old railway line. He thought about leaving the bag by the wall, but there was nowhere dense enough to cover it from plain sight. As he crossed the line he scanned the horizon ahead for any golfers, but there was only an area of practice ground on this part of the course and no one appeared to be about.

Ash could feel the sweat running down his back as he made his way over the large section of rough grass and undergrowth towards the old green keepers' hut, which didn't look like it had seen a coat of paint since the days when he'd had his golf lessons here. Although he had played the course a few times since then, he had never been in this part of it before. There were a few golfers several hundred metres away. But he knew they wouldn't be able to notice him, as they were just specks in the distance.

As he neared the hut he stepped into a large pothole and stumbled and fell forward winding himself as he hit the ground in a sprawl.

'Ooof!' He cried out. Closely followed by, 'Bollocks!'

He quickly picked himself up and surveyed the mud on the knees of his trousers and bits of grass and undergrowth that were now stuck to him.

'Oh Shit! Bollocks!' He said again.

He continued as carefully as he could but he was acutely aware that time was pressing.

When he reached the hut it was unlocked and he briefly considered leaving the bag inside, but decided against that in case one of the staff happened to come by. The old mower and roller next to the hut didn't look like they had been used in years, but he didn't pay much attention to them as he noticed the undergrowth was particularly dense about 25 yards from the back of the hut and he decided that the bag would be completely hidden if he left it there rather than behind the old machinery.

So he paced out twenty five strides from the hut back in the direction he'd just come from. Then as he stood in the thick undergrowth he chose a spot that was very overgrown, but where the ground seemed to form into a hollow. He used the heel of his shoe to dig at the ground and also pulled at clumps of the heavy grass to create even more depth, before placing the bag in the ready-made hole and then pulled the surrounding undergrowth over the bag to cover it.

His heart was racing again and he knew that he had to get a move on, so he took a few paces back and then turned to check that he'd successfully hidden the bag.

When he couldn't immediately see it he initially panicked and quickly walked back. But as he reached the spot he lost his footing and fell over again. This time though he fell against the mound of earth and undergrowth he'd just created and the bulk of the bag hidden underneath struck him squarely between his legs and he went down in a heap.

'Aaargh! Jesus!' He cursed. The awful creeping pain that follows a blow in the nether regions spreading inside him.

'You twat!' He cried, looking down at the state of his trousers.

But he at least felt slightly better knowing that he'd definitely now remember where the bag was as he noted its position in line with the hut.

But to be doubly sure he took out his phone and photographed the scene, taking in the view from where he'd hidden the bag back to the green keepers hut and the machinery next to it. He thought this reference point would be his insurance to locate the bag whenever he was able to return for it later.

Then he ran back the way he'd come. This time he was able to avoid falling over.

He brushed himself down hurriedly as best he could when he reached his car and then drove back to Senior's house as instructed. He tried not to consider anything other than what Danny Perkins had said and prepared himself to act as normally as possible.

Chapter Twelve

'Where the hell have you been and what the fuck happened to you while you was there?'

Danny Perkins followed up his question with a scowl, as he stood hands on hips in the driveway of the Senior's house staring at Ash's dishevelled appearance on his emergence from his car.

Ash had rehearsed a few potential responses on the journey back. He tried number two.

'Don't ask!' He said in as calm a voice as he could muster.

'But I am, Ashley!' Perkins persisted.

'I got caught short and needed to stop for a slash. But when I found a spot that was out of the way enough, I stepped into a pothole and fell over!' Ash hated setting himself up for his colleague's derision, but he felt that he didn't have much choice.

He got the response he expected from those present. Most of whom relished the opportunity to openly laugh at him.

When the laughter had died Perkins said, 'well I hope you didn't piss yourself, because you're taking me back once we've got everything in the cars.'

They took everything they'd catalogued and accounted for out of the house and loaded it all into the boot of both remaining cars.

Ash had seen Sue inside the house and she smiled and winked at him when she knew she couldn't be seen by any of his colleagues.

'Phone me as soon as you can, babe.' She whispered to him. 'I'm very pleased with you.'

He tried to look puzzled in response but couldn't risk a conversation with her there and then. So he nodded to her and carried some of the seized items back outside.

He heard her shout to Danny Perkins, 'Don't forget, lardy. I've got a receipt for everything you've taken and I'll want proof that you're entitled to keep any of it. You'll definitely be hearing from my Lawyer.'

Perkins bit his tongue before replying;

'Mrs Senior, I can assure you that everything we've taken away will be examined and investigated and anything that does not form part of the case against your husband will be returned to you.'

Then, as he left the house and was out of her earshot he said, 'fucking bitch!'

'Yeah, granted Skipper and no argument. But she has got a cracking pair of tits!' Said Lewington.

'Not real ones though, I'll bet.' Perkins replied.

'Real enough.' Ash thought to himself.

He hadn't stopped to consider this before now, but the penny had just dropped that Sue would have been given an inventory of all items removed from the house, which of course would include the amount of cash seized.

But, as his brain was currently full of a myriad of thoughts, he wasn't going to concern himself about that until he spoke to her later.

The rest of the day passed interminably slowly for Ash.

They had returned to the station and booked in everything seized from the house. Then he wrote his report about his part in the search and mentioned the list of items he'd brought down from the upstairs room.

He hadn't counted the money in the sports bag that he'd given up as evidence. But he was told back at the station that it amounted to £260,000.

A further £156,000 had been seized from the floor safe upstairs, in addition to files, bank statements, business account records, investment and share information, a myriad of other documents and also 2 hand guns and ammunition for both.

The horde was completed by the computer equipment, phones and other media devices they had also removed from the rest of the house.

He had no further opportunity to go back for the money until late afternoon, after spending all day involved in tying up his and his colleagues part in the search of Senior's property.

Once he'd finished at the station he sat in his car and prepared to phone Sue Senior on the mobile he'd used earlier.

He pondered on whether her mobile number would be tracked as part of the crime squad operation, but reasoned that Sue wouldn't be of interest to them. Especially now that arrests had been made and potential evidence seized.

But, to be on the safe side, he still changed the sim card before making the call

'Hello.' The female voice was instantly recognisable.

'Hi Sue, it's Ash.' He said.

'You clever boy.' She replied. 'You gorgeous, clever, boy. How did you manage it?'

He wasn't prepared to lay all his cards on the table so early and did not want to have to give up a large chunk of the cash he had only just gained. So he played dumb.

'Manage what, babe? I phoned to tell you that everything has been handed over to crime squad officers and that our team have no further part to play in their operation.'

It's not everything though, love, is it? Sue replied. 'We both know there was a load of money in those bags and as I only put about a hundred grand of it in the safe and the police inventory record shows another two hundred and sixty was accounted for in a sports bag, that leaves a fucking big shortfall. Now you know how much I like you Ashley, but don't think for one minute that you can rip me off, or I'll have to start telling tales about you!'

Ash knew he'd have to play it straight with her, or at least straightish. There was still room for him to keep some of the money for himself, as he was fairly sure she was being truthful about her knowledge of the amount in the bags.

He certainly couldn't afford her finding out later from Ron just how much there had been, as Sue could cause him a lot of problems.

'Whoah! Whoah! Whoah! Calm down, Suze! Don't get your knickers in a knot. You know the only thing I'd rip off you is your clothes, babe. I'm just playing with you. It's been a bitch of a day. But I did manage to get one of the bags out and I'm going to pick it up now.'

'Sorry, babe. But I've not exactly had an easy day of it either.' She replied. 'That's more like it though, darling. Where did you leave it? In a locker somewhere?'

'If only.' Ash said. 'I had absolutely no time to think. I got called back to yours just a few minutes after I'd left. So I had to hide it on the golf course.'

'On the golf course! That was a bit risky. Wasn't it?'

'I had no choice, love! Time was against me and finding anywhere else suitable wasn't possible. I'm just going to retrieve it now. I'll phone you when I've got it. But I'd suggest you meet me somewhere, just in case anyone is watching the house?'

'Yeah, ok then, babe. We can sort that out later. I'll wait to hear from you. Well done though, you clever boy.'

They ended the call and Ash sat in his car feeling exhausted and a bit deflated. He considered how on the one hand he wouldn't now be getting several hundred grand all to himself and would still have to be accountable to someone.

But he also realised that he'd got way ahead of himself, wrapped up in the excitement of seeing all of that money, as he'd never have been able to have kept it all anyway.

He also felt pretty confident that Sue would be generous in splitting a good proportion of the money with him. As well as the fact that he could skim twenty or thirty grand off before admitting to her how much was actually in the bag.

Even if the true total ever did come out he could claim that one or more of the other officers must have pocketed some of it.

Plus, there was the added bonus that Sue would be equally generous in other ways that Ash was already well aware of.

The obvious alternative facts that she could cause him untold grief with Ronnie Senior's associates and in addition shop him to the police for his connection with her husband was the clincher for him to play along with her.

It had still been a good day, as he was going to be a lot better off financially than he'd been the day before.

Ash drove back out towards the golf course, but decided to take a random route, while checking constantly in the rear view mirror to make sure that he wasn't being followed.

Once out of town he drove to the same lay by that he'd parked in earlier. He watched the road for a couple of minutes, but apart from the odd one or two passing vehicles there was no cause for alarm.

He made his way back towards the green keepers hut, again scanning the horizon for any golfers or staff from the course. But as before, the area seemed deserted.

As he approached the hut he felt a sense of unease. He couldn't see how he could be being watched. But he still felt as if something wasn't right.

Then he noticed the pile of scrub where he buried the bag earlier. It looked different, as if someone or something had disturbed the ground and there was no sign of the bag.

His stomach started churning as he walked around in circles, feeling a growing sense of panic. He was sure he was in the right place and remembered the photograph he took earlier. He lined up the view from the photo to where he was currently standing and then looked down at the scruffy undergrowth that had definitely been disturbed.

He struggled to think straight and started kicking at the ground and flailing around, just in case he'd remembered the location incorrectly. But he knew in his heart that he was in the right place and the bag had gone.

He felt sick. Who could've taken it, he mused, as the anger rose inside him.

He pondered over whether one of his colleagues had had the same idea as him and maybe followed him and waited till he'd gone. He was angry, disappointed and worried all at the same time. How would Sue react now, he thought?

He swore and kicked at the ground again and then he noticed the most stupid looking hat that he'd ever seen amongst the undergrowth and scrub near the hole where he'd buried the sports bag.

He wondered if the hat had been there earlier, but he was almost certain that it wasn't. He then wondered how the hell anyone could have wandered by such a remote spot.

He picked up the hat and swore at it.

Then from out of the mists of his memory he recalled seeing it before. Or at least he remembered seeing one very much like it, as it was the object of some ridicule to the group he was playing golf with towards the man wearing it.

Ash scoured his memory and focused on the occasion. Then he recalled it exactly. The Feathers Golf Society Pairs Match Play final about three years before.

This was closely followed by the mental image of the man wearing the hat. It was Rob Gordon.

'Bog.' He said aloud. Then more menacingly, as he tightly screwed the hat up in his hands, over and over. 'Bog!'

Chapter Thirteen

'So Bog, just what ARE we going to do with £645,500 in twenty and fifty pound notes?' Asked Kenny to his mate, who was sitting opposite him on the floor of the Lounge in Kenny's house.

'I can't believe it, Ken.' Rob said. At least the tenth time that either of them had repeated that phrase in the last sixty minutes.

'We didn't mix it up with the other money that Bertie left, did we?' He continued.

'No.' Kenny said, assuredly. 'That's over there on the table.' He pointed across the room. 'You put it there, you dick!'

'Did I?' Rob queried. 'Must've done it on autopilot then.' He smiled a big silly grin.

'I can't believe it.' Rob said again.

'Neither can I, mate.' Kenny beamed back at him.

They had been counting the money for the best part of the last hour and both had repeatedly said things like, 'bloody hell' and 'Jesus! More?' As each bundle of notes was produced out of the bag, they looked at it and each other incredulously, with stupid grins on their faces.

'It must be stolen money though, Ken, surely?' Rob was all at once worried again.

'Yeah, it must be. But if we say nothing and more importantly do nothing for a while, then who is going to know we've got it?' Kenny was trying to reassure himself as much as his mate.

'I want to believe that so much.' Rob replied. 'All the time we were playing earlier, I kept running through how it could've got there and why? Like we've said, it has to be dodgy. But in that case, whoever left it there isn't exactly about to go to the old bill to report it missing, are they? It just might be right place, right time. But we've got to be careful and say nothing to anybody and we've got to put it somewhere out of the way.'

'What? Like on a golf course?' Kenny offered, smiling.

'Nah. You know what I mean.' Said Rob. 'I just can't fathom why they would've hidden it there in the first place though?'

'Ours not to reason why, my son.' Said Kenny, sagely. 'Ours just to spend it wisely, bit by bit.'

'Not for a while though, eh?' Rob stressed. 'And we can't do anything flash to draw attention to our sudden windfall.'

'No, I know we've got to be very careful.' Agreed Kenny. 'But I think we've settled now that we are going to keep it mate, yeah?

Rob nodded as if deep in thought. Then, clapping his hands suddenly he said; 'Right, what are we going to do about the others?'

'I dunno, Bog.' Kenny replied thoughtfully. 'We're mates and all that. But if it was the other way round do you think Bertie, or Dino would be looking to weigh the rest of us in?'

'I dunno? I doubt it, mate?' Rob said from a pained expression. 'But it's an awful lot of money and it could do a lot of good for quite a few people.'

'I know.' Kenny replied. 'But the more people that know, the more likely it'd be that the story would get out and that would only bring trouble with it. Big trouble as well!'

The guys looked at each other pensively. But Rob nodded his assent.

Kenny continued. 'Ok. So if we're agreed that we say nothing and see how it pans out, what are we going to do in a bit then when we meet the others?'

Rob thought for a few seconds before replying; 'Well, I think we should just play along as it was intended to go when the wind up was planned. Remember, none of them knew anything about it and even if Bertie lets them in on it, they'll still be expecting you to have fallen for it, or it would have come out at the course.'

Kenny looked a bit put out. Well actually he looked again as if he had trapped wind, but the cause of his discomforted expression was the same.

'I'll still look like a complete plum though, won't I? And they'll all take the piss.' He said.

'Maybe they will.' Rob smiled at him. 'But at least you'll have the satisfaction of knowing the real situation. Plum or not, you'll still be a rich one!'

'Yeah. You're right of course. I'm just being a dick.' Kenny grinned at his friend. 'I can't believe it, mate.' He said again.

'Me neither, pal. We'll just need to be careful and not get carried away tonight.' Rob said, still smiling.

'Yeah. Watch each other's back and check what we're saying.' Ken replied.

Rob's mobile rang at that moment, as if on cue.

'It's Bertie.' Rob said. 'I'd better answer.'

'Hello, Mr Bassett.' He began, raising his eyebrows to Kenny as he spoke.

'Hello, mate. How did it go?' Bertie replied anxiously. But, before Rob could answer, he continued;

'Did he buy it?'

Rob thought for a second or two then responded;

'Yeah. It all went to plan. He wasn't sure what to make of it at first. Which wasn't helped by me falling over and nearly breaking my bloody neck!'

Bertie guffawed at the other end of the phone.

'That must've been so funny? I wish I'd seen it.' He laughed.

Rob continued; 'Yeah thanks! Anyway after a minute or so's indecision, we just agreed to take the money and decide what to do later. We never mentioned it again, apart from a few raised eyebrows, until after we'd dropped Kev off. But by then Ken was pretty set on us keeping quiet as it must be dodgy money and we both said how we couldn't let the story get out or it would bring trouble back on us. To be honest though mate, I just want to spill the beans as soon as possible tonight.'

'Yeah, fair enough.' Said Bertie. 'But we've got to have a bit of fun with him first though, eh?'

'Yeah, ok. But nothing too bad?' Rob reasoned.

Bertie was keen to get his money's worth though. 'No, nothing too strong. But we want a bit of a laugh out of this. I can pretend that the police have been in the pub asking questions about some stolen money. I'll get Gracie onside and he'll back me up. Then perhaps, you get one of the notes out to buy a round or something? Then I'll prime Gracie up to look at the note and spot that it's dodgy and pretend to want to phone the police. That'll get Ken's bum twitching!'

'Ok.' Rob replied. 'That sounds alright, without going too far. See you in there shortly.' He ended the call.

Rob looked across at Kenny and told him the other half of the conversation.

Kenny took it on the chin regarding what Bertie had said.

Rob smiled at him. 'That should be quite straightforward. If you just play along and act surprised, it'll soon be out of the way.'

'Yeah, that's all very well.' Kenny countered; 'But you can imagine all the snide comments from some of the others when they find out I wasn't going to say anything about the money?'

'But that'll be easy to deflect.' Rob argued. 'You just have to say that you wasn't sure what to do, or say, about finding a lot of money on a golf course and how would they have reacted, or something to that effect. You can also say it was as much my idea as yours to keep it.'

'Yeah, I suppose.' Ken agreed.

'We'll just need to work out how we play it when it comes out though.' Rob said. 'You know? Have our act all worked out?'

'We're normally pretty good at that sort of thing though, Bog.' Kenny said.

The two of them thought it through for a few minutes and outlined a little double act for later.

'Changing the subject back to reality and I'm sorry to bring it up again, Ken,' ventured Rob; 'But what ARE you going to do about Mo? You HAVE to talk to her about that letter you found.'

'I know, mate. We've not been speaking much lately and this problem has obviously not helped things. Mo just seems to have been in denial. Her Mum died of Cancer a few years ago and it wasn't pleasant. I'm sure that's what's caused her to be so secretive about this.'

'Well I know it's none of my business,' Said Rob. 'But, for what it's worth, I'd say that you have to speak to her as soon as possible.'

'Yeah I will, pal.' Said Kenny. 'Thanks, Rob.'

For the second time that day, his mate's use of his name rather than his usual habit of calling him by a nickname struck a chord of emotion in Rob and they looked awkwardly at each other for a moment or two, before giving each other a slightly awkward hug.

It had been an emotional day.

'Right then.' Said Kenny, returning to normal. 'We'd better get a wriggle on and get to the pub. Do you want to borrow a shirt rather than go back to yours to change?'

'Thanks for the offer, mate.' Rob replied. 'But I don't think one of your shirts would fit me too well, do you?' And as an afterthought; 'Besides, I don't look great in orange! But then again, neither do you!'

'Bollocks!' Came the predictable reply.

Chapter Fourteen

Ash had been driving around aimlessly for the best part of an hour. His head was spinning from all that had happened during the day.

He'd phoned Sue Senior to tell her about the money being missing. Although she'd gone ballistic and didn't believe him initially, she had at least calmed down and responded more positively when he said that he thought he knew who might have found it.

He'd told her that he would try to find out more that evening and get back to her.

'Make sure you do.' Sue had said before ending the call.

Not long afterwards Sue made a call herself.

'Yeah, that's right. Ash said that the money wasn't there when he went back for it. I'm not sure if he's lying or not, but he did sound really stressed and pissed off and he also said he thinks he knows who might have found it. He said he's got to tread carefully though.'

She ended the call with; 'Alright darling. We'll see what he says next before deciding. I'll be in touch when I know more.'

Ash pulled up outside his house just before six o'clock.

He was surprised to see Dean Willis turning to leave outside his front door and Ash's partner Kirstie waving to Dean as he walked up their garden path.

Ash got out of his car as Dean reached the front gate.

'Alright, Dino?' Said Ash. 'Were you looking for me?'

Dino turned to Ash. 'No, mate. Kirstie phoned about me putting up some lights for you. I'm coming back first thing Monday, before I go to another job I'm on all next week.'

Ash was initially angry but tried to hide his surprise. 'Oh yeah, she's been on at me to put them up for ages. Just haven't got round to it.'

'Oh right. I would've done them for you in the morning, only I'm away all day tomorrow with some of the guys from the pub.' Dino winced inwardly as he said it.

'Are you?' Said Ash. 'What's that in aid of?'

Instantly regretful and trying to backtrack, Dino replied; 'We only arranged it the other day. A lot of the lads other halves are away this weekend, so we thought we'd do something too.'

Ash again did his best to hide his discomfort at not knowing this bit of local news, as he liked to think he was at the centre of all local events.

'I've been a bit busy the last week or so and haven't been in the pub. Who's going?'

Dino wasn't best pleased at having put himself on the spot as Ash wasn't the most popular bloke locally.

He hedged for a second or two before replying; ...'erm, just the usual suspects. Bog, Kenny Bradley, Speedo, Bertie Bassett, Starfish. You know the crowd. And I think Gracie's coming as well.'

'Sounds like a laugh.' Said Ash. 'Where are you going?'

On the defensive now Dino mewed; 'Only to Cleethorpes. It won't be too involved. Just a bit of fun...maybe?'

'It's a good crowd though.' Ash enthused. 'What are you doing? Going by coach or something?'

'Yeah.' Dino half heartedly replied, knowing what was coming next.

'I'm off this weekend.' Said Ash. 'Are all the seats taken? It sounds like a bit of a laugh and I'm sure I could swing it with her indoors.'

'I'm not sure about the coach size, Ash.' Dino lied. 'Gracie booked it through his mate who did the coach when we went to Newmarket last year. I don't think it's a full size one.'

'Oh right. Well, I'll be in the pub in a minute anyway, so I'll ask Gracie and see if I can squeeze in. As long as that's alright with everyone?'

Dino's heart sank. More than a bit miffed with himself and backed into a corner he replied; 'Yeah of course. If there's room it'll be fine.' He lied again.

'Are you going to The Feather's now, Dino?' Asked Ash cheerily.

'Eh no. I'm nipping home to change. I played nine holes up the road straight from work, so I want to freshen up before I go to the pub.'

'Oh. Alright, mate. No doubt I'll see you in there a bit later and I'll buy you a beer. Thanks for the heads up about tomorrow.' Ash smiled at him.

'Yeah right.' Climbing into his van and feeling like he'd just been subjected to a Police investigation, Dino said; 'Bollocks' under his breath as he closed the door.

Ash went in the house and saw Kirstie in the Kitchen.

'Hi.' He said. 'I just saw Dean Willis leaving. What did he want?'

She looked at him and rolled her eyes. 'I saw you talking to him, Ash. So I presume he's already told you that he's going to put the lights up that I bought weeks ago. I phoned him earlier because I couldn't stand waiting any longer for you not to do it.'

She waited for a second and then continued;

'What? Did you think our stories wouldn't match or something? Did you think he was my fancy man? Actually, I wouldn't mind if he was, for all the interest you show in me.'

'Oh don't start all that crap again, for god's sake!' Ash exclaimed. 'I've had a bitch of a bloody day and then I have to come home to a nagging.'

'Makes a bloody change for you to come home at all lately.'

'What are you on?' He replied. 'Get the vodka out early tonight, did we? Well you'll be pleased to know that I'm going to the pub because I need a drink.'

'Oh great!' Kirstie replied. 'What if I want to come too?'

'You know where it is, love. I'm sure you're more than capable of finding your own way once you've put on four ton of make-up and a bottle of fake tan!'

'Bastard!' She shouted.

'Oh yeah.' Said Ash over his shoulder as he walked to the front door; 'I forgot to mention that your new boyfriend Dino has invited me to a day out with the boys from the pub tomorrow. I would've stayed in and put those lights up. But as you've got that covered now...' He slammed the door as he heard Kirstie shout;

'Wanker!'

As she calmed down she consoled herself that enough had been said between her and Dino lately for her to have something to look forward to on Monday morning and hopefully beyond then if all went well. The curtain had fallen on her and Ashley Richardson some time ago and it was high time she told him to leave. She would pick her moment and have the last laugh on him.

Chapter Fifteen

Ash walked into the bar at The Feathers, which was fairly full of early evening drinkers and diners.

The Landlord, known universally as Gracie, was at the far end of the bar engaged in serving as well as bantering with several of his customers.

It randomly occurred to Ash that, after all the years he had been using The Feathers, neither he, nor, as far as he was aware, any of the other people he knew who frequented it, actually used Gracie's real first name. He was just known as Gracie by everybody, after the old time singer Gracie Fields with whom he shared the same surname.

'Why on earth am I thinking that?' Ash thought to himself. He was acutely aware that he had far more pressing concerns at that moment. But, with that in mind, he needed to speak to Gracie about tomorrow's planned trip.

He squeezed by a few people around the bar as he made his way towards the far end to engage with him. Ash nodded and smiled to one or two familiar faces as he passed by.

'Evening, Mr Fields.' Ash smiled as Gracie turned towards him.

Gracie smiled back at him and said half jokingly; Mr Fields? Is this an official visit then, Ashley?'

'No, of course not, mate.' Ash rankled at the use of his full Christian name, but took it on the chin. 'I was just being respectful. You alright then...Gracie?'

'Yeah, I'm alright, thanks. Living the dream.' He smirked at having put Ash on the back foot, as he wasn't one of his favourite people.

'What can I get you? A Campari, is it?'

'Maybe later.' Ash played along. He perused the list of house Bitters on a chalk board behind the bar. 'But for now I'll try a pint of Sheep Dip, please.'

Ash wasn't really a Bitter drinker. But he wanted to integrate with the regular crowd tonight. The beer he'd chosen was the strongest on the list, which appealed to his sense of machismo.

'Have you drunk it before, Ash?' Said Gracie. 'We only got a barrel of it in on a sale and return as a try out. But it's a bit too rich for my blood.'

'No, I haven't. But I like strong beer.' Ash lied.

'Fair enough.' Gracie said. 'I was just going to say, did you want to try a taster, before I pull you a pint of it?'

Ash bridled at the thought that it might be too strong for him.

'Thanks Gracie. But I'll take my chances. I'm sure it'll be fine.'

Gracie pulled a pint of a dark treacle coloured beer and put it on the bar.

'Anything else, mate?'

'I might have some bar food in a bit.' Ash said. 'But that's it for now. Do you want one?'

'Bit early for me yet, thanks.' Gracie smiled. 'That's £3.90 then.'

Ash handed over his money and took his first sip. It was very bitter and very strong and he hated it. But he kept a straight face.

'Not bad. Not bad at all that.' He said, a little too enthusiastically.

Gracie was a generous man and even though he wasn't that keen on Ash, he gave him an opportunity to save face.

'It's a bit of an acquired taste, I think. Are you sure you don't want to change it for something else?'

Ash couldn't bring himself to admit that he hated the strong tasting beer.

'No, I really like it.' He lied again.

Gracie smiled to himself. 'Muppet!' He said under his breath as he turned to serve another customer.

Ash stood at the bar with his pint, trying to force it down. He looked around, but none of the Friday night crowd that Rob Gordon hung around with was in yet.

He fell into conversation with a few of the early evening crowd who were friends of his Dad's and he nodded and smiled in the right places. But at least half of his brain was focused on how he could get the money back without dropping himself into all sorts of trouble.

He reasoned that if Rob had the money, he'd either have handed it in by now, or have hidden it somewhere else. The most likely place being at home.

Ash's dilemma was how he could find out more when there was no way he could be seen to know anything about the money. He thought about inventing a story about the police looking for money that had been hidden somewhere locally by a gang they now had in custody. But that could leave him...

'Are you having one then, Ash, or what?'

His thoughts were brought back to reality as Charlie Stock, one of the crowd he'd been supposedly speaking to, stood in front of him waving an empty glass.

'Earth to Ashley.' Smiled Charlie.

'Ser...ssorry, Charlie.' Said Ash. 'Miles away, mate.'

'What's that you're drinking? I'll get you another.' Charlie persisted.

Ash recovered; 'No, let me get you guys one, Charlie.'

'No! It's my round.' Charlie insisted. 'What'll you have?'

'He's on Sheep Dip.' Gracie offered mischievously from behind the bar.

'Just a half then, please.' Said Ash, defensively.

'Nonsense!' Charlie laughed. 'Us old timers might be going shortly, but you've only just come in. Pint of Sheep Dip for Ash then please, Gracie. And one for yourself.'

'Thanks Charlie.' Gracie smiled at the old man. 'Just a half of Old D though. It's going to be a long night for me. And a long day tomorrow too.'

He pulled Ash's pint and put it on the bar in front of him.

'Enjoy, Ashley!' He smiled. 'Glad you like it.'

'Cheers, Charlie.' Said Ash, weakly. He downed the remains of his first pint and raised the full one towards Charlie and the others in his company.

'About tomorrow, Gracie.' Ash said. 'Dean Willis mentioned to me about the planned day out just before I came in. He said you might still have some space left on the coach?'

Gracie dithered on purpose. 'I'm not exactly sure on numbers, pal. The boys haven't confirmed how many are going yet. But they'll be here in a bit and we'll know then.'

'Fair enough.' Ash said.

He was under no illusions about his popularity. But he'd shared some laughs with most of the guys in the past and although he hadn't been one of the crowd for some time, he figured he could make a show of fitting in for a day if it got him some time to find out more about the money.

He continued; 'It'll be a laugh though, no doubt.'

'Yeah. Very likely given that lot.' Gracie said, as he turned to serve people at the far end of the bar.

Chapter Sixteen

By seven o'clock Ash was beginning to feel the effects of his third pint. Gracie had insisted on buying a round for Charlie and the other old boys before they went home and he'd included one for Ash out of mischief, which he told him he'd put in for him, as Ash still had most of his second pint to drink at that point.

When Charlie and his mates eventually headed off, Ash ordered himself a bar meal to combat the effects of the beer. By the time he'd finished his burger and chips he was back on a more even keel.

He'd mulled over what he should and shouldn't do several times and spun it around in his head, until he couldn't think straight.

He considered if he'd be better staying at home tomorrow and maybe trying to find a way of breaking into Rob Gordon's house to search for the money, as he'd surmised from what Dean Willis had said earlier that Rob's wife was probably away for the weekend. But Ash figured that Rob might well have hidden some, or all of it elsewhere, if he hadn't already handed the money in.

The possibilities outweighed him, so he settled again on trying to spend time around Rob and the others to see if anything became obvious. He couldn't afford any slip ups.

He made sure he was served next by one of the barmaids and ordered a bottle of Lager. He didn't want to give Gracie the satisfaction of knowing he'd had enough of the strong ale.

A short while afterwards, Alan 'Bertie' Bassett and Dean Willis walked in and were closely followed by a couple of the others who drank in the crowd with Rob and Kenny. They were all full of smiles.

'Gracie!' They echoed.

'Boys!' Acknowledged Gracie. 'Have you had a good day?'

A few laughs emerged from the other end of the bar as Bertie mentioned some of the events from earlier on.

Ash moved towards them to say hello as he heard him say, 'Bog fell over in the rough after he'd hit his ball miles left from the first tee. I wish I'd seen it! He did look surprised though when he caught up with us. Kenny was with him, so you can imagine the stick he must've given him. You know what those two are like!'

Ash took their collective good mood as his cue to join them.

'Hello, chaps.' He said, smiling.

'Ash.' Bertie replied, looking round. 'How you doing?'

'I'm alright thanks, Bertie.' Ash grinned. 'Sounds like you guys had a laugh earlier?'

Ash saw that Scott Flintoff and Kevin 'Speedo' Morris were amongst the group with Bertie and Dino.

'Hello Starfish.' Ash said to Scott.

Scott raised his eyes at the greeting, as the chuckles started around him.

'I'm still trying to live that down, thanks, Ash.' Scott said, looking more than a little embarrassed.

The others giggled.

'Never mind mate.' Ash said. 'We've all had our moments.'

'Oh yeah!' Speedo exclaimed. 'I'd forgotten all about that.'

'Hello, Kev.' Said Ash. 'On the ball as ever I see?'

Scott had been christened by his so called mates as 'Starfish,' ever since a night when he was very much the worse for wear after a day spent celebrating a win on the horses and had been found being profoundly ill in the toilets at The Feathers.

That alone was embarrassing enough for him as he'd neglected to lock the door of the cubicle. But it had been compounded by the fact that he'd presumably decided to be ill when he was already halfway through what must have been his original intention for visiting the loo, as his trousers and underpants were around his ankles and the first view his rescuing 'mates' saw of him was his bare backside perched above the toilet, while his head was very much inside the pan.

Dean Willis had dubbed him 'Starfish' on the spot, based on the unflattering image of his rear end. The full story, plus the new nickname, had soon spread amongst the pub's regulars.

Scott had had to re-live that moment many times since then whenever he bumped into people he hadn't seen for a while, or when one of his mates just felt like reminding him of his embarrassing experience. Tonight being no exception.

Ash and the others laughed at the memory, to Scott's great discomfort.

But Speedo had a perplexed look.

Eventually he said to Scott, 'I remember Dino calling you ''Starfish'' and everyone laughing once we'd revived you a bit. But I still don't get why he called you that? I thought you looked more like a Praying Mantis, myself?'

After a moment's reflection this was a cue for more laughter, although this time even Scott joined in.

'What?' Speedo enquired.

Chapter Seventeen

More of the guys appeared over the next half an hour. Some of them had already begun their evening's festivities in one or two of the other local hostelries and the overall mood was one of impending fun.

Kenny and Rob came in together just before eight.

'Evening, Ladies.' Rob smiled to the welcoming throng.

'Evening, Mr Gordon. Evening, Mr Bradley.' Gracie beamed at them from behind the bar.

'Good Evening to you, Mr Fields.' Rob smiled back.

'Indeed! Always a pleasure, Mr Fields.' Echoed Kenny.

'Not so sure about some of your customers, though.' He continued, looking at his mates.

'Hello, Bog.' Said Ash, smiling warmly at Rob.

'Ash.' Rob replied with a nod.

Ash nodded to Kenny. 'Mr Bradley. How the devil are you?'

'I'm very well thank you, Ashley. Living the dream.' Kenny replied, knowing how Ash disliked being called Ashley.

'I can see that, Ken.' Ash responded. 'Good living, eh?' He patted Kenny's belly.

'At least I haven't grown through my hair though, eh, Ash?' Kenny responded and patted Ash's thinning forehead.

'Ouch! Touché,' I'd say Ashley.' Gracie offered from behind the bar.

Despite his initial annoyance at being bested, Ash grinned broadly at Kenny.

'I've just got 'em in, so what can I get you boys?' Ash said to Rob and Kenny.

'Cheers Ash. I'll have a pint of Old D.' Said Rob.

'Me too please, Ashley.' Kenny responded. 'Cheers.'

'Two pints of Old D coming up.' Said Gracie. And then to Ash; 'You've forgotten to get yourself one, mate. Are you still on Sheep Dip?'

'Erm, no Gracie.' Ash blustered. 'I've only just eaten and I'm a bit full for now. I'll just have a bottled lager, please.'

Gracie smiled as he turned to get two glasses.

Once the drinks were served, Ash wasted no time.

'Bog. I understand from Dino that you've got a bit of a trip planned tomorrow. I was just wondering if there's any chance of a seat going spare for me to tag along? Unless you're fully booked, of course.'

Dino was in Rob's eye line over Ash's shoulder and from behind Ash he raised his eyes and mouthed to Rob; 'Sorry mate.'

Rob started to respond, but Kenny was straight out of the blocks.

'What's all this? A trip tomorrow? How come I didn't know anything about it?'

Ash raised his eyebrows and was unusually humble; 'Oh shit! Sorry. Have I just ruined a surprise or something?'

Rob continued with a slight pause; 'No...It's ok. Just a bit of a change, Ken. We thought after all your nagging about us doing something this weekend that we'd pretend not to be interested. But we've organised a coach in the morning to take us on the piss for the day.'

'Well, bugger me!' Ken smiled. 'I take it I am invited?'

Rob was quite impressed with his mate's acting.

'Of course you are, mate. The whole gang is coming.' He responded. Then nodding to Ash. 'I think we can manage to squeeze you in as well. As long as you pay Gracie your bus fare.'

'Excellent!' Ash beamed. 'Be good to catch up with everyone again. First time for ages.'

'Yeah. Should be a good day.' Rob echoed, albeit less enthusiastically.

'Where are we going then?' Said Kenny.

'Sunny Cleethorpes!' Several of them responded in unison.

As the noise levels increased with the gathering throng of people, Bertie pulled Rob to one side for a minute.

'D'you think we should hold off saying anything about the money for now, being as knobhead's latched onto us?' He said, gesturing with his head towards Ash at the bar.

Rob thought for a few seconds. 'No. It should be alright. We haven't done anything wrong have we?'

'No, I know. But I just thought he might get a bit sniffy and want to know where it came from and that. He just makes me nervous.' Bertie frowned.

'I know, mate.' Rob agreed. 'I wouldn't trust him as far as I could throw him either. But like I said, we've done nothing wrong.'

He heard himself saying the words, but he also felt uneasy at the close proximity of a policeman. Especially one with an iffy reputation like Ash. And obviously for completely different reasons than his friend.

Rob looked across at Kenny and raised his eyebrows towards Ash. He knew that Kenny hated him more than anyone.

Kenny smiled back though and mouthed; 'Fuck him!'

Rob smiled and felt better.

Chapter Eighteen

As the night progressed alcohol became a useful leveller in regard to Kenny and Rob's mood. Bertie had done as he'd mentioned earlier and roped Gracie into the wind-up planned for Kenny.

When Rob was about to buy a round, Gracie feigned a conversation with Bertie and Dino about the police being in the pub earlier.

The guys were all draped around the bar and most were within earshot.

Ash showed interest straightaway.

'Yeah, that's right, Bertie. They came in about half five about some stolen money they were looking for. They said there'd been a robbery earlier and some money had gone missing. About a hundred grand, I think they said.'

Kenny's mind was in overdrive, as he knew this was part of the wind up he was supposed to know nothing about. But the close relationship it had to the real situation that he and Rob were in was surreal and it was hard not to blur the lines.

But to his credit he acted his part well and showed faux nervousness, even though in reality it was driven by genuine anxiety about the real money.

'A hundred grand eh? Blimey! Nice pay day for somebody.' Kenny even added a little nervous laugh.

Rob was very impressed.

Ash however went into overdrive.

'Who was it, Gracie? Plain clothes officers? Detectives?'

'No it was uniformed coppers.' Gracie embellished. He was keen to get his part over with and could do without the added element of a real life copper who obviously wasn't in on the wind up.

'What did they say about the robbery?' Ash probed.

'Just that they were looking for some stolen money from a robbery, like I just said.' Gracie repeated.

Then, remembering another bit of the detail that Bertie had given him to say, he added;

'They said it was all in £50 notes. And they said it was a hundred grand.'

Ash's mind was in a whirl. But he kept his composure outwardly. What if he'd been seen earlier? But if that was the case, he'd have been arrested hours ago? Perhaps someone had seen him and only just reported it and the enquiry was at an early stage? But why were they so specific about it being a hundred grand in £50 notes? He'd got loads more than that in the bag? Had Rob Gordon kept all but a hundred grand and then put in a call to the police? He was brought back to earth by what happened next.

Rob couldn't wait any longer to get his bit out of the way as this was all too close to reality for him and he was struggling to keep it together.

He remembered back to when he'd tried to plan a surprise party for his Wife Sally's fortieth birthday and the panic it had caused him leading up to it with all the white lies he had to tell her beforehand. That had been bad enough, but this was ten times worse and he just wanted to get the big reveal out of the way, so that he and Ken could get back to keeping their far bigger secret under wraps.

He took a £50 note from his wallet.

'Never mind all of that, Gracie.' He managed to say without stammering.

'I'm dying of thirst here, mate,' He smiled at the Landlord. 'Let's get 'em in again, eh?'

Kenny gave him a pantomime stare as if to say; 'What are you doing?'

It was very well done.

Gracie started pulling pints, but Ash looked suspiciously at Rob's £50 note.

Something wasn't quite right here, Ash reasoned. He also caught the faint traces of smiles on Bertie's and one or two other faces around the bar.

'One yourself too, Gracie.' Rob smiled thinly.

'Thanks, Bog.' Gracie beamed. 'Call it £35 mate.'

Rob handed over the £50 note and Kenny felt the need to give a little cringe. But this wasn't picked up by anyone.

Only Bertie, Gracie, Rob and Kenny knew the full details of the wind up at this point, but most of the other guys, excluding Ash, had been primed for a bit of a wind up at Kenny's expense and Bertie had given a little more detail to a couple of them when he'd primed Gracie for his supporting role, prior to Kenny and Rob coming in.

Gracie theatrically held the note up to the light. 'Hope you don't mind, mate?' He said to Rob. 'But under the circumstances there might be one or two dodgy £50 notes in circulation locally given what the cops were saying earlier.'

As he examined the note, Ash looked around and was pretty sure now that this was staged. But this just made him more confused and more than a bit edgy. He felt his temper rising and fought hard not to lose it.

He heard himself blurt out; 'Why? Did the officers say the money was dodgy then?'

Gracie embellished again; 'Not necessarily. But you never know. Hang on a minute.' Gracie exclaimed. 'This note is dodgy. It's got no watermark or thread through it. Where did you get it, Bog?'

Kenny answered for him; 'It was at the cash point on the way back from the golf course, wasn't it, Bog? You asked me to stop in the village because you needed some cash, didn't you?'

Rob decided enough was enough and went into the reveal that he and Kenny had discussed earlier.

'No, Ken. This is one of the £50 notes that you gave me for my Driver after we got back from the golf. He bought my driver off me.' Rob explained to the gathered little crowd.

Kenny acted it as best he could.

'Was it?' He said in partial surprise. 'Then I must've got a dodgy note from the cash point when I went earlier.'

'Have you got any others, Ken?' Asked Bertie. 'Just how much did you get out of the cash point?'

Seeing Kenny's pained expression, Bertie decided to let him off lightly.

'Was it a hundred grand in £50 notes?'

'You bastards!' Kenny said in mock desperation. 'You all knew all along. Didn't you?'

Ash was now completely dumbstruck. What the hell was going on here?

'I wanted to hand it in.' Kenny whined. He was actually enjoying his bit of Amateur Dramatics now. 'It was Bog's idea to keep it!'

As the laughter started and echoed amongst the rest of the guys, Ash looked at Rob and said; 'What the fuck is going on here?'

The reveal was explained in full by Bertie, who was quite proud of his little scam.

Kenny took a bit of ribbing from his mates. But he was easily able to turn it round by saying; 'Well, what would you have done, if you suddenly found a hundred grand on a golf course? I was actually a bit scared!'

That last bit of course was very true. He still was. But somehow this had helped settle his nerves a little and he felt a bit better

Rob explained his part in it to Ash and the others in as brief an account as possible. But Bertie had been more than ready to provide full details.

Ash felt calmer initially. But he still couldn't rationalise where the real money was.

However, with Bertie's subsequent description of where he'd left the fake money and the mention of the old mower and the green keeper's shed, it was obvious now to Ash that

Bertie, Rob and Kenny had, by a remarkable coincidence, all been in the very same area where he'd buried the sports bag in the undergrowth earlier on.

Knowing them as he did, Ash was sure that Bertie's only part in this had been in hiding the fake money. He doubted Bertie's ability to have been capable of finding the bag he'd left and say nothing. He reasoned that had Bertie found it, he would've handed it in and would also have told the world and its wife about it.

However, he thought Rob Gordon and Kenny Bradley could well be capable of something else.

Ash now felt sure that between them they had taken the money he'd hidden and he determined that he would have it back whatever it took.

Ash smiled at Rob. 'Nice one, Bog. Well played out.'

But something in his smile gave away a more sinister meaning to Rob.

Rob smiled thinly back at Ash, but his insides felt cold and he could feel his heart hammering in his chest. He had one clear thought in his mind;

'He knows.'

Chapter Nineteen

'I don't know how he knows, Ken. But I'm telling you, he knows.'

Rob and Kenny were in the Gents toilet a few minutes later, after Rob's urgent insistence that Kenny joined him.

Kenny repeated the comment he'd only just made;

'How can he possibly know?'

'I could see it in his eyes, mate.' Rob whispered. 'It was like he could see what I was thinking.'

'Well he must have bloody good eyesight then.'

Kenny was still a little light headed from getting the reveal about the fake cash out of the way.

'Look, Bog.' He continued; 'We are still sitting pretty. We don't know for sure that Ash is on to us. And even if he is, how can he know without having had something to do with the money being there in the first place?'

'I dunno!' Rob whispered loudly. 'But the fact that I think he knows is more than enough to be taking in right now, as far as I'm concerned.'

Ken surprised Rob with his calmness.

'Look, mate.' He reasoned; 'If Ash thinks he knows about us having the real money, then he must also be a part of it being there in the first place, like I said just now when I was talking and you obviously wasn't listening! And if so, that means he must be mixed up in something iffy. He can't prove anything and he can't say anything. Not without giving himself away! So we just have to play it straight and say nothing more about it. The money's safe where we've left it for now, so just play dumb. Which shouldn't be too hard for you?'

Rob ignored the insult.

'Do you really think that we've left the money in the best place, Ken? I can't help thinking we should've put it somewhere more out of the way.'

Kenny raised his eyebrows and replied;

'It's hidden in plain sight, pal. Well, plain sight if you happen to be in my back garden, anyway. And I thought we'd agreed on that?'

'Yeah, I know we did.' Rob whispered more quietly this time. 'But I'm just worried now that I'm sure that bastard knows somehow that we've got it.'

'Maybe. But he doesn't know for sure what's happened, does he?' His mate countered.

'Well he's hardly going to forget about it, is he?' Rob whined.

Again Kenny's response was calm.

'No, he's not. But he's not about to go and get a search warrant, is he? And in the mean time, it buys us more time to think about what we're going to do.'

He continued; 'Granted, it isn't as straightforward as we'd have liked. But as long as we keep an eye on him, then, for now we don't have to do anything........But for Christ's sake, let's go back to the bar, or they're all going to think we're up to something else!'

Rob at least now felt a little less anxious.

Chapter Twenty

The rest of the evening played out much like many other Friday nights spent in The Feathers.

Most of the talk amongst the group centred on tomorrow's trip and also on reminiscences of previous outings that they had shared over the last few years. And as the beer continued to flow, so did the inevitable mickey taking.

'So talk us through your plans for spending that hundred grand again, Ken.' Bertie teased.

'Bollocks, Bertie bloody Bassett!' Kenny predictably replied. 'I told you, it was a complete panic. Bog was in on it and even he sounded nervous, and he's not that good an actor. So it was for real alright!'

'Alright. Keep your knickers on!' Laughed Bertie. 'I just wish I'd seen your face, that's all!'

'What ARE you going to spend it on though, Ken?' Enquired Kevin 'Speedo' Morris. '

The guys all looked at him with a mixture of disgust and pity.

'You complete Dufus!' Kenny finally replied.

'Well I only asked.' Speedo said, with a slightly hurt look on his face.

'Moving swiftly on...' Bertie interjected, 'What time are we kicking off tomorrow?'

'About half nineish.' Rob replied; 'Or at least that's the time I told Gracie to tell his mate to be in the car park with his coach.'

Gracie nodded from behind the bar.

'That'll be about right though.' Bertie replied; 'Even if we get away a bit after then, we should still be in Cleethorpes by just after eleven. Then we can get straight on it!'

'Indeed. That is the plan mate!' Rob smiled.

'And Ken'll be pissed about half an hour later!' Dino boomed to anyone within earshot.

'Ha, ha, ha.' Said Kenny, ironically. 'I nearly broke a rib then pal! You're so funny.'

Dino smirked at him.

Gracie leaned over the bar smiling;

'Boys, I bunged an extra couple of quid on the asking price just to cover my costs, but I'll lay on some coffee and bacon sarnies in the morning to set us all up. So best that everyone's here by nine.'

'Nice one, Gracie!' They all echoed.

'Also, best we all settle up now.' Rob said; 'We don't want any unpaid debts, do we, Starfish?'

Scott Flintoff raised his eyebrows.

'Bloody hell, Bog! That was all a complete misunderstanding last time.' He whined.

'I thought Dino had paid for me. I told you!'

'Yeah whatever, pal.' Bertie intervened; 'But like Bog said, we don't want any unpaid debts...or misunderstandings....or trying to get money out of people tomorrow night when'....He paused to look directly at his selected targets.... 'people might be puking up in an alley, or sticking their head down some pub boghole with their arse in the air!'

Kenny and Scott, the two main targets looked sheepishly at each other, amidst the laughter and general ridicule at their past misdemeanours.

'I paid earlier!' Ken said.

Ash felt the need to have a dig at Kenny too.

'What, with some of your funny money, Ken?'

Although Kenny was a major culprit for winding up others, he was never particularly good at being on the receiving end, even with people he liked. But taking abuse from Ash was more than he could bear.

He felt the anger rise inside him and though he knew he should just smile and let it go, he couldn't quite manage to stop himself.

'Well I guess you'd know all about funny money, Ashley. Wouldn't you?'

Ash's own anger and frustration at how the day's events had played out boiled over.

'What the fuck is that supposed to mean, fat boy?'

Ken reared up. 'I'll tell you wh...'

'Whoa! Whoa! Whoa!' Gracie loudly interrupted; 'Now now boys. Let's keep it civil!'

He gave Kenny a look. But Kenny was already biting his tongue and staring at the look of horror that Rob was fixing him with.

Gracie continued to Ash;

'Ashley! I'm surprised at you. An officer of the law!'

Ash looked at Gracie's smiling countenance and immediately went back to his normal smarmy persona.

'Sorry, Gracie. Just a bit of banter.' He smiled at Kenny; 'That's all it was, Ken. Wasn't it?'

Ken again looked sheepish. 'Yes...that's right. Sorry, Gracie.'

Gracie smiled; 'No harm done, boys. Another drink anyone?'

Ash smiled thinly at Kenny.

Kenny smiled back and then looked back at Rob who mouthed to him;

'You twat!'

Chapter Twenty-One

The party broke up about twelve as most of the guys decided to call it a night and Gracie pointed out to those that hadn't had enough, that he most certainly had and that they had a big day in front of them tomorrow.

'Apart from anything else, Starfish...' He said to a now visibly swaying Scott;

'I don't want to be fishing you out of my bog and trying to dress you again. I'm still trying to rid myself of the image of your bumhole sticking up in the air, from last time!'

There was a chorus of guffaws from those surrounding Scott.

'Tell you sssomething though...' Slurred Scott. 'I didn't half feel rough that night and it wasn't all down to drink either. My arsh the next morning....ooow!'

'Yeah alright, Scotty.' Bertie interrupted. 'Too much information, old son!'

Scott looked at his mates and nodded.

'It was bad though. I sshaw it in the mirror. It looked jusht like a Japanese flag!'

There was a general chorus of disapproval, accompanied by a collection of goodnight wishes as they left the pub one by one.

As Kenny and Rob crossed the car park, Ash called from behind them;

'Bog! Thanks again for letting me tag along tomorrow, mate. It'll be a good laugh.'

They turned as Ash caught them up.

'That's ok. There's enough room, so the more the merrier!' Rob replied, as convincingly as he could.

'Sorry about earlier, Ken.' Ash smiled. 'I didn't mean anything...I was just having a laugh with you.'

Kenny had more than recovered his self discipline now despite the intake of several beers. Although he hadn't quite mastered full control of his voice.

'Ner need to shay shorry, Ashh. Fault wash all mine. Let'sh furgetit. Like you shaid, we'll all have a laugh tomorrow, eh?'

'Err..today, actually.' Rob said, looking at his watch.

'I'm off home to bed.' He continued.

'Don't fancy a nightcap, either of you?' Enquired Ash hopefully.

'Nah. I think we'll be having more than enough tomorrow, without starting the day feeling rough.' Rob said and continued; .....'Besides we've got to give lightweight here a fighting chance of making it through the day without embarrassing himself too much!'

He laughed and threw his arm around Kenny and led him away.

Kenny just smiled an ironic smile.

'Yeah I s'pose so, mate.' Ash conceded. 'Good call. See you about nine for round two. Night!'

He smiled and wandered off in the opposite direction towards home.

'Yeah, night!' They chorused not quite together.

'I fink we justh about carried that off alright.' Kenny offered when they were out of earshot.

'Carried it off? What? With you saying about him knowing all about funny money? You are a dick sometimes!' Rob glared at him.

'I know, I know,' Kenny admitted. 'But he justh getsh under my shkin sho much!'

'Why DO you hate him so much, Ken? I know he's flash and a bit smarmy. But he really does get to you, mate. Doesn't he?'

Kenny nodded and shrugged more or less at the same time. Which somewhat affected his balance and caused him to stumble forward.

As Rob steadied him, Kenny smiled wryly at his mate. He suddenly felt the full effects of the evenings' drinking.

'Shorry pal. I know I've been a bit of a dick. We....we... we just have history, I shuppose.' He looked at Rob a bit watery eyed.

Before Rob could answer Kenny continued;

'He'sh just sho fucking flash! Eshpeshially round women. And he'sh been more than a bit over familiar with Mo before.' And then almost to himself as he looked into the distance, 'I think she fanshies him.'

Rob felt uncomfortable at this revelation. As he often did in such circumstances. But for once he spoke with clarity and understanding;

'Look mate. You've got a lot on your mind at the moment. Try not to get too far ahead of yourself. There's no way your missus fancies that twat any more than Sally does. I've heard them taking the piss out of him at the way he is around all the girls. And let's face it, when all's said and done our wives are ten times more sensible than we are about things, aren't they?'

Kenny came back from his thoughts with a smile.

'Well I wouldn't go that far! Haha...Yeah! Coursh they are. I'm being shtupid. Thanksh, Bog. You're a good mate.'

They both laughed and exchanged a brief hug before setting off toward home.

'But we can't afford for that to happen again, mate.' Rob said pointedly. 'You have to keep it together tomorrow!'

Then he quickly added, more to himself; 'We'll both have to keep it together tomorrow.'

'What can I shay, pal?' Ken replied. 'You're right. Coursh you're right!'

After a few more wobbly paces he continued. 'But we will! Itsh far too important not to!'

When they reached Kenny's house Rob again repeated what he'd said to Ken earlier.

'Do you think the money will be safe where it is?'

'I honeshtly can't think of anywhere better for now, mate.' Kenny replied.

He continued; 'I mean...even... God forbid, if shum..one broke in, they aren't likely to be shearching round in my composht heap. Sssspchially given all the crap on top of it!'

Rob nodded. 'Ok. Maybe there is nowhere better for now. But we'll have to move it soon, because Ash and for all we know anyone else he's involved with, are not just going to forget about it. So we should put it somewhere further away from us as soon as we can.'

Kenny nodded his agreement but couldn't help adding as a smiling afterthought; 'Like a golf courshe?'

Rob's look needed no interpretation; 'That wasn't even funny the first time.'

They said their goodnights and parted.

Chapter Twenty-Two

Ash leant against the back wall of The Feathers. Although he'd had a few drinks over the course of the night his mind was clear in regard to his most pressing of thoughts.

He had no idea what to do next though.

If he questioned either of the guys about the money, it would be obvious to them that he was involved in it being on the golf course in the first place.

Staying behind tomorrow and attempting to break in to their houses was at best a big risk with a whole lot of variables and at worst a disaster if he was seen.

Even if he did gain entry to either house there was no guarantee that he'd find anything, as it wasn't likely that they'd left the money anywhere in plain sight.

They may well have put it somewhere else?

His frustration was mixed with the fear he felt at having to go back to Sue Senior empty handed. She could quite easily implicate him in a whole world of trouble and the likelihood of a whole world of pain to go with it.

He decided to face it head on and phoned Sue.

'Hello, Ash.' Her familiar tone sounded harsher.

'Hi, Suze.' He replied. Trying to sound as in control as possible.

'Well? What have you got to tell me then?' Came her impatient response.

'I'll be totally straight with you babe. I..'

'That'll make a fucking change, Ashley!' She interrupted.

Sue continued. 'I've been waiting all evening for news from you. Any news. Fuck me! Can you not imagine the type of fucking day I've had?' Her voice breaking slightly at the end of the last sentence.

Hearing the change in her voice, Ash relaxed slightly and smiled to himself before replying, turning on the charm as he did so.

'Of course I can, babe. I know it's been a completely shit day. Especially for you! But there's no point in us falling out over events that have been completely out of our control. We have to stay as calm as we can to think what we can do to get the money back.'

'You'd better not be shitting me, Ash!' Sue hissed.

He decided to throw himself on her mercy.

'No! I'm not, Sue. I'm as fucked off about this as you are. Honestly! I had the bloody money. I got out of your house without being seen. I was absolutely cacking myself that someone, ANYONE, would see me. But once I was away in the car I really thought we'd cracked it. But since I got called back and had to find somewhere to hide the money, then it's all gone to shit!'

'Why did you choose a bloody golf course, you idiot?' Sue sounded slightly more reasonable.

'Look. I couldn't take a chance on bringing the money back with me. It would've been too risky. So I had to find somewhere quickly and somewhere that on any number of other fucking occasions would've been as safe as possible a place to have left the bag.' Ash hated the pleading tone of his voice.

'Ok. Ok.' Sue sounded less harsh; 'I can just about live with that for now. But how can you be sure that those guys you know have actually got the money?'

'I know for sure now that they were playing the course this afternoon and I also found out that by some poxy coincidence that they were really close to where I left the bag. And I also found a golf hat that I know belongs to one of them.'

'What? I'm struggling to take this all in. This must be the most ridiculous coincidence ever!' Sue sounded angry again.

She continued. 'If you are trying to cheat me.....'

But Ash had lost it now and had nowhere else to go.

'Look! Believe what you bloody want! I know how ridiculous this all sounds! But how the hell could I make something like this up, eh?'

'Alright. I'm sorry.' She replied. 'So these guys you know. Are they dodgy then? I mean, are they, I dunno? Are they ordinary people? Or are they crooked types? I mean, who takes a bag full of money that's been left on a golf course, for Christ's sake?'

'I have no idea what they were thinking, or for that matter, still are thinking, Sue.'

He explained about the trip away to the coast, which set off another round of disagreement, before Sue finally calmed and agreed with his plan.

'All I can do for the next day or so is stick close to them and see if they give anything away. Breaking in to their houses isn't really an option as it's too random and the money may well be elsewhere anyway.'

'Jesus. What a bloody mess!' Sue said, wearily.

'I know babe, I know.' Ash said, as much for his own peace of mind as for hers.

He continued; 'But these guys won't have any experience of this sort of thing, so they're bound to screw up somehow or other.'

'And that's your considered opinion, Ashley, given all of your great experience of losing a shed load of money, is it?' Sue added, with more than a trace of sarcasm.

'If you've got any better suggestions, I'm happy to hear them, love.' He countered. But continued more contritely; 'But as I said just now, we're not going to get anywhere by arguing and playing the blame game. This is a mess, I know. But it can be sorted.'

'Well, keep me informed then, Ash. Because there is no way that I'm giving up on what must be at least half a million quid!' Sue replied defiantly.

'Of course I will, babe.' Ash was back in usual smarm mode. But he smiled inwardly at her calculation of the amount of money, as he suspected it to be a lot more than half a million, given the amount Sue declared earlier that she'd put in the safe and what she'd said was in the inventory.

They ended the call with Ash promising to provide regular updates on any developments and Sue sarcastically signing off by wishing him a nice time at the seaside.

Sue then sent a text and shortly after received a call. During the short conversation she said; 'He's pretty certain that these guys have the money. But no clue yet as to where they might have put it. No, I don't think there's any point in you risking breaking into their houses while they're away. But it might be worth keeping an eye on them tomorrow though, like you said.'

Chapter Twenty-Three

Ash arrived home feeling mentally exhausted but couldn't stop thinking about the endless possibilities of where the money now was.

The house was quiet and he heard the muffled sounds from upstairs of Kirstie sleeping soundly as he stood in the passage. This was the first opportunity he'd had to properly run through what had happened without any distractions.

His conversation just now with Sue had at least allowed him to rationalise some of his thoughts even in the face of her anger and disappointment.

He cast his mind over the events of the day again.

He immediately discounted that anyone had seen him leave the bag on the golf course based on the incredible coincidences that he'd found out about that evening.

Although he'd have thought it unlikely that ordinary guys like Rob Gordon and Kenny Bradley would ever have kept a bag full of money, he also knew that the sight of all that cash could easily turn the mind of any otherwise law abiding citizen.

Given how close Rob and Kenny had always been he was sure that there was no way both of them could not be involved in this.

For one thing it would have been nigh on impossible for Rob to have literally fallen over the money and then secrete the sports bag without Kenny seeing him.

He wondered if he should've searched for longer on the course to see if they had put the bag somewhere else. But he soon determined that it would be highly unlikely for someone to make such a find and then decide to leave it behind and return for it later, thereby taking the chance of it not being there on their return.

And as he wasn't aware of any report of the money being handed in, or anything to that effect being mentioned this evening he was certain that they must have both removed and kept it.

But where to?

The course wasn't far from the industrial estate where he knew they worked. So it was feasible they may have called in there and left the bag in a locker without arousing any suspicion had they been seen?

Obviously they could also have just taken it home. But the element of doubt, added to the risk factor of being seen breaking in to one or both houses, rendered that option as being a total last resort.

He'd also only just recalled that both their houses had excellent up to date alarm systems, as he now remembered both guys installing them a couple of years and also doing installations for other people from the pub and the golf society.

His frustration at being so close to thousands of pounds gnawed at him endlessly. But he resolved to ingratiate himself to both guys on the trip away and try to disarm them and force at least one of them to slip up.

He knew that he couldn't divulge too much information about police work. But he reasoned that he could mention something about the arrest of Ronnie Senior's gang, as the story would be all over local news over the weekend and he could perhaps accidently on purpose let slip about the gang having money hidden?

A plan began to come together in his mind.

He determined to mention some details tomorrow about the police being aware of a large amount of money being missing somewhere in the local area, which was part of the investigation following the raid and subsequent arrests made on Friday.

He planned to drop this into conversation once the guys had had a few drinks to check their reaction and observe their behaviour afterwards.

At least this germ of an idea gave him enough satisfaction to call it a night and he climbed the stairs after gulping down a rather large Brandy.

'I'm coming for you, guys.' He said under his breath.

Chapter Twenty-Four

When Rob got home his mind was in a complete whirl. He suddenly realised that he hadn't spoken to Sally since she'd left earlier and although it was late, he figured that the girls would probably still be up enjoying themselves.

He needed to hear her voice just to help settle himself, so he rang Sally's phone and just as he thought the call was going to voicemail he heard a familiar voice answer.

'Hi, love!' Sally shouted. Half drowned out by the commotion of voices and music in the background.

'Hey, Darling.' Rob smiled as he replied. 'Are you having fun?'

'Hello, you!' Rob smiled at the sound of Sally's slightly drunken reply. 'Yes. All good thanks. We've had a lovely day. Train journey up was a right laugh. We had half the carriage joining in with our party games. And we've just gone on from there really. How about you? Did you get up to much?'

The more Sally spoke, the more Rob realised she had probably had much more to drink than was good for her. But he was happy she was having a good time. Sally had been a bit down since their youngest Daughter Liv had gone off to Uni and this weekend would be a good pick me up for her.

He thought it best not to divulge the full details of the day just yet though.

'Nothing out of the ordinary. We played nine holes this afternoon. Me, Ken and a few of the others. Usual crowd. And then we went to The Feathers tonight. Same old, same old.' He replied.

'I dunno. You lot are so predictable! Did you succeed with your wind up of poor Kenny?'

Rob had given Sally some of the details of the guys' plans before she'd left.

'Yeah. After a fashion.' He hesitated. 'You didn't say anything to Mo. Did you?'

'No! But she wouldn't have said anything anyway, I told you. Are you alright love? You sound a bit flat. I thought you'd be all happy being with your mates and having the weekend off.'

'I...I'm fine Sal. Just feels a bit weird being at home alone, I s'pose. Yeah, we had fun and Ken took it well in the end. But I won't keep you now, as I can hear everyone's having a good time there. I'll phone you in the morning before I leave..... If you're up!'

'Cheeky bugger!' Sally replied. 'You know I'm always up at Sparrow's fart!'

'Better than being up Dawn's crac...' Rob stopped himself, not quite in time.

'Oooooh! You can tell someone's been around his friends!' Sally laughed.

'Sorry, love! Have a great night and I'll speak to you in the morning. Love you loads.' Rob signed off.

'Night, night, lovely man. Love you too.' Sally replied, closely followed by a chorus of 'night, night, lovely man' from an obviously inebriated crowd of excited females close behind her.

'Night ladies.' Rob laughed, ending the call.

He smiled to himself and felt better having spoken to his wife. But in the pit of his stomach he felt ill at ease with the events of the day. As exciting as finding the cash had been, it had brought with it a range of issues that he was having trouble with rationalising now, having had additional time to think.

Having all that money between just him and Kenny was such a big secret to keep. The more he thought about the ramifications of that, on top of the worry of Ash almost certainly knowing their secret, was becoming an increasingly heavier burden for him.

He thought hard about telling Sally everything in the morning, as she was his barometer in all things and he pretty much knew in advance what she would say. That knowledge alone was enough to send him off to bed feeling very uneasy.

Chapter Twenty-Five

Kenny congratulated himself on the quality of the Fish Finger sandwich he'd just finished off. He smiled as he sipped his second cup of coffee, which then proceeded to burn his lip as it slopped down his shirt.

'Owww! Bollocksh!' He exclaimed as he placed his cup on the coffee table in front of him as best he could before holding his hand to his newly sore lip.

'Ouch! Twat!' He berated himself.

He'd thought hard about phoning Mo with his news since he'd got home. But a combination of not wanting to bother her in the midst of whatever she and her mates were doing and his urgent need of finding something to eat had delayed him until now.

He knew that she would probably still be up, as the girls trips had always been fairly full on affairs in the past. But given the distance he'd felt from Mo in the last few months, he was somehow reluctant to just phone and chat. This in turn made him feel sad, as they'd always been really close till the last few months.

He resolved to change things from now on and to spend more time concentrating on making her happy. Especially if there was something unpleasant to overcome first.

He sat looking out at the darkness of his back garden for several minutes, sobering up a little until he finally found the courage to phone Mo.

He heard the ring tone at the end of the line and was aware of how nervous he was and was almost relieved when her voicemail eventually kicked in.

After her busy message finished and the tone sounded for him to leave a voicemail, Kenny hesitated for a second before launching into; 'Hello love. S..ssorry for phoning so late. Hope you've had a good day.' He hardly recognised the tone of his voice and he felt incredibly emotional all of a sudden.

He continued; 'We've had a bit of a day ourselves. I'll talk to you more when we finally speak properly. But I hope you're ok. I...I...' He didn't know what to say next, so ended the message by repeating himself; 'I hope you're ok and I'll speak to you tomorrow morning. Night then.'

Then after a few more seconds; 'Love you.'

He ended the call and sat back down on the sofa. It occurred to him that he hadn't realised he'd stood up at some point while making the call.

He felt suddenly very flat and was aware that he'd shed a few tears.

'Pull yourself together, you dick!' He said aloud.

He walked over to the French doors and looked out at his garden and could just make out the shape of the Conifers at the bottom of the garden in the Moonlight. He rested his head on the glass of the door and looked in the direction of his shed and next to it the compost heap in the corner of the garden where he and Rob had hidden the bag full of money. It all seemed a long time ago. He replayed the events of the last few hours and the highs and lows of emotion.

He thought he'd feel over the moon. But instead he felt sad and more than a bit worried.

Chapter Twenty-Six (Saturday)

Ash hit the alarm button on his clock a little harder than he intended to. But at least it stopped the interruption to his dream.

He quickly refocused his thoughts though, from trying to undo Scarlett Johansson's bra in the land of fantasy, to the more mundane reality of his real world situation.

The first thing to deal with was the after effect of last night's drinking, which was causing his head to throb and pound like a team of drummers, banging on metal pipes.

'Whattimeisit?' Kirstie's sleep filled voice enquired.

'Half past seven.' He answered grumpily, as he got up. 'Go back to sleep.'

Her reply was unintelligible.

After two glasses of cold water had washed down two Paracetamol and two Ibuprofen, Ash showered and started to feel more human.

He had allowed himself a bit of time to assess the situation before walking to The Feathers.

He reasoned again that there was no point in staying behind to attempt a break in to either of Rob or Kenny's houses and replayed yesterday's events over again in his mind, which did nothing for his mood. But it did strengthen his resolve to regain the money.

With that in mind, he remembered to do something that might come in handy later on in trying to get the truth out of either of them.

Then, although he knew that there would be coffee and bacon sandwiches available at the pub, Ash felt the overriding need for some extra ballast to ward off the potential effects of a long day's boozing, so he made himself some breakfast.

Afterwards he got ready and left the house, with Kirstie still asleep upstairs.

'Lazy cow!' He said under his breath as he closed the front door a little harder than was necessary.

The sound of the slamming door brought Kirstie out of a particularly pleasant dream into a reality that she'd already had more than enough of.

She jumped out of bed and peered out of the bedroom window in time to see Ash walking away towards the pub.

'Goodbye, Ashley.' She said.

Chapter Twenty-Seven

As Ash walked into the bar via the back door of the pub there were already a selection of regulars, either seated at nearby tables, or standing at the bar, that were universally tucking into Bacon sandwiches and sipping coffee.

The aroma of the bacon and coffee filled the large bar room and just about masked the usual early morning smell of a busy pub's previous night.

In any case, the scent of breakfast food and drink was guaranteed to generate a good mood amongst the guys.

'Morning all,' offered Ash as he approached the bar, already noting that neither Rob Gordon or Kenny Bradley were there yet.

'Morning, Ash.' Answered Bertie Bassett, through a mouthful of sandwich.

The greeting was echoed by several of the other occupants of the bar.

Bertie swallowed the remainder of his mouthful and continued;

'Help yourself.' He pointed to the bar where Ash saw several sandwiches on a large platter, next to smaller side plates and mugs and flasks of coffee.

Ash picked up one of the flasks and began to pour it into a spare mug, when the top of the flask fell into the mug, closely followed by a deluge of coffee which flooded the counter.

'Oh, bollocks!' Ash angrily exclaimed.

'Oops! Didn't I fasten that properly?' Kevin 'Speedo' Morris, half smiled in his embarrassment from along the bar.

'You twat, Sp...' Ash angrily started, but was halted by Gracie as he came through from the kitchen with another platter of sandwiches.

'Whoa there, Ashley! Is that any way to start the day?'

Ash tried to recover his composure, but Gracie wasn't quite finished winding him up.

'You really should keep a lid on that temper of yours, old son. That's the second time I've had to intervene in your troubles in less than a day. I hope you're going to behave yourself today?' Gracie smiled in enjoyment as he watched Ash squirm.

'I'm sorry, Gracie.' Ash said quietly. 'Just a bit embarrassing, that's all. Have you got a towel I can clear up the mess with please?'

Gracie was happy to oblige and Ash mopped up the spillage. Those around the bar smiling at his discomfort.

The uncomfortable silence was broken by Bertie;

'Why don't you pour yourself another coffee, Ash?'

Ash cringed inwardly at the surrounding guffaws, which acted as a release valve around the bar. But he managed a weak smile and replied;

'Perhaps I'll get Kev here to pour it for me. Is that ok mate?'

Although he was notoriously slow on the uptake Speedo could sometimes be unintentionally funny.

'Well I suppose I couldn't make a worse job of it than you just did, Ash!'

Speedo's reply, although not meant to be sarcastic, was the catalyst for more laughter.

Although this time it at least provided Ash with a way out of his discomfort, when he said; 'Bloody hell! Bested by Speedo. This day can only get better!'

Even Gracie laughed.

The bar filled gradually in the next few minutes as everyone arrived, except a notable few yet to show, which included Rob and Kenny.

'Coach should be here by now. Shouldn't it, Gracie?' Enquired Bertie.

Gracie rolled his eyes and replied;

'Bertie, did I, or did I not tell you for about the tenth time last thing last night, that I'd told Mick not to bother getting here till half past nine, 'cos I bloody knew there'd be at least a couple of stragglers we'd be waiting on? One of which will always be Bog. As he'd be late for his own friggin' funeral!'

'Oh yeah, sorry mate.' Bertie said holding his hands up. 'Bit pissed last night and the end was a bit of a blur.'

'He'll be here soon though.' Said Gracie. 'Cos Mick is the opposite of Bog. Tell him a time and he'll always arrive earlier.'

'Does that mean he'd be digging his own grave for his funeral, rather than be late for it? Unlike Bog?' Said Ash, trying to be funny.

For once Speedo answered first.

'Well he couldn't, could he? 'Cos he'd be dead.' He said earnestly.

Ash rolled his eyes and died inwardly as his attempted joke had fallen flat, while Speedo's stating of the obvious had attracted a few laughs.

However Speedo being Speedo then rather spoilt his semi golden moment.

'And also, how do you know that Mick doesn't want to be cremated?'

Amidst the groans and sniggers, Ash looked at him and said; 'you're right, Speedo. I don't. Silly me, eh?'

Still not finished and with a furrowed brow, giving the appearance of someone in deeply serious thought, Speedo finally said;

'Does Mick want to be cremated, Gracie?'

Although most of the guys knew Kevin Morris well enough by now to not be surprised by anything he said, he still managed to find new ways to ridicule himself in their company on a regular basis.

Again amidst groans of derision and a few, 'oh, for fuck's sake, Speedo' comments, Gracie, ever calm in a crisis, smiled sweetly at his friend and said; 'Do you know what Kevin? I don't? Shall we ask him when he gets here mate?'

Speedo's puzzled expression added to the general laughter and even Ash thought that Gracie was quite the wit.

However Ash had also been clocking the time and wondered why both Rob and Kenny had still not appeared.

He was just speculating that they might be on to him and may be moving the money when the two of them, accompanied by Scott 'Starfish' Flintoff appeared through the now open doorway.

'Morning Gentlemen and you Bertie Bassett!' said Kenny, cheerily.

'Thought you'd all slept in...or changed your minds.' Bertie replied, amidst a general chorus of 'Morning' greetings.

'No way!' Rob replied. 'Big day out, accompanied by one or two friends to assist me with our care in the community project of looking after elderly folk like your good self, Mr Bassett! Wouldn't have missed it for the world.'

Bertie had just stood up to take off the fleece top he'd been wearing, which revealed a rather loud and garishly patterned Hawaiian style shirt underneath, which attracted some immediate attention.

'Jesus, Bertie! Can you turn the volume down on that thing you're wearing?' Kenny volunteered.

Before Bertie could muster a response he was bombarded from all sides.

'Why are you wearing one of your missus's blouses, Bertie?' Scott added.

Rob felt the need to contribute too.

'Gracie! Can you turn all the lights off please, mate? I'm getting blinded by the light coming off Bertie's shirt.'

Gracie looked across the bar at the vision of Bertie and laughingly added; 'That's a horror, mate!'

Bertie to his credit smiled back at them all before replying; 'I just knew I'd get that sort of crap from people who have no sense of style.'

The guys continued their general round of mild mickey taking while finishing off the sandwiches and coffee, until the unmistakeable noise of a large vehicle pulling into the car park outside stirred them into action.

'Right. Come on guys!' Bertie said, as he sprang to his feet. 'Let's get this show on the road.'

'I'd better just go for a quick waz before we set off, Lads.' Said Scott, apologetically. Then quickly added; 'Sorry,' as he copped some general abuse.

'Bloody hell Starfish!' Bertie said. 'Turn up late and then you still faff about! Just make sure it is a waz and not anything worse, as we're not coming in to rescue you again after last time!'

Scott was more resilient to the banter when he was sober and passed it off with; 'Change the record Bertie! That old chestnut again?'

But as he went through the door towards the Gents toilet he heard a comment from behind him;

'Never mind old chestnuts. We saw enough of those things last time!'

The guys eventually all climbed aboard Mick's old coach and after Gracie had confirmed once again that he had sufficient staffing cover in place at the pub all day, they set off.

Ash made sure he sat as close as possible to Rob and Kenny and therefore selected the seat behind them in the rapidly filling coach.

A few moments later, as the coach lurched forward, Ash's head appeared above the back of Rob and Kenny's seats, as he leant forward.

'Morning, chaps.' He said, smiling a little too much. 'I was beginning to think you two had changed your mind and made alternative plans.'

Rob smiled weakly. But Kenny was more on the front foot.

'I believe we got here before the coach, Ashley. And it doesn't take long to scoff a bacon sandwich and slurp a coffee. I've got to spend all day with you lot and as lovely a thought as that is, I had more important business to attend to at home.'

For a second Ash was worried and felt a sinking feeling in his stomach, until Rob explained;

'He was having an extra long dump, which I unfortunately heard most of while I was banging on his front door!'

'Best way to start the day!' Kenny said triumphantly.

'Although I might've overdone it with the reading material, as I'd nearly lost all feeling in my legs when I stood up!'

'Ugh! Too much information, mate.' Came the general chorus from several of his mates.

Chapter Twenty-Eight

The atmosphere inside the coach was one of general good cheer, bonhomie and expectation of the day ahead.

As the guys got into their stride, the banter and accompanying laughter had taken the volume up a notch in the coach, from the slightly subdued atmosphere in the pub earlier.

Ash though, was anxious to find a way to crack Rob and Kenny's resolve.

In addition to his certainty that both were equally involved with the disappearance of the money, an additional element had just occurred to him which had increased his already heightened stress levels.

He thought back to the spat he'd had with Kenny in the pub the night before and remembered Kenny's reaction to his comment.

At the time, he just assumed that Kenny was reacting to being wound up and Ash's comment was the straw that broke him. But the more he thought about it, the more it occurred to him that Kenny had made a connection between the money and Ash.

If that was indeed the case it made the whole situation more difficult for him, as it meant that it wasn't just a case of getting the money back now. It also meant that if Kenny and also presumably Rob, somehow knew the money was connected to Ash, then even if he did get it back he would also have to deal with the fallout of them both having that knowledge of his involvement too.

He found it hard to think straight and realised he was panicking.

He decided to go for broke.

Standing suddenly and leaning over the seat in front of him again, he said to Rob and Kenny;

'Did you guys hear the local news this morning, about the arrests we made yesterday on the industrial estate?'

Given the amount of background noise on the coach from chatter, laughter and engine noise, they barely heard him.

'Sorry Ash. What did you say?' Rob answered.

Ash leant further over the seat.

'I said did you hear the local news this morning, about the arrests we made yesterday on the industrial estate?'

'No,' they answered pretty much in unison.

Ash tried to sound as matter of fact as possible and continued; 'I'd have mentioned it last night, but didn't want to say anything until the news went public. Yeah, we made some big arrests of a local crime gang, who were mixed up in all sorts.' As usual though, Ash wanted to inflate his status in anything he said.

Bertie, sitting opposite Ash, overheard him.

'I thought they said on the news that it was the Regional Crime Squad that had made the arrests, in some sort of operation against the gang.' He intervened.

Ash, although slightly flustered, came back; 'Yeah, that's right it was. But as usual, our team had to do all the donkey work for them. The RCS just get the glory in the news.'

'So were you involved then, Ash?' Bertie replied.

Ash bristled. 'Yeah. Course! We seized a load of cash, computers and other stuff from the gang leaders' house. But the word is there's still a lot of cash hidden somewhere local. Although no further information has come out yet as to where.'

He looked closely at Rob and Kenny as he spoke to see if there was any reaction.

There wasn't. Although Rob wasn't looking directly at him.

Kenny though was fairly quick off the mark.

'Blimey! Be a nice find for someone if they stumbled across that by accident eh?' He said, laughing a little strangely in a high pitch voice.

Bertie laughed and replied. 'Absobloodylutely!'

Rob could feel his stomach clenching and thought for a moment that he was going to be sick.

'So, how do you know about the hidden money, Ash?' Asked Bertie.

Both Kenny and Rob were relieved that Bertie was taking the lead on quizzing Ash as, at that moment, anything that involved them having to speak to him about the money was pushing their powers of trying to keep cool, calm and collected way beyond the point of no return.

Although Kenny had initially thought that 'fighting fire with fire' was, as he'd described to Rob earlier on the phone, their best strategy for appearing oblivious of any knowledge of the money to anything Ash said or did today, he was now struggling to keep on top of his feelings.

His initial reply to Ash moments before had all been fuelled by adrenalin and bravado.

But the combined effects of hearing himself saying stuff about how great it would be for someone to find a load of cash, as well as the horrified look of panic on Rob's face as he said it, was stretching things much further than he now felt capable of dealing with.

As for Rob, Kenny could visibly see that his earlier banter in the pub and the pretence at normality had given way to fear and apprehension, given the tense look on his face.

He tapped his mate's leg and mouthed to him to keep it together.

Ash meanwhile had hesitated in his reply to Bertie's question.

He'd not fully thought through how this conversation would pan out, as he'd really only visualised having it with Rob and Kenny and the slight pause as he turned to look at

Bertie was sufficient enough to allow further inquisition from him.

'I mean, I didn't hear anything on the news about any money being hidden locally.'

However the additional question also gave Ash sufficient thinking time to regain his composure and he answered as confidently and condescendingly as he'd have liked to have done in the first place.

'Well you wouldn't have done Bertie, old son. It's not common knowledge yet and not in the public domain. But I can tell you that we already know enough to more than suspect that a substantial sum has been left somewhere, in the hope that it doesn't come to light.'

He smiled smugly and continued;

'But we know,' (he emphasised the word 'know' a little more strongly than he'd maybe intended to, as he looked back again at Rob and Kenny somewhat theatrically and then back to Bertie for additional effect), 'because we have knowledge of how much money should've come to light.'

'Really? So what happens next, then?' Bertie persisted, expectantly.

'Well, obviously, I can't go into too much detail.' Ash replied, continuing;

'But suffice to say, every lead will be followed up and it will all come out in the end.'

Although his confidence wasn't exactly brimming as he looked at the semi blank stares from both Kenny and Bertie.

However Rob wasn't looking quite as matter of fact and seemed to be ill at ease, which at least gave Ash more satisfaction.

'You alright, Bog?' He enquired.

'Y..Yeah.' Rob said in a flat tone. 'Just a bit travel sick I think.'

Kenny intervened sharply by saying; 'You'll be alright mate. Just need a hair of the dog probably? Bit of a livener will sort you out!'

Rob smiled weakly. But realised he needed to sharpen up. He was still taking in what Ash had said and trying to come to terms with it.

He tried to think clearly, in the general hubbub of mixed conversations going on around him.

If the police did know there was some money missing, then perhaps someone had admitted under questioning that they had hidden it somewhere? Maybe they'd even admitted leaving it on the golf course? In which case, Ash already knew that they had all been on the course yesterday.

But if that was the case then......

'Well do you Bog?'

Rob's thoughts were brought sharply back to reality by Bertie's question.

'S..sorry Bertie. What did you say?'

'Bloody hell, Bog. Wake up!' Exclaimed Bertie. 'I said do you know any decent boozers in Cleethorpes? I haven't been there for years.'

'Neither have I, mate!' Rob snapped impatiently. 'I thought we'd said that the other day, when we arranged this?'

Then, seeing the look of deflation on his friend's face, he softened and continued;

'There's bound to be loads to choose from, though. I think Dino and one or two of the others know a bit more about the town.'

'Oh. Ok. I'll have a word with Dino in a minute.' Bertie's puppy like nervous energy was something Rob could do without at the moment.

He was relieved that Ash had at least for now sat back down and from his reflection in the window, Rob could see him looking at his phone.

'Calm down, mate.' Kenny said in a concerned whisper.

Rob indicated with an incline of his head and eyes towards Ash and whispered back;

'What if the police do know about the money and where it was hidden?'

Kenny whispered back, after first checking in the window reflection that Ash was preoccupied and not listening.

'I think he's fishing, mate. Just chill out for a bit and we'll talk properly when we get out.'

Rob nodded. But his stomach was in knots.

Chapter Twenty-Nine

The pressure on Ash was also ramping up. His phone vibrated in the pocket of his Jeans to indicate that he'd received a text.

As his personal mobile was in his jacket pocket, he was aware that it was probably a text from Sue Senior, as she was the only person he'd contacted via the burner phone since he'd changed the sim card in it yesterday afternoon.

The text was fairly straightforward and reflected Sue's obvious mood when she sent it.

'Any news? You promised to keep me updated. Don't fuck about!'

Given the amount of grief that she could bring him, Ash felt an immediate tightening in his stomach as he started to type a reply.

'Nothing new yet. Think their bum's are twitching though. Have to be careful, so bear with me.' He pressed the send button.

He kept the phone in his hand, as he expected a fairly quick response and sure enough, within a minute the phone vibrated again.

'For Christ's sake! Ring me ASAP.' As Ash read the message, he swallowed hard.

He looked around for any other vacant seats and was both surprised and relieved to see two empty rows at the back of the coach.

He got up and shuffled out into the aisle, holding onto the back of a seat to steady himself in the moving coach.

Bertie looked up from his morning paper. 'You ok, Ash?'

'Yeah. Just have to make a call to work.' He replied.

He swayed a little unsteadily down the aisle holding onto the tops of seats and smiling unconvincingly at any of their occupants, until he reached the back of the coach.

Once in situ in the back row Ash phoned Sue, who answered almost immediately.

Ash got in first. 'Sue, I'm on the coach, so I can't talk easily.' He half whispered, cupping one hand around the phone. 'What's up?'

'I'll tell you what's up Ashley. The fucking game is probably up! Ron's brief was on the phone just now. He said Ron's been put through the wringer under questioning all day yesterday and again in the night, when they evidently received more information.

Those bastards know way more than he reckoned and have obviously been tipped off about loads of stuff. Some shitbag has grassed for sure! They know that money has gone missing and they also now know that the stuff in those lorries was fake gear. So someone is taking the piss majorly!'

'What? Oh Jesus, Sue! Who the hell was Ron dealing with? It must have come from them? Especially if the drugs were fake.'

Sue's voice betrayed her anxiety and she sounded genuinely worried.

'Clive wasn't telling me much. He just confirmed the amount in the Inventory your lot gave me yesterday and asked if I'd managed to hide some away. Ironically, Ron was concerned enough about me to get him to call me to say that, if I had managed to do that, then I should be extra careful now as they know how much Ron was supposed to be paying for the drugs and therefore know what the shortfall is!'

Ash's brain was in overdrive. But he thought quickly.

'Just think for a minute, Sue. Did Ron ever mention any names, or give any idea who he was doing the deal with? Or at least who the go-between was? Because he said to me on the phone, just before he got busted yesterday, that the deal was done through an intermediary?'

But Sue didn't take any time to think.

'I have no idea. I knew he was doing a big deal and like I said to you yesterday, I thought he was biting off way more than he could chew. But he never gave me any details. That's never been his way. He's obviously been stitched up though!'

Her voice broke at this point as she continued half sobbing.

'Tell me you're not mixed up in this, Ashley? If I we get wind you're involved in this, then you know you will end up in worse shit than anyone.'

Ash's heart was hammering.

'Sue! For Christ's sake! I know we've all been mixed up in some dodgy stuff.' He was struggling to keep his voice to a whisper. 'But I would never have done anything like this, even if I'd been party to any information. Jesus! I even tried to warn Ron about the raid, as soon as I knew anything!'

He could hear Sue crying as she spoke again.

'I know...I know! I'm sorry, babe....It's just that at the moment' ...She broke off crying again.

'I know you're really going through it, darling.' Ash whispered soothingly, desperately trying to calm her.

He continued; 'Right now I can only guess how alone you feel. The only good part of this, is that it sounds like Ron has got his brief to phone you out of concern for you, rather than to accuse you of anything.'

Sue sounded calmer as she replied;

'Yes, you're right. That makes me feel more guilty obviously. But I'd warned him so many bloody times, not to keep on taking stupid risks! We were ok money wise. We had a good life. He was just so bloody flash and stupid! Stupid bastard!' She almost spat out the last bit, as her anger returned with more emotion.

As Sue ranted about her Husband, an obvious thought had only just occurred to Ash.

Until now, he'd imagined Ron to be largely out of the picture, locked away in custody as he was.

In his own desire for the money, Ash had completely overlooked the fact that the shortfall of cash from what Ron had known to be in his house prior to his arrest, in comparison to what had been in the inventory from the police from what they'd seized, would of course have been apparent to Ron from his conversations with his Lawyer.

He felt a large lump in his throat and had to fight hard to stay in control of himself.

'Look, babe. I wish I was there right now to try and help make sense of this with you. I really do. But the best I can do at the moment is try to get more information about what's happened to the money. As I've said, I'm sure it's been taken by these ordinary Joes in some stupid bloody coincidence and I don't know any other way right now to try and get it back, without it all coming out and screwing it up for all of us. Do you?'

Sue was becalmed and sounded exhausted as she agreed with him.

Before he rang off he had to ask one final question.

'How did you leave it with Clive, when he asked if you'd managed to organise getting the money that wasn't seized out of the house?'

'I was straight with him. I had to be didn't I? I said we'd managed to get one of the bags out of the house without it being noticed. You said Ron had told you how much...'

'Yeah, yeah. That's fine.' Ash interrupted. 'Ron told me roughly what was in the bags. I just wanted to make sure we were on the same page, that's all.'

Ash ended the call genuinely making protestations of affection for her and desperately trying to reassure her that he was doing all he could to make things right.

As she ended the call Sue wiped her eyes and composed herself.

'Some performance that, Suzie! You should be an actress love.'

She turned to face her admirer and smiled.

Chapter Thirty

'It wasn't all put on, though.' She said. 'I am worried that we're getting in deeper and deeper, Mike.'

Detective Sergeant Mike Phelan put his arms around her and held her close to him.

'I know baby. It's all gone a bit tit's up. But at least we can let lover boy do all the leg work for now. If he's right about these mugs, then we can let him take all the risks for us. As much as I detest blokes like him, I have to say that I do believe his story. As ridiculous as it sounds!'

Sue smiled thinly and said, 'Yeah, I suppose I do too. As much as he's a liar and a definite player, he sounds genuinely pissed off and worried. And if he knows these guys, then he's out on a limb in trying to get the cash back, without giving himself away. And we need him to do that at least, before you do the dirty on him, eh?'

Phelan smiled smugly; 'Yes, I am looking forward to doing that.'

Sue smiled in response. But her expression changed as another thought suddenly occurred to her;

'If your team does know there is a big shortfall in cash, Mike, then they're not going to take long to pay another visit here, are they?'

'Well apart from the lovely view of your garden from this room and the fact that you're such a welcoming host, why else did you think I was here, Mrs Senior?'

Phelan continued;

'I told my guv'nor that I might be able to catch you off guard if I called round on a Saturday morning, on the pretext of asking you some questions about your business turnover and average profits, so we can consider what to ignore from the total money seized so far.

He doesn't think you are wrapped up in this and apart from your loyalty to Ron getting in the way of you providing anything massively useful to us, he's doubtful that you know specific details about his business ventures anyway.

Your old man is an old school misogynistic villain, who keeps his business affairs very separate from his family affairs.'

Sue shrugged her shoulders in concession and smiled wryly;

'Well I suppose that much IS true!'

Phelan explained; 'I told him that if anything incriminating came out, then I'd continue our chat at head office.'

'So, you going to grill me then, copper?' Sue sounded calmer now.

'Absolutely, Mrs Senior. Things are going to get very hot for you in a minute!' He said, pulling her towards him again amorously.'

Her shriek and subsequent giggling was stopped by the sound of the doorbell.

Sue looked perplexed.

'I wasn't expecting anyone and the Postman's been by already.'

Sue peered out from behind the curtains in her dining room just as the doorbell rang again and was accompanied by a loud banging on the door.

'There's two strange looking blokes outside, Mike. Big geezers. Are they from your lot?'

Phelan joined her at the window, and also peered through the gap in the curtains.

'No, nobody I know.' He said, slightly concerned.

They looked at each other worriedly.

'You'd better answer it I suppose, Sue.' Phelan said, uncertainly.

Sue gulped a little and made her way to the door. She forced a smile as she opened it.

'Hello. Can I help you?' She said pleasantly to the two men on her doorstep.

'You must be Missus Senior? Sooo, isn't it?'

The slightly smaller of the two men answered, in a foreign accent that Sue knew to be Dutch.

Before she could answer both men stepped toward her.

'I sink weet bedder come in and talk to you ant your frent Mike over dere.' The same man said.

Sue's expression portrayed an obvious concern to Phelan, as the two large men brushed past her. The larger of the two extended his muscular right arm to push the front door closed, before shepherding Sue across the hallway towards the worried looking policeman, who stood watching them in the Lounge.

'Hello Mike. We meet at last,' said the man who had done all the talking so far.

Phelan felt a cold shiver down his Spine, as he now recognised the Dutch accent.

'H..Hello Rinus.' He replied, more nervously than he'd have liked. 'What are you doing here?'

Rinus Krol smiled patiently at Phelan.

'Oh, come on Mikey! Shurely you wass ecspecting a visit from us, after all our conversations, no?'

Phelan felt a horrible sinking feeling in his stomach and the look he gave Sue Senior did nothing to quell the profound uneasiness she was now displaying to him.

Chapter Thirty-One

Ash looked around him after retaking his original seat. His frustration was sky high. Almost simultaneously, he felt so close and then immediately, so far away from the money.

Sue's news and her subsequent emotion had actually punctured his usual persona of indifference.

He realised that the situation had escalated now and he felt very uneasy at the news of senior officers being aware that a large amount of money had supposedly gone missing.

This was doubly increased by his stark realisation that Ron could be equally aware too.

Although at least in Ron's case he wouldn't know the current situation until told otherwise.

He figured though that, given Senior was in more than enough trouble already, the interviewing officers would hardly be likely to think that he'd be withholding evidence about any missing money.

It might depend on Ron's state of mind when questioned as to whether he could bluff it out about the full amount of cash in his house, in order to allow Sue the opportunity to have arranged to dispose of a large chunk of it.

But Ash assumed the officers interviewing Ron would very likely assume he would've had all the money for the drugs in one place though, (as he had confirmed to be the case to Ash on the phone yesterday morning).

If so, that meant that they would now be aware that the money had almost certainly gone missing from Senior's house, given that the remaining money had been found there.

He felt more and more concerned about the events of yesterday and the impending possibility of the investigation now leading the officers towards him.

'You alright, Ash? You look a bit unwell.' Dean Willis, now sitting opposite him, enquired.

'It's just work stuff, Dino.' He replied, almost to himself. 'Just a bit complicated.'

'Oh right.' Dino said over his shoulder, immediately wishing he hadn't asked in the first place.

He turned back to another conversation and the accompanied laughter, from the seats in front of him.

Ash was left alone with his thoughts and peered out of the window trying to fathom things again.

He assumed that the interview with Ron Senior would've been done in stages and maybe reconvened as new information had come to light.

He would no doubt have been charged early on, as there was overwhelming evidence against him. But that fact would also have restricted much of the bargaining room of the interviewing officers in offering inducements to him to provide them with information, as Senior knew he would be facing very long jail time.

Ash figured that by now they would be turning their attention to where the money had gone and that he reasoned would lead back to the search of Senior's house and also to Sue.

Either way, Ash was sure that he would be under scrutiny as part of the team involved in the search. And once they'd confirmed where the rest of the seized money had been found and who had searched that room, it was inevitable that he would be under suspicion and questioned.

Right now, in Ash's mind, the missing money became a secondary issue. At least for the time being he knew that he had to rehearse how he would deal with any investigation coming his way and try to distance himself from any further scrutiny.

The increased laughter in the rows in front of him did not break his concentration and he continued to look aimlessly out of the window.

Speedo was the subject of derision again just a couple of rows ahead of him.

'What are you on about, Speedo? Gay lesbians?' Gary Chivers, sitting next to him said incredulously.

'What do you think I mean, Gaz?' Speedo responded. 'There were two gay lesbians on telly the other night. Like I just said.'

'Why aren't they just lesbians?' Gary asked. Continuing; 'That's just like saying two female women! If they were lesbians, then they're just lesbians.'

'No. Lesbian lesbians are women who look like lesbians and like women. But these women in the film on telly were lesbians who also liked men. So they were gay lesbians!' Speedo responded.

Gary, who to be fair had not known Speedo for that long, looked increasingly puzzled and impatient.

Those in the surrounding seats who watched on amused at the spectacle did nothing to ease his failure to understand what he was dealing with.

'Let me try once more, Kev.' He said. 'Lesbians are, as you know, women who prefer women to men sexually. But if they also like men too then they are bisexual.'

'Or greedy!' Offered Dino, sitting nearby.

'Don't confuse him anymore than he already is, mate!' Said Bertie, laughing.

'Well I've always thought of it as either straight or gay.' Speedo said earnestly. If a woman likes another woman they are a lesbian. But they are a gay lesbian if they also like men.'

'Well, what about a bloke who prefers other blokes, but also occasionally likes women too?' Gary persisted.

'Then he's gay, gay I suppose.' But as he said it, even Speedo looked confused.

'As opposed to a straight gay?' Dino suggested.

He Continued; 'Who would I guess under Speedo's definition be a man who likes men? Or if a bloke just liked women, he would be straight, straight. Is that right Kevlar?'

Speedo rolled his eyes before replying; 'Well now you're just being silly!'

This was the cue for more laughter and derision.

Chapter Thirty-Two

Mick pulled the coach into the large car park of a service area, having finally given in to calls to stop for a lavatory break.

As the coach drew to a stop most of the guys stood up to get off, but Gracie stood in their way in the aisle next to the driver.

'Right guys!' He announced loudly. 'No messing about here. Ten minutes for a quick piss and a fag, for those who must have one. Then back on the coach. Right?'

His comment was met with a chorus of, 'ok, mate,' or similar responses from the collective.

The guys disembarked and either stretched a bit and made their way towards the main service building, or in a few cases, took cigarettes and lighters from their pockets to light up.

As they crossed the car park Kenny and Rob nodded to each other as they surveyed Ash's face back on the coach.

Kenny whispered to his mate, 'I wonder what's wrong with him? He's not even getting off.'

Rob felt a whole lot better surveying Ash's gloomy expression.

'Jesus! He does looks worried, doesn't he?' He whispered back.

He continued; 'What was all that stuff he said about the police knowing there was money missing?'

Kenny shrugged. 'Like I said on the coach, I think he's fishing, mate. He obviously must've put it all together from last night. If he knows from the wind up about the fake cash that we were only yards from the real money and thinks we've taken it, then it must've been him that hid the sports bag there in the first place. It's just the sort of dodgy thing he'd do. But if what he said earlier wasn't all made up and the police really do know there's money missing, then I bet he's shitting himself!'

Rob took some comfort from that. But he was already regretting not telling all to Sally this morning when he spoke to her. He'd agreed not to say anything after Kenny had phoned him first thing. But in his opinion they were still wrapped up in something that was way beyond anything he could feel comfortable with.

'Look, Ken.' He said, as he steered his friend to the side of the service area away from the others and out of sight of Ash on the coach.

'I know you think that money may be of some use to you right now, mate. But whatever it is that Mo might have wrong with her can still be treated by normal means. Surely you know that she wouldn't want any part of this?'

Kenny had also avoided any mention of the money in his brief and somewhat stilted conversation with Mo this morning. It had all been pleasantries and as both of them were nursing hangovers, they hadn't said anything of note. To be honest his uneasiness late last night had not left him and in truth he regretted the situation he and Rob were now in.

'It's so much money though, Bog!' Kenny said. 'Life changing. And it could make such a difference.'

But Rob had had enough.

'But it's not worth this sort of pressure, Ken! This ain't us. We're ordinary blokes. Not high flyers and certainly not crooked bastards. We don't need this!'

He continued softly;

'Look, mate. Whatever it is with Mo, Sally and me will help in any way we can. But you've got to talk to her and get it out in the open. It might not be as bad as you think. And god forbid, if it is then you and Mo can confront it together. But not like this with all the additional worry and fear this brings.'

Kenny started to object. But Rob was firm.

'I want out, Ken. I can't handle this sort of pressure. And now after proper thought it all just seems so wrong. It's dodgy money from dodgy people and we need to hand it in, or put it back where we found it. But phone Mo, Ken!'

'We can't just hand it in though, can we? We can't just turn up at the police station and hand over a bag containing over 600 grand and say, ''there you go.'' They'd be very suspicious and ask all sorts of questions and...'

Rob interrupted. 'We can actually. But we don't even have to do that. We could just call the police from a pay phone and tell them there's a bag of money and leave it there.'

'But it's six hundred and odd grand, Bog!' Kenny said, resignedly.

'I don't care! Phone Mo mate and sort this out.' Rob said walking away.

'And hurry up about it!' He called over his shoulder. 'We haven't got long and I need a piss!'

'I'll see you in a minute.' Kenny said, as he got his phone out.

As the guys meandered their way across the car park towards the service area building's main entrance, a large black SUV pulled up in an available space and four noticeably large men got out and headed in the same direction.

Chapter Thirty-Three

Kenny's mind was in turmoil. He knew that Rob was right. He knew in his heart and in his gut that keeping the money not only felt wrong, but it was wrong. He also knew that if his wife knew about it she would in no uncertain terms tell him to get rid of it.

But, although the excitement of yesterday had given way to the fear and uncertainty of today, he was still somehow reluctant to give up on his new found wealth.

However, he had to know what was going on with Mo, as she was the most important person in his life and the not knowing if she was ill and suffering from something awful was driving him crazy.

He nervously pressed the call button on his phone as he stood alone behind the main building of the service area.

After several rings he was about to give up. But then he heard Mo's familiar voice.

'Hello, Ken.' She sounded surprised.

He felt more nervous now than he had the first time he'd plucked up the courage to ask her out twenty odd years before.

'Hi, Mo, it's only me.' He said cautiously.

'Are you alright?' Mo asked in a concerned voice. 'You sound worried.'

'I am, love. I'm worried about you. I...I..I should've said something about this before now. But I know that something's the matter.' He started to feel his emotions overflow.

'I'm fine, you silly sod! Why do you think I'm not? We're having a really good time and everything's great. I thought that you'd be in your element today with all your mates?'

'I found the letter, Mo. The one from the Hospital. In a draw in the bedroom. I was looking for some papers and there it was.'

'What letter? Oh.... wait a minute. You mean the one about the missed appointment? I wondered what I'd done with that. I me...'

'Yes, that one!' Kenny interrupted. His voice now trembling. 'Why didn't you tell me something was wrong? Why did you suffer on your own? I can't bear the thought of anything happening to you, Mo! You mean everything to me. I love you so much!'

He was crying now

'Oh, darling!' Mo said soothingly. Then more in a tone that Ken recognised; 'You've got completely the wrong end of the stick! Did you happen to see the date on the letter? It was over six months ago!'

'W..What? No! I just read it and froze. I meant to say something a few weeks ago. But you hadn't said anything and I just thought the worst and..'

His voice tailed away as the emotions came back again and he imagined life without Mo.

'Oh you poor thing!' She said comfortingly. Then less so;

'You are a silly sod, though! I told you months ago I was having pain when I was peeing and I went to the Doctors. I remember telling you he thought it was a Urine infection and they took a sample to check it out, which they sent to the Hospital. But he gave me some tablets and it cleared up in no time. The appointment was cancelled as it had been made in error after my test results confirmed nothing more serious than the infection. I told you all that ages ago!'

'No you didn't!' Kenny said indignantly.

But from somewhere in his memory he felt a cause for uneasiness.

'Kenny Bradley. I bloody told you about the whole thing! But as per flippin' usual you had your head stuck in the paper sat in front of the telly and took no bloody notice, did you?'

The penny suddenly dropped.

'You did tell me.' Kenny vaguely recalled it now. 'I'm sorry. I'm a dick!'

'YOU'RE sorry you're a dick! So am I.' Mo replied. But she was laughing by the end of the statement.

'Oh, Ken! For the first time in ages, I think I've got my Husband back! I love you, you silly bugger!'

They exchanged loving comments and both of them got emotional as Mo took in the weight of her Husband's unnecessary worrying and his outpouring of emotion and love just before, while Ken basked in the relief he felt, now that he realised his Wife was ok, fit and well.

He also immediately thought to himself; 'Sod the money!'

Kenny could see Gracie in the distance pacing around the coach and knew he had to go.

'I'm so glad you're alright, love.' He said. 'Have a great time up there in the land of the Jock and I'll see you tomorrow. Love you so much.'

'Blimey! This is the nicest you've been for ages!' Mo said.

'Funny thing is, I was only thinking yesterday on the way up here, that for someone who makes so much noise and says so much, so little of it is of any consequence! But then you go and completely take me by surprise like this. You're a silly sod! But you're MY silly sod! I love you so much, Ken.'

Kenny was already walking towards Gracie with his hand up in apology. But as he closed to within a few yards of him and wiped away the last of his tears with the back of his hand, he said to Mo;

'Maureen Bradley, I am so lucky to have you as my Wife and I love you very, very much. But you are a cheeky cow!'

They said their goodbyes and Gracie spared him the bollocking for being late.

However, as they got on the coach Gracie loudly announced to everyone, 'well he kept us all waiting, but at least he loves his Missus!'

Then he whispered quietly to Ken;

'I'm glad you've finally realised just how lucky you are, mate. She's the making of you!'

Kenny was still brimming with emotion and turned to his mate, gave him a big hug and said misty eyed;

'Thanks, Frankie. You're not wrong there!'

As Kenny passed them in the aisle, Gary Chivers, having overheard his reply, said to Speedo sitting next to him;

'Frankie? Why'd he call him that?'

Speedo looked at him with a puzzled expression and replied;

'Because it's his name. Why else?'

Gracie/Frankie turned round in his seat to face them and smiled.

'Gary mate, you didn't think that Gracie was actually my name, did you?'

He and Speedo laughed and Gary, a relative newcomer to the village, laughed too.

'Nice one, Frankie!' He said.

Gracie fixed him with a semi serious stare.

'Gracie to you though, sunshine!'

Speedo, enjoying a joke at someone else's expense for a change, continued to laugh.

Kenny having made it back to his seat turned to Rob and gave him a big hug too.

'She's fine, mate! Absolutely fine. All good.'

He fought back the welling up sensation in his eyes and throat and smiled.

Rob felt the relief of his best mate like a wave and genuinely felt similarly, as he and Sally adored Mo as a dear friend.

For the first time that day the two of them experienced a temporary respite from the pent up anxiety they had caused for themselves.

Kenny checked that no one was paying attention, before quietly saying to Rob;

'Ok. Now we're on the same page. We don't need it. We'll return it as soon as we get back.'

The shared look between them confirmed their mutual understanding.

Chapter Thirty-Four

Rinus Krol smiled. 'It's all under control, Sooo. Don't worry, eh?'

Sue Senior stared blankly back at him before replying;

'Easy for you to say Rinus. I've been keeping so many balls in the air lately and the stress of that'....

'I know, I know, baby ' He interrupted. 'But it will all soon come togedder. We will soon sort out dis liddle problem wit the money and den all dese guysh won't be a bodder for uss no more.' Rinus smiled reassuringly.

'But what about Mike Phelan? He knows everything.' Sue said concernedly.

Rinus smiled before replying reassuringly;

'Mikey will do ecsactly as he has been tolt to do. He knows that he is in a difficult posishun, as we know also everysing about his part in dis.'

'But he also knows our part too, Rinus. Except for the bit about you and me. And when he gets wind of that as well, then he's likely to become much more copperlike.'

Half an hour previously Mike Phelan had left the house without a backward glance after Rinus, assisted by the presence of his very large Dutch compatriot Bruno, had 'reminded' him of his part in their plan.

Rinus also told him that he'd already arranged for a carload of his 'assosshiates' to follow the coach carrying Ash and the other guys to Cleethorpes.

'Sooo, baby.' Rinus laughed. 'As much as you are widout doubt a beautiful and secsy woman, you have to realise dat his main interest will be in de money he sinks he will make out of dis. And you won't be staying arount here anymore in any case once we haf de money.'

Sue still looked uncertain.

'Relax baby, eh?' Rinus continued.

'A penthoush flat in Amshterdam. Holidays in de sun whenefer we like. Cars, money and everysing else you coult ever want are all waiting for you. Dat is your future, Sooo.'

'Well, I do rather like the sound of all that, Rinus.' Sue smiled.

'But,' She said laughing in a pseudo imitation of Rinus's accent, 'I sink we are going to haf to get you some elocooshion lesshons to improof our communicaishun, eh?'

She screamed playfully as he grabbed her amorously.

'We don't neet worts to communicate properly, Sooosan!' He laughed.

Chapter Thirty-Five

Kenny and Rob both felt a massive burden had been lifted from them as they sat back in their seats taking in the chatter and noise around them.

They were both fully aware that they still had to decide on how best to get rid of the money. But their joint relief at having decided to relieve themselves of the responsibility for it was, at least for now, a long way back to a resumption of 'normal life.'

Ash though had retreated into his own world of deep thought and concentration.

He ran and reran all of the information from Sue repeatedly as he tried to fathom the best way forward from here.

He had no doubt that he would be under deep scrutiny and the waiting for confirmation of that brought gut wrenching concern that took him back to his schooldays.

Although he had repeatedly faced troubling times since then in both his personal and professional life, he had always faced that off with confidence in his self assurance and ability to lie his way out of trouble. But this situation was completely different and he felt exposed and without as yet a plausible defence.

It reminded him of the times at school when he hadn't yet acquired the self confidence that came in his mid teens. He remembered crying in front of his Headmaster when his truancy had come to light and noted that the compassionate response he'd received from the Head had been effective in sparing him from anything more than an understanding mild rebuke and then a series of one to one meetings with his Housemaster to make sure he was ok.

He recorded that as being the start of his realisation that people could be manipulated as the situation demanded.

But crying was definitely not a way out here.

It increased his anger towards Rob and Kenny as he figured that, even if senior officers had become aware that money had gone missing, without their meddling in his plan he would've still actually been in possession of the money and able to conduct things with more of an idea of what to do next. He could maybe have got away with all of the cash and started a new life somewhere.

'Maybe I still could?' He found himself mumbling under his breath.

At the moment he could see no way of plausibly answering any questions and deflecting suspicion away from himself. So his focus started to shift back to his total need to obtain the money and keep it for himself.

It strengthened his resolve to heightened levels. Although he knew he would have to outrun both the police and criminals too, he backed his cunning and his knowledge of the criminal world to be able to elude any pursuers and get out of the country with the money.

He visualised life somewhere where he could live on his wits with a clean slate and the backing of substantial cash behind him.

'That's the dream. Now I have to make it a reality.' He muttered.

As he snapped back to conscious thought he noticed Kenny Bradley, a couple of rows in front, laughing at a comment that Ash hadn't heard.

But the sight of one of the main causes of his current woes with a big smile on his face was almost more than he could bear.

'You're so going to regret what you've done fat boy!' He said, a little louder than he'd intended.

Chapter Thirty-Six

Speedo was again the centre of attention.

'So what was that big foreign bloke talking to you about then?' Enquired Dino.

'We were just talking about music mostly. I was looking at some CD's in that place in the service area and he asked me what sort of stuff I liked. He was interesting.' And then as an afterthought he added, 'not like you lot!'

Dino laughed and was accompanied by Bertie and several of the others.

'What d'you mean mate? "Interesting," and not like us?' Dino persisted, knowing that wasn't what was meant.

Speedo sighed a heavy sigh before replying.

'He was interesting as a person, Dean. We talked about music. He knew a lot and we also liked similar stuff. It made a nice change to talk to someone like that. Whereas you lot are nothing like that, and we never talk about anything interesting. Because mostly, you just want to take the piss!'

'Well that's us all told off!' Kenny called from a couple of rows back laughing as he did.

'Oh mate!' Dino said, sounding almost sincere.

'Well, it's true.' Speedo said flatly. 'When do we ever talk about anything interesting?'

An awkward silence reigned for a good ten seconds before Bertie responded first.

'Oh bollocks Kevin! Who's rattled your cage? That big bloke probably fancied you, or something.'

There was general laughter amongst a few of the guys. But Speedo just shook his head.

But Gracie, seeing the look on his mate's face, felt the need to interject.

'Gaz.' He called to Gary Chivers. 'Can we swop seats for a minute mate?'

His accompanying look to Gary conveyed sufficient conviction for Gary to immediately oblige.

Gracie slotted in beside Speedo while the other guys in the neighbouring seats quietened down and talked amongst themselves to allow Gracie a bit of time and space, as they all felt more than a bit uncomfortable.

'Hey mate.' Gracie said quietly. 'Come on now. Nobody meant anything personal. Perhaps just a bit too much? But only said in jest. Alright?'

It occurred to Gracie that as much as he'd known Speedo (Kevin) for over 20 years, he barely knew the guy besides a few random circumstantial conversations across the bar over all those years.

It made him feel almost guilty of letting his regular customer down and being a sincere bloke at heart, he resolved to change that.

It turned out that there was quite a bit more to Kevin Morris than was apparent on the surface. From their short conversation Gracie discovered a guy who was lit up by music and the arts in general in a way that he'd never really known, or ever pretended to understand.

But once Speedo opened up a bit and began talking about the things that really interested him, Gracie saw a new guy unfold before his eyes.

Unfortunately this also made Gracie feel more than a bit shallow, given the time he'd assumed to know 'Kevin' and he wondered how many other of his regular customers at the pub he'd maybe also mentally pigeon holed as a certain type of character and had possibly completely misjudged.

Again he made a strong mental note to try and change his way of thinking.

'I knew you were into your music, mate.' He eventually managed to say, when the flow of words from Kevin finally began to slow. 'But I never knew quite how much, obviously! You're a dark horse mate!'

Kevin smiled a sardonic smile and said;

'Look. I enjoy the company in the pub and most of the time I don't care about not really getting what the crack is. I suppose I only half listen to what's going on. I live on my own and I suppose I'm sort of in my own little world. It's ok though. But don't say anything to anyone. It's their bloody loss if they don't really bother to get to know someone I suppose. We've all got our own funny little ways!'

Gracie couldn't help himself after that comment though; 'Well, yes! But you certainly have sometimes, mate!'

They both laughed at that.

'Between you and me though,' Kevin whispered. 'I sometimes play my own little game of pretending not to understand, just to wind people up. But it wouldn't do to let them know.'

Gracie smiled wryly. 'Well, your secret's safe with me, mate.'

Although he wasn't absolutely sure that that was always the case.

Chapter Thirty-Seven

Behind the coach, several cars back, a large black SUV containing four also very large Dutchmen tracked their progress, having left the car park at the same time.

'What was you saying to dat guy in de store back dere Rudi man, eh?' Enquired the driver of the vehicle to the equally tall and broad man sitting next to him.

Although extremely large, Rudi Rensenbrinck was very softly spoken and he whispered a barely audible reply, given the conversation between the other two guys in the back of the vehicle, the music that blared from the radio and the traffic noise emanating through the partly open window next to the driver.

'We was just discussing music, dat's all.' Rudi smiled serenely.

'He was a nice guy.' He added.

Marco Neeskens (the driver) grinned at his friend.

'Awww. Do you haf a soft spot for your new liddle frent, Rooodi?' He half sang his friend's name as he said it.

Rudi again smiled.

'Maybe? He likt der same kint of stuff as me. I set we may see him and his frents later, as we are also headet to der coast.'

Marco patted Rudi's knee before replying. 'Just remember we are here on business eh? Aldough I guess we hat to get to know these guysh as well as keep an eye on dem like Rinus wants.'

'Ecsactly!' Rudi beamed. 'Just like Rinus wants.'

The two younger, but equally large men in the back caught the last bit of their conversation.

'Fuck all dat! We just wanna get dis money back. Dat's what Rinus wants.' Said Danny van Basten, from his seat behind Rudi.

'Yeh, dat's right.' Agreed Johann van den Bent, who was sitting next to Danny.

Marco glanced disapprovingly at them over his shoulder.

'Guysh, shut der fuck up ant calm down eh? Dere is no neet for aggression, unless it becomes absolootely necessary. Ok?'

Danny and Johann looked suitably chastened. They had been the recipients of admonishments from Marco before and both of them knew better than to get on the wrong side of their colleague.

'Ok.' They replied, more or less in unison.

'Gootl I'm glad dat is all understoot.' Marco's countenance changed back to his more familiar geniality

He continued. 'Like I set as we left just now, I saw dat guy Ash on dere coach. When we get to Cleethorpes we will have a liddle wort wit him to make sure he knows wat to do.'

There were nods all round and Marco broke into a big smile and said;

'Like dey say here in the UK, It's all goot!'

Danny laughed and said; 'Yeah, but maybe not so goot for dat guy Ash, eh Marco?'

Marco didn't turn round, but replied; 'We'll see. We'll see.'

Chapter Thirty-Eight

A while afterwards Mick pulled into the coach park near the sea front at Cleethorpes, amidst a few cheers from the occupants.

There was general excitement amongst the guys and the noise level had risen steadily as the coach had gotten closer to their destination.

Gracie again called everyone to order and they all disembarked and gathered outside.

Ash was in complete turmoil and went through the motions of joining the others.

Given the news from Sue he now wondered if this was all just a waste of time and he began to regret not having stayed at home to be closer to where the money surely was.

Being around all of the jollity and banter going on in front of him was the last thing he needed at that moment and he stayed on the periphery of the now fully disembarked group and tried to gather his thoughts.

Kenny and Rob however felt as if a large burden had been removed from them.

Their smiles and laughter of the previous day when they had been counting the money had returned for a completely different reason and they were both genuinely happy to be with their mates on a day out.

They were still fully aware that they had a task to finish in regard to completely relieving themselves of the responsibility of the money they had secreted in Kenny's garden yesterday evening.

But, despite having had no opportunity as yet to discuss exactly what they were going to do with it next, they had both been mulling that over on the coach on the journey from the service area and were equally keen to talk about that as soon as they safely could.

'Right Gents. Let's get on it!' Shouted Bertie.

He clapped his arm around Dino's shoulder and continued;

'Lead on Dino, and take us to the nearest boozer!'

The smiling throng set off from the car park and made towards the seafront.

Ash hung back a little in his melancholic mood and watched the other guys in their groups of twos and threes as they happily ambled away.

He reasoned that he had to pull himself together and was just about to stride away in pursuit when he felt a large hand on his shoulder.

He froze, as somewhere in his mind he visualised this to be his moment of arrest.

But as he turned to face the owner of the large hand he was met with the spectacle of a very large guy wearing amongst other things, a black polo shirt that seemed to have muscles escaping from it everywhere. The giant was smiling down at him.

'I believe you are Ash. Is dat right, eh?' Said the smiling giant in a strong European accent.

'Err...yesh..I..I mean yes.' He found himself replying nervously.

'Who...how d'....Ash's attempted continuance was interrupted.

'Eassee man. We're frents.' The giant extended the arm that was not still gripping Ash's shoulder to indicate three other giants in similar looking attire, who stood a few feet away.

'We're here to help you, man.' Said one of the other giants.

'H..hel..help me?' Ash stuttered a small reply.

The original giant clapped Ash on the back, nearly knocking him over and laughed.

'Yeah man, eh? Help you in your task to retrieve de money!'

This time the smile was a little more menacing.

'Who ar...'

Again Ash's reply was stagnated by an interruption. This time from the second giant again.

'Like we just set, Ash. We're frents. Our boss is keen for us to help you fint de money dat is missing.'

Ash's mind was in complete meltdown. But he pulled himself together sufficiently to finally say;

'Look guys, forgive me, but I don't know you and I'm here with friends.'

Ash indicated towards the fast disappearing group in the near distance.

Giant two also fixed him with a more intense look this time.

'Ash. We know who you are. We know all about you. We know about your ''relashionship'' wit de unfortunate Mr. Senior.'

The more pleasant and slightly less disturbing demeanour returned.

Smiling at Ash he continued;

'Look. We know dat sings haf got a liddle more complicatet. But we can resolf dis situashun ant get de money back. Den everysing will be fine again. Ok?'

Ash fleetingly considered asking them who their boss was, but decided this wasn't the place or the time for any heroics. Especially as he was as scared as he'd ever remembered being.

He stumbled briefly through a repetition of the events of yesterday and how the money had been missing on his return to the golf course. Although he hated the pleading tone of his voice, he sincerely hoped they believed him.

They told Ash to catch up with the others and advised of a plan for them to join up with the group, where they would 'accidently,' bump into him and his 'frents' in a while and sort 'sings' out.

They gave him a number to contact them on once he and the others were settled somewhere.

Seeing Ash's vexed expression, giant number one semi playfully cuffed him round the shoulder, propelling him a few feet sideways.

'Like I set just now, take it eassee, man.' He laughed. 'It's all goot, eh?'

But just to reinforce the intent as Ash walked away he said;

'But don't try anysing stupit, eh? Make dat call soon, Ash.'

Chapter Thirty-Nine

Ash's chest was pounding. As he walked, or part jogged after the others, he swore he could almost hear his heart beating.

His mind was still trying to process what had just happened. But he knew for sure that he had never felt this much fear and dread before. All thoughts of outrunning villains as well as the police had disappeared. He was genuinely petrified.

Still breathless, he caught up with the guys as they stood outside a Wetherspoon's pub around the corner from the Coach park.

'Right. Whip money boys! £20 each for now. Ok?' Bertie smiled and clapped his hands as he spoke.

'Are you alright holding the whip again please, Gracie? You're by far the most reliable of us,' he continued, whilst fixing Kenny with an icy stare.

Gracie nodded his assent.

He was well versed in this particular role and had performed it on several occasions over the past few years, having replaced Kenny, after he'd disgraced himself by managing to lose a not inconsiderable sum when he inadvertently left it on the bar of a pub in Leicester on one of his more infamous drunken lapses.

Kenny caught the inference and Bertie's look.

'Oh, for gawd's sake!' He whined. 'Are you still going on about that? Talk about ancient bloody history! A bloke makes one mistake...'

'Wasn't just the one though, was it?' Bertie acidly interrupted.

'Whatever!' Kenny said quietly, backing down, as he accepted the truth of past misdemeanours.

'And make sure it's real money you're putting in as well Kenny Bradley! None of those dodgy notes from yesterday.' Bertie added, to the amusement of several of the group.

'Oh, I think I've just busted a rib from laughing.' Came Kenny's ironic reply.

The guys all handed over the required cash to Gracie and they went into pub number one of their Cleethorpes experience, The Coliseum.

There was already a fair crowd both inside the bar and in the seating area outside.

'Blimey! We've got a welcoming committee, lads.' Said Dino, as they tried to find the closest route to the bar.

'It's match day, mate.' Said an old chap queuing at the bar, on overhearing Dino's comment.

'Oh right. I was wondering why so many people were wearing black and white shirts!' Said Dino, taking in the surrounding scene.

'The mighty Mariners!' Bertie informed him.

The old chap turned around and smiled.

'Not so mighty these days...come to think of it, not so mighty any day!' He said, laughing.

Bertie and Dino laughed along with the old chap, who bore a striking resemblance to an older version of Kevin 'Speedo' Morris.

Dino and Bertie both noticed it simultaneously and neither could suppress their amazement.

Fortunately the old gent had turned back to the bar and managed to catch the attention of one of the bar staff and didn't hear the exchange between them.

'Bloody hell! It's Speedo's Dad!' Dino laughed.

'Dead ringer!' Bertie agreed excitedly.

Dino looked quickly over to where Gracie was endeavouring unsuccessfully to sandwich himself between people who were drinking at the bar in a forlorn effort to get served and then tapped the old guy in front of him on the shoulder.

'Excuse me, mate. Sorry to be a pain, but are you on your own?'

'Y..yes.' He replied, sounding a little surprised.

'Well, would you mind if we took over your order please? There's a few of us and it'll save us time. And there's a free pint in it for you too.'

The old guy gave Dino a look as if he'd just given him the best Christmas present ever and willingly agreed.

He took his pint from the barman and said, 'my mate'll give you the rest of the drinks.'

Dino smiled at him and pressed on with the multi order, simultaneously attracting Gracie's attention and enabling him to extricate himself from the human sandwich that he was now the meat in.

As Gracie shuffled round to them, trying to avoid stepping on the toes of the assembled throng and potentially starting a fight with what appeared to be the entire content of the Grimsby Town Supporters Club, he shouted across to be heard over the noise around the bar;

'Nice one, Dino. I thought we'd be waiting ages!'

Dino couldn't help himself. 'Thank Speedo's Dad here.' He indicated the smiling, older aged Kevin Morris lookalike standing next to him.

'Eh?' Said the old guy.

Bertie obligingly endeavoured to explain by pointing to Speedo, who stood several feet away staring open mouthed at a vision of himself, twenty odd years into the future.

Bertie shouted to him. 'Say hello to your Dad, Kev!'

The old guy, who they soon found out was unbelievably called Maurice, took a big gulp of his beer before exclaiming, 'bugger me, you look more like me than my own kids do!'

Speedo (Kevin), still open mouthed, finally summoned up the strength to reply.

'You could be my Dad!'

Then, as an afterthought, 'ARE you my Dad?'

Maurice looked at his new found 'Son' and exclaimed hesitantly, 'I..I..I dunno mate!.. How could I be?'

As more of the guys took in the spectacle of the older Maurice and the younger Morris they became the focal point for sustained comments and good natured banter.

Gracie said to Bertie and Dino; 'Is this for real?'

'I have no idea, mate,' Bertie replied. 'But take a look at them. It could be!'

Kevin was more than a bit overwhelmed.

He said to Maurice, who had by now introduced himself, 'I..I never knew my Dad, you see, and you look so much like me. My Mum and my Grannie brought me up. So you might be! Somebody is!'

This admission made him a little unsteady, and the ensuing conversation between him and Maurice did nothing to dispel that.

After Kevin mentioned where he was from and had divulged a few further details, it slowly triggered Maurice's memory of events years before. And following what seemed like an eternity of the two men looking at each other in silence, everything eventually came back to him.

'Shirley Morris.' He finally said. 'Is that your Mum's name?'

'Y..y..yes, it is. Kev replied. His voice wavering.

It turned out that Maurice had worked all over the county years ago, before finally settling in the Grimsby area. But from what Kevin had told him, he'd recalled long buried personal memories and it transpired that Maurice and Kevin's Mother had been in a short term relationship while he'd worked in her locality all those years before.

Maurice was also taken aback.

'I never ever knew she was pregnant, honestly I didn't! If I'd known....' His voice tailed off as he thought about that time in his life.

'Shirley Morris.' He said again. This time a little misty eyed.

Bertie, Dino and Gracie, although uncomfortable initially as the reality of the situation began to dawn in front of them, were now all spellbound at the revelation.

Kevin though was overjoyed at the connection.

'Yes, Yes, that's definitely my Mum!' He beamed.

'She always was independent.' Maurice said, and then repeated, 'if I'd known..'

Kevin interrupted the man who he now knew WAS his Father.

'It's ok. I never missed out. Mum's always said it was what she wanted. She's never blamed you, and never tried to find you.'

Maurice was now very teary eyed and Kevin shook his hand and then instinctively gave him a hug, saying, 'this is my Dad, guys!'

The boys hugged their mate and shook Maurice's hand. Word soon spread to the others, which gave rise to more congratulations and the cue for more drinks to be ordered.

A table became free and Kevin and Maurice were able to sit down to properly 'catch up,' while the story of their incredible coincidental meeting and how it had all occurred spread among the group.

'Bloody hell! You could not make stuff like that up, could you?' Bertie said, as he regaled several of those who had been largely oblivious to what had just happened.

Kenny and Rob were among that group. They had initially huddled together on entering the pub to try and discuss how they would dispose of the money. But with Ash in close proximity and then all of the fuss about Speedo's family reunion, they had not yet had a chance to talk.

They briefly congratulated a beaming Speedo and his Dad Maurice and then took their opportunity to slip outside the pub with their pints in hand, with Ash temporarily nowhere to be seen.

Chapter Forty

Kenny got in first.

'I think we either put it back where we found it, or we leave the bag in a phone booth somewhere.'

Rob looked a little vexed at that.

'Yeah, I've been thinking about that again though. A public phone is just too random. Anyone could find it and that might just lead to more problems! And depending on where it is, there's also the chance of us being picked up on CCTV! '

Kenny frowned. 'Oh Jesus! I hadn't thought of that. Ok. But we can't take it to the police now....unless we pretend we've only just found it on the golf course, if that's where we'd say we found it?'

'Bit convoluted that, though.' Rob pondered. 'We'd have to turn up for a game and then pretend we'd just found it and take it to the Pro shop and get them to phone the Police. And what about Ash? He could still twist things against us somehow.'

'How?' Kenny said, still looking around to make sure Ash was nowhere nearby.

He continued; 'Ash couldn't say anything to the police about where we found it, could he? And if we were handing a bag full of money in, they would hardly be interested in us afterwards. Either way, it wouldn't be our problem anymore, would it?'

'No, it wouldn't.' Rob agreed. 'But by coming forward to the police, we'd be officially connected with that money and that would filter back to Ash and who knows who else, if he's mixed up with anyone?'

Rob's last comment caused a look of anguish to appear on Kenny's face.

'I hadn't even considered him being in with anyone else, Bog. Bloody hell! Perhaps we should just leave it back where we found it and not say anything?'

They rolled their eyes at each other and prepared for further thought.

Inside the pub, Ash, whose heart was still pounding, along with a hammering in his head, was going through the motions of normality in front of the others.

He was actually pleased at that moment to be as unpopular as he knew he was amongst the group, as it gave him some time and space on his own to consider the current situation.

He gauged that the group would not be moving on anytime soon, so he made a call to the number already put in the burner phone he'd proffered to the giant who'd slapped him about in the car park.

After two rings the call was answered by the now familiar European voice.

Ash gave the name and location of the pub and then made a call to Sue Senior.

Chapter Forty-One

'Who the hell are these gorillas, Sue?' Ash half pleaded down the phone.

'How am I supposed to know, Ash?' Sue's deadpan response sounded flat.

'I don't know!' He said, sounding at the end of his tether. 'But they said they were here to "help" me get the money back! How would they even know about the money?'

Sue stuck to the same stonewall replies she'd used since first answering Ash's call. She said she didn't know how four European guys could know about any missing money.

'Well they certainly do know!' Ash hissed, trying to keep up the pretence of looking calm in the crowded bar.

The noise level was as bad inside the pub as it had been when he'd started the call in the seating area outside, before thinking better of it and coming back in. None of which was helping Ash's mood.

Sue offered a possible explanation finally.

'They must work for the guy Ron was dealing with? He would've been expecting Ron to be paying a million quid for those drugs, wouldn't he?'

Ash thought briefly before replying. Something didn't sound right.

'I dunno, Sue.' He said hesitantly. 'But anyway, how would they know that the police hadn't seized that cash as part of the raid?'

Sue went back on the defensive.

'I don't bloody know, Ash! But they obviously do! Maybe one of your lot is in with them?'

But an alarm bell had rung in Ash's head at her earlier reply when she'd mentioned how much Ron was supposed to be paying for the drugs, as he had never mentioned the amount in the bags to her prior to the search and neither of them had mentioned an exact sum since. He suddenly had the impression that Sue wasn't being entirely truthful with him.

He ended the call having avoided saying anything else about that though, as he knew he'd be dealing with the four heavies again imminently.

'What dit he say?' Rinus asked.

'He was panicking. He said your guys spoke to him a little while ago and scared him a bit. They're going to join him and the others in whatever pub they're in, any time now.'

Sue pondered before continuing;

'What did you tell them to do, Rinus? These guys are ordinary blokes.'

'It's fine, baby. I just tolt dem to get close ant speak to dose udder guysh as well as Ash, ant play it by ear. I wantet to get dere take on sings. I don't trust dat weasel Ash.'

Sue thought about her conversation with Ash.

'I think I just screwed up though when I spoke to him. I said about the money for the drugs being a million quid, didn't I?'

Rinus looked at her puzzled.

'So what?'

'Well, Ash and me had never mentioned the amount that Ron was supposed to be paying for those drugs. We only ever said it was a load of cash, or something like that. But I just blurted out about it being a million quid and I think he noticed.' Sue chewed her lip and looked worried.

'Don't worry, baby. As far as Ash knows, you coult have fount out from Ron's Lawyer, or even from Ron. Dat is no big deal.'

'What are your guys going to do to him and those other guys that he said have taken the money, Rinus?'

Rinus sighed.

'Like I just set. Dey will play it by ear, Soo. I sink dat Ash is a lying bastard anyway. We already know dat, don't we?'

Sue didn't reply. Her mind had wandered. All of the events of the last twenty four hours were taking their toll. Although she'd been fully complicit in the web that had been woven, it was a lot harder to live through than she'd imagined when it had been planned and first suggested to her.

'Soo, what are you worrit about, eh?' Rinus took hold of her arms.

Sue looked him in the eyes.

'I just don't want a load of bloodshed. The worse this becomes, then the more grief there'll be after. Especially with coppers and ordinary people involved.'

'It won't come to dat, baby. My guysh are not idiots. Dey will fint out whatever dey can. We know dat dis money is not far away.'

'It MUSN'T come to that, Rinus!' Ok, Ash and Mike Phelan are bent coppers. But they're just trying to make money in the same way as we are. Ron maybe deserved his come uppance for his greed and his wickedness over the years. But these other guys, IF Ash is right about them finding the money, well..they don't deserve anything bad to happen to them.'

Rinus smiled reassuringly and put his arms around Sue to calm her. But as she looked over his shoulder she wasn't sure whether or not he was being sincere.

Chapter Forty-Two

Sue Senior had lived her life till now entirely on her wits.

Yes, for sure she enjoyed a good time and had made the absolute most of her ability to charm men.

But from the very start she had experienced a tough upbringing.

She was the second eldest of five children in an Irish family and the oldest of the three girls.

Her Father had been an abusive drunk, who made his living on building sites as a Labourer and spent the vast majority of his wages in the pubs in their local area.

Her Mother had done her best for her children and had worked in between and even during her numerous pregnancies, to provide food and clothing for them.

But it had never been a safe and secure family environment to grow up in and Sue and her Brothers and Sisters had often witnessed violent scenes between their drunken Father and their Mother.

As Sue grew up, her Mother relied upon her to take on a lot of the domestic chores as well as the care for her younger siblings and it became second nature for her to put their needs before her own.

But, even from her earliest memories, Sue had always taken a pride in her appearance and how she and her two younger Sisters looked outside the house.

Her Mother, broken down by the continual abuse she'd experienced from her Husband, became very ill in her mid thirties and passed away when Sue was only thirteen.

Sue had idolised her Mother as a child, but as she grew she became annoyed that her Mum didn't stand up to her Father, or at least report his behaviour to the authorities.

After her Mother died, her Father took up with another woman, who he promptly moved into the house. But she became his drinking partner rather than any sort of Step Mother to the children.

By this time Sue had become aware of the changes in her shape and appearance that Puberty brought on and the ensuing popularity this gave her with boys.

She always tried to look after her Sisters and little Brother, but had no rapport with her older Brother Michael, who'd already been in trouble with the police and was often not at home, eventually ending up in Prison.

Her Father and his Partner's behaviour became so bad that Sue and her siblings were taken into care by the local authority.

But almost immediately, she and her Sisters had to face the tragic loss of their little Brother, who was killed in a road accident aged only eight.

The care home that Sue and her sisters were admitted to was not somewhere they felt safe and they eventually managed to persuade their Social Workers to allow them to move in with their Grandmother and one of their Aunt's on her Mother's side of the family.

By that time Sue had begun to enjoy being the centre of constant male attention at school and after she and her Sisters moved in with their family, she felt freed from the constant need to look after them and started to make her own way.

She left school at sixteen and started a full time job at the Hairdresser's that she had worked part time at for a year before leaving school.

She was also by then in a relationship with an older boy, who she became pregnant by soon after.

Given her situation and her doubt of how serious the relationship was, she had an Abortion. She didn't realise at the time but, the effects of that procedure later proved to be the cause of her not being able to have a child later in life.

Although she worked hard and became very much in demand as a Hairdresser, her personal life was always very turbulent and there were a succession of boyfriends before she met up with Ronnie Senior.

She had been immediately attracted to him, due to both his cheeky chappie character and the bad boy rumours that followed him and his Brothers around in the local area.

Ron was really taken by Sue and for the first time in her life she felt both loved and looked after. When he asked her to marry him, she didn't hesitate to say yes and for a long time afterwards they were besotted with each other.

Ron always had big plans and due to him Sue was able to start her own business, as both a hairdresser and beauty consultant.

She had always been well liked, both by girls at school and women she met and became friends with at work after that, as she had always stuck up for people being bullied and ill treated.

Her caring nature towards women suffering at the hands of a man, fuelled by her own experiences growing up, made her increasingly popular as time went on.

Because of her relationship with Ron, who, along with his older Brother Frank, had by then risen to leading their own gang and commanded a grudging level of respect from their rivals in the local criminal society, she was handy for women to know if they were being treated badly by an offending man.

Ron saw Sue as almost an equal in the way she conducted herself in business and he didn't hesitate to support her financially, especially given the opportunity it gave him to launder money from his own affairs through her books.

Like Sue, he had come from humble beginnings and she provided him with the first real stable relationship in his life, other than his bond with his older Brother.

But as time went on, Ron's criminal ambition and greed grew as he strived to become even more powerful. As a result, Sue and Ronnie's relationship inevitably changed.

Although they remained fiercely loyal to each other for a long time, due to their abiding respect and admiration for each other, her liking for a good time and a party lifestyle and his burning desire for power took them in different directions.

Sue felt they had a secure enough financial base to live a really good life, without needing to take any more risks.

But Ron thought that, if he tried to 'retire,' or take more of a back seat, he would lose his identity and his own inflated sense of status.

She grew tired of Ron's obsession to do more and more 'deals' and she became more aware that his relationships with numerous unsavoury characters had noticeably changed him into a colder and increasingly more ruthless man.

Given the deprivations of her turbulent childhood, long term security and stability were vitally important to her. She also retained a hatred of injustice and seeing what she described as, 'bad things happening to good people.'

So, in frustration at his stubbornness and also having witnessed him become colder and harsher towards both her and others around him, Sue had begun to return the affections of other men, as she had never been short of admirers.

She had realised that Ron was riding for a fall some time ago and had tried to warn him to call time on his criminal activities and become a purely legitimate businessman, like his Brother Frank had done. But when he refused to see it that way, she then made the decision to look after her own interests.

Right now though, with her stomach churning, she stared over Rinus's shoulder at the wall behind him. As she replayed events from both her distant and then more recent past, Sue wasn't really sure about anything anymore.

Chapter Forty-Three

Marco Neeskens was more than accustomed to being stared at when he entered a room full of people.

Being a tall, muscular, imposing looking guy had its benefits in many respects.

True, he wouldn't have been a suitable candidate for close undercover work with any need to remain inconspicuous. But that had never been the type of work that he had either sought, or carried out.

As he and his three associates made their way through the throng of people sitting and standing around in the crowded area outside the bar that Ash had said they would find him in, it was a bit like the Red Sea parting for Moses, as people made way for them to pass.

Despite his bulk and his ability to use his size and strength to his advantage, Marco was by nature a calm and measured individual who liked to get on with people. Even when things became difficult, he much preferred to resist rising to anger, unless all else failed.

Although in such circumstances, he was more than accomplished in administering an appropriate level of summary justice to match whatever was needed to resolve any given situation.

Like his good friend Rudi, who had been at his side for many years during their many 'business experiences,' Marco had hidden depths.

Their current companions Danny and Johann though, were not as yet worthy of his trust and he and Rudi were mindful of the need to keep tabs on them.

As they scoured the faces of the people inside the bar, Marco and Rudi made sedate progress through the parting crowd, smiling and nodding their thanks to people who made way for them to pass.

Ash noticed them as they entered from outside, as the daylight behind them was fleetingly eclipsed by the two giants standing side by side and then again by the pair of equally large men who entered immediately behind them.

He made his way over to them and they met near the bar.

Ash briefly put them in the picture about the crowd he was with and without making it obvious, pointed out Rob and Kenny as the two guys that he believed had taken the money they were all interested in.

'Look guys, if we're to make this in any way believable, I think I should introduce you as colleagues from the Dutch Police.

I can say that we've worked together before and are now involved in a joint case between English and Dutch Police? That would be a lot easier to explain how we know each other and for you being here now.'

While Marco and the others were taking that on board, Ash continued;

'It would just be too random otherwise, for four guys from the Netherlands to suddenly just latch onto a crowd of guys they don't know. Especially this crowd!

So are we agreed then, to say that we're working in partnership on the same case?'

Marco looked at Rudi and both men smiled and agreed.

'Yeah, dat sounts like a plan, Ash.' Marco smiled, continuing; 'Let's see where dat leads us. If anyone asks, we can say dat you invited us, ok?'

So Ash led his newly created Dutch 'friends' over to where the nucleus of the group stood and tapped Gracie on the shoulder.

'Hey, Gracie. I've got four new recruits for the whip.'

He introduced them as work colleagues and left the guys to introduce themselves as they liked.

The feel good factor from Speedo's unbelievable meeting with his Dad had created such a buzz, that most of the group took no real initial notice of the four new guys.

No one that is apart from Rob and Kenny. Who, having come back inside the pub, properly congratulated Speedo and spoken at more length to Maurice, had started to chill out. But were now looking at each other wondering what on earth was going on.

Speedo though was more animated that any of his friends and acquaintances had ever seen. Even when he'd had more than his usual quota in the past, he was usually a quiet drunk who withdrew more into his own thoughts.

But his unexpected and highly emotional meeting with his Father, fuelled by three quick pints, had caused an unexpected level of confidence to emerge.

And when he surveyed the four huge guys who'd just joined their party his smile grew even wider, as he noticed the smiling face of the man he'd spoken to briefly at the Roadside Services a while back.

'Hello again.' He said. 'Do you remember me?'

Rudi's smile also grew broader as he replied;

'Of course. Hello again. I believe I set we may meet again at der coast?'

Speedo stood awkwardly from the cramped table he sat behind, almost dismantling a few of the semi full pint glasses from the surface.

'Easy Kevlar!' Said Bertie, who from his standing position next to the table, managed to stabilise it without issue.

'Oops, sorry! Thanks, Bertie.' Speedo smiled at his mate.

Fixing Rudi and his three equally large friends with a friendly grin, He continued;

'My name's Kevin, by the way. And this gentleman,' he said, indicating his new found Father, 'is my Dad, Maurice. Pleased to meet you. We didn't get time for proper introductions earlier.'

Speedo's mates had never seen him so animated. But most of them assumed him to understandably still be on a massive high of emotion.

Rudi though was touched by the welcome.

'I am very pleast to meet wit you, Kevin. Pleast also to meet wit you, sir.' He nodded to Maurice, who was sitting next to the chair that Speedo had just vacated to stand.

'My name is Rudi.'

Maurice nodded and smiled at Rudi.

More drinks were bought and Ash felt the need to fill in Gracie and Dino, who'd got the drinks, as to who the four Euro giants were.

'There's been a development in a case I'm involved with.' He said grandly.

'Can't say too much, but these guys are from the Dutch Police and they're working in partnership with us.'

'Oh right.' Gracie replied, without the slightest trace of interest. 'Thanks for letting us know.'

He turned towards Dino and raised his eyes and mouthed silently; 'Twat!'

Chapter Forty-Four

Bertie was keen to get the day on a proper footing and suggested they should all invest in what he described as, 'a flutter on the gee gees.'

'What about it eh, chaps? You never know. This could be our lucky day?'

The general feelgood factor amongst the majority of the group, fuelled by a few pints, was the clincher.

Bertie and Dino had already scanned the Racing section of Bertie's newspaper during the journey earlier and they were primed with suggestions for the proposed bet.

'If we all bung in a tenner each, we could do a decent sized Lucky 15, or a Yankee?' Bertie said to his mostly bemused audience.

But with Gracie and Dino's assistance, aided by another round being delivered, courtesy of the addition to the whip money via the Dutch contingent, the momentum gathered.

'Are we all up for it, then?' Bertie said enthusiastically.

'Come on guys! What have we got to lose?' Dino contributed.

'Erm...a tenner, probably!' Gary Chivers responded.

'Oh come on Gaz! It's not like you can't afford it, is it?' Dino countered.

Gary was a Senior Manager in a large Construction firm and was known to be on a very good salary

'Go on then.' Gary laughed, and threw a ten pound note on the table in front of Bertie.

The Dutch giants had until then been fairly anonymous to the group and had stood on the periphery surveying them without much comment.

'Are you guys in as well?' Bertie enquired to Ash, who was the closest to him of the group including his Dutch 'colleagues.'

Johann broke ranks initially.

'What, more money to pay?' He whined.

Marco and Rudi glared disapprovingly at him.

'Don't be such a baby. It's only a bit of fun.' Marco said mockingly.

Johann, shamefaced, got his wallet out and produced an impressive amount of notes.

Rudi, on seeing the notes and already tiring of both Danny and Johann's attitude, decided to tease him further.

'Fuck me! Ok moneybags. Since you haf brought all of your pocket money from your Momma wit you, you can pay for us too, eh?'

'Absolootely!' Marco agreed.

Johann wanted to say something, but thought better of it on seeing the thinly veiled humour replaced by more serious looks from his older and more experienced countrymen.

He leant across and extended a heavily muscled arm, and threw four ten pound notes on the growing cash pile in front of Bertie.

Ash bit his tongue just in time, as he had considered asking Johann to pay for him as well.

'Dat's bedder man! Cheer up, eh?' Marco laughed.

But the air of tension between the Dutch men was clearly evident to the other guys, and they also decided against any supporting banter.

Most of the guys had no real interest in Horse Racing, and were happy for Bertie, Dino and Gracie to finalise the selections for the group. The bet was then placed by Bertie via his phone, as he held accounts with several bookmakers.

'Ok guys. We're on!' Bertie announced after getting off the phone.

After another drink, Maurice, who only originally came in for a couple of beers prior to going to watch Grimsby Town, got unsteadily to his feet.

He and Speedo had exchanged numbers and addresses and preliminary arrangements had already been made for

Kev to meet his half Brothers and Sisters, once Maurice had broken the incredible news of their meeting to his family.

'I'd better be getting along though, Son.' He said.

'If I drink anymore, I'll only end up embarrassing you and myself in front of your mates.'

Speedo looked at his Dad and then gave him a big hug.

'You could never embarrass me, Dad. This is the best day ever. And believe me, you've got nothing to worry about, as I've seen quite a few of these blokes in all sorts of a state in the past!'

'Blimey, what's happened to Speedo?' Dino said. 'He's turned into a wit all of a sudden.'

Maurice said his farewells and with best wishes from the guys he made to depart.

But not before the giant Rudi had made his way over to wish him well.

'I've only just hert from the guys dat you two only met today for der first time? Dat is a wonderful coincidence!'

'Yes it is.' Agreed Maurice.

And seeing his boy looking a little emotional and a bit tipsy, Maurice said to Rudi, 'look after him for me please and keep him out of trouble.'

Rudi smiled a beaming smile and gave the tiny Maurice a bear hug.

'Dat will be my pleasure, Maurice. I'll make shure dat he comes to no harm.'

'Thanks, Rudi.' Said Maurice gratefully.

'Doesn't he have a beautiful accent, Son?'

Speedo/Kevin looked up at his new Dutch friend admiringly and eventually replied;

'Beautiful, yes. What's that saying Dad, about beauty being something to do with the beholder?'

As Maurice started to reply, Speedo's recall came back to him and they spoke in unison;

'Beauty is in the eye hole of the beholder, isn't it?'

Dino turned to his mates and said, 'Oh, wait a minute! There he is. Speedo's back in the room!'

Scott Flintoff quickly added; 'Yeah and Maurice is definitely his Dad!'

Chapter Forty-Five

The Dutch contingent had started to integrate more with the group now and got to know who was who.

Marco and Rudi had previously agreed to take Danny and Johann respectively under their control, prior to the integration exercise and Ash also made more of an attempt at normal conversation.

He still felt totally bemused at how events had unfolded and had a distinct feeling that he was the planned victim of a major set up over the money.

The emergence of the Dutch guys had left him feeling even further from the missing cash. But for now, he aimed to return to his original plan of seeing if anything came to light from Rob and Kenny as the day wore on and they hopefully became a bit more relaxed through the effects of drinking. He knew that he'd have to tread carefully now though and see how things unfolded.

But the Dutch guys were more direct in their approach and had begun to mention the reason for their presence in the UK in their general conversations with the group.

'You must be wondering why we haf just suddenly showt up here, no?' Marco said, smiling his most engaging smile to a small group that included Kenny and Rob.

Marco had a certain presence that disarmed people and drew them to him, and he was an easy man to like in many ways.

Kenny caught Rob's nervousness and made a tense face at him, trying to encourage him to focus.

However, Bertie's desire to be in the thick of most conversations bought them a little more time to compose themselves.

'Well, it's obviously something quite serious for the Dutch Police to be needed over here. But, I presume you're all off duty now, though?'

'Yes, of course. But we neet to fint out about some money dat has gone missing in der area near where you guysh liff.' Marco said conspiratorially.

'A large amount of money, too.' He continued.

'It goes widout saying dat if you guys hear or come to know anysink about it, dat you let de police know rightaway, eh?'

'Of course.' Kenny felt confident enough to offer.

'What was it dat Ash was telling me a liddle while ago, about you guys and some fake money, yesterday?' Marco said laughing.

'Oh, that was all a joke. A wind up. Do you know what a wind up is?'

Kenny surprised himself as he found the confidence to discuss the 'safer' parts of their experience the day before.

'Yes, I am familiar with a "wint up." We haf a lot of your English sayings in our country. Who was being der victim of dis "wint up?" '

'I was.' Kenny smiled wryly.

'My lovely mates here decided to put some fake money out for me to find, hoping that I'd keep it.'

Marco laughed.

'Ant, dit you keep it? Errr, sorry. Kenny isn't it?'

Kenny felt a little uncomfortable, but did his best not to show it.

'Y..Yes, I did. At first.'

Marco nudged Danny and they both laughed, which induced Bertie and one or two of the others to join in.

'It's the sort of thing we often do to each other, though...isn't it guys?' Kenny half pleaded for support.

Rob felt the need to help his mate.

'Absolutely! We've all been the victims of things like that over the years.'

Marco laughed briefly and then looked again at Kenny.

'Tell me dough, Kenny. Woult you always keep any money you fint randomly like dat?'

After a brief silence Marco laughed again and was joined by Danny and the others, except for Kenny and Rob, who smiled ruefully.

When the laughter had subsided, Kenny replied.

'No, I wouldn't. Especially after what this lot put me through, yesterday!'

This was the cue for more laughter.

But Kenny felt more than a bit shaken by the conversation.

Chapter Forty-Six

The guys decided to take a break for food shortly afterwards, in order to pace themselves for the long haul ahead of them.

'What are we doing then?' Scott and a couple of the others chorused to Bertie and Dino.

'Well, I think we need some nose bag now. Otherwise the day will go quickly downhill.' Bertie answered.

'Nose bag? What is dat?' Queried Marco to Rudi.

'I sink he means to eat. I've hert it set before here in Englant.' Rudi answered.

Marco drew Rudi to one side.

'I've just been speaking to dat guy Kenny. You know, one of the two guysh dat pussy Ash tolt us hat taken der money.'

Rudi nodded.

'I askt him about der fake money dat Ash mentiont, ant den I put him on der spot a bit, as I askt him if he woot always keep any money he fints.'

Rudi raised his eyebrows and waited for Marco to continue.

After a pause, Rudi said impatiently, 'ant what dit he say?'

'He set, he woot not. But I'm not so sure. He seemt nervous.'

Rudi pondered this for a few seconds and then replied.

'Dees guysh all seem "normal," dough. You know, like...everyday types of people.'

Marco shrugged his large shoulders.

'Yes, I woot agree wit you Rudi. But, who is to say how someone woot react if dey really dit fint a lot of money? Be dey an everyday type of person, or not. But of course, dat also depents on Ash, ant if he is telling the truth or not?'

'Yes indeet. Ant I certainly don't trust HIM,' Rudi replied, continuing;

'But, because dese udder guysh are so "normal," it is probaply understantable dat dey might get nervous when questiont by a giant like you!'

'Hmmm, maybe? But I haf to agree wit you about Ash.'

Meanwhile, Bertie canvassed the group for a general consensus on what they wanted to eat and Fish and Chips won the straw poll by a hefty margin.

He turned to Dino for some local knowledge and the guys finished their drinks and headed the short distance to a restaurant around the corner from the pub.

'We'll try and get in at Steel's.' Said Dino.

'There's plenty of choice for food places. But it's always good in there. Although we might have to wait for tables for all of us.'

After joining a queue at the door, most of the group were eventually able to get seated at various tables. But a few guys decided against queuing and went elsewhere, with the plan to meet up after eating.

An hour later, after large quantities of Jumbo Haddock and Chips had been consumed by the majority of them, they felt ready to tackle the arduous task of further enjoyment.

Rudi and Johann had sat with Gracie and Speedo, as Rudi and Speedo's burgeoning friendship had dictated they should sit together.

As he finished his meal Rudi exclaimed; 'alsof er een engeltje over je tong piest.'

Johann smiled and agreed.

Seeing the obviously puzzled look on Gracie and Speedo's faces, the now calmer Johann, mellowed by both alcohol and Rudi's continued observance of his behaviour, explained;

'He was saying dat he loves de foot. As do I. It is a saying we haf in Dutch when we like what we are eating.'

Rudi provided further clarification;

'It translates as somesing like, "a small angel is pissing on my tongue"!'

Gracie laughed. But poor Speedo looked puzzled.

Rudi, anxious to put his new friend at ease, explained clearly again until the penny dropped.

Bertie called across from a table opposite;

'Result boys! We've just had a nice winner. 10/1!'

He then had to explain to several of the crowd, that it was only the first of their four bets. But it meant there would be some return on their earlier wager.

Dino, now more at ease with the Dutch contingent, asked them what football teams they supported, and having established their interest in the 'beautiful game,' he suggested heading for the beach to participate in a spot of 'international football.'

Ash was noting the body language of the four Dutch guys, and trying to gauge their thoughts and feelings.

Kenny and Rob had become more subdued since the arrival of the strangers, and had only had the chance for whispered and snatched conversations since.

'You're both bloody quiet!' Bertie chirped at them, continuing;

'What's up? You've hardly said a word in the last hour or so.'

Kenny managed a riposte;

'Can't get a bloody word in, with you rabbiting on, mate! Anyway, talk me through this winner we've had. 10/1? Big price wasn't it?'

'Yeah. That was a surprise to me too.' Bertie replied. 'It was only 7/2 when we picked it out. But the odds went way out. Nice one though, eh?'

Kenny kicked Rob under the table, prompting him to reply.

'Y..Yeah. Absolutely. I presume you backed it best odds guaranteed?'

'Course I did. Always do.' Bertie confirmed.

A few minutes later they settled their bill from the whip money, which had been replenished prior to coming into the restaurant and they headed down to the beach.

Phone calls were made to arrange a meet with the stragglers who had dined elsewhere.

A football was purchased from a souvenir stand on the seafront and preparations were made for the afternoon's main event.

Chapter Forty-Seven

Marco made a call to Rinus, to update him on their progress so far.

'Dat's right. Both Rudi and I are of the same feeling. Ash cannot be trustet. Dese guys all seem preddy normal to us so far. Dey sink we are Dutch police officers, but dey are all quite lait back.'

Rinus told Marco to keep on until they were certain who was, or wasn't being truthful, and to use their initiative and discretion in how to play it.

'Make shure you get to the boddom of this Marco, ok? No fuck ups! Ant if you sink dat Ash or any of the others are holding out on you, den apply whatever means you sink fit to get dem talking!'

Marco was grim faced when he got off the phone.

'What dit he say?' Enquired Rudi.

'Sometimes he just pisses me off! He states the fucking obvious, and den says to me, ''no fuck ups!'' Does he sink we are stupit? And den he says to use our initiative and discretion in leaning on Ash, or any of the others if we don't believe them! Sometimes, Rudi...'

Seeing the anger and frustration in his friends' expression was not a new thing for Rudi. Their boss was a difficult character to deal with.

Danny and Johann, although fairly new to their association with Rinus, had also had experience of ill feeling amongst his underlings, and both raised their eyebrows to each other in uneasiness at the situation.

Their earlier bravado had evaporated since they'd met up with the English guys, who they found to be affable and fun to be around.

'So what do we do now?' Rudi asked Marco.

'We haf to be careful whatefer we do. Don't forget dat Ash is a police officer. For shure, someone is lying. But, also, we can't just start beating on people to fint out who.'

'Are you in guys?' Dino called across to the Dutch contingent.

They turned in his direction and he held up the recently purchased football to clarify the situation.

'Are you playing?' Dino elaborated.

Rudi answered for the group.

'Yes, of course.'

Marco made a face to indicate that he wasn't really in the mood, but Rudi ignored his unwillingness.

'Come on Marco! We neet to keep in with dem socially, ant given your moot, you coult probably do with a liddle ecssersise anyway to get it out of your system.'

So the game was on, and the guys split into two teams, with two Dutch men in each.

Ash, although initially reluctant to join in, then changed his mind when he realised that nearly everyone else had agreed to play.

Gracie had persuaded Mick, the coach driver, to meet up with them and join in too. Mick duly being keen to, 'go in goal.'

There was the usual mickey taking and good natured banter as the game got underway. The ranks of the teams were soon swelled by a group of guys on a day trip and a couple of other local people who asked if they could join in.

After a few minutes of running around on the sandy beach, several members of the group were starting to blow hard and breathe heavily.

The pace of the game had slowed to a virtual walking pace, due to the physical condition, or lack of condition, of most of the participants.

But the younger guys and one or two of the fitter, older ones, kept up appearances for the pleasure of the three or four dog walkers who had congregated to spectate.

Kenny had also initially volunteered for goalkeeping duties when the teams were being decided on. But he'd been overlooked, due to his previously witnessed general lack of agility and suitability for the role, and he'd therefore adopted a sort of roaming position where he vainly chased after the ball, but rarely ever touched it.

Rob, on the other hand, was pretty fit and healthy and he'd retained most of the footballing skills he'd enjoyed since childhood.

Several times he attempted to bring Kenny into the game by either passing the ball to him, or just ahead of him, to enable him to run onto it. But this hadn't worked out too successfully, and the game went on around Kenny and the others of his age, lack of fitness and mobility.

His big moment came though when Danny fired across a ball which hit Kenny on the side of his head as he lost his footing and slipped forward on the sand, and flew beyond Gary Chivers' despairing dive, inside the perceived 'post' made of a pile of coats and jumpers and into the goal, to put his team one up.

Kenny's 'diving header' immediately drew gales of laughter from both sides. But Kenny was having none of it.

'Did you see that?' He shouted.

'Did you bloody see that? What a goal, eh?' He asked no one in particular.

Although as he got to his feet, he realised that he had a faceful of sand. Some of which had gone in the corner of his eye.

He didn't appreciate the lack of concern for his discomfort as he bemoaned his painful eye, but everyone was still recovering from their bouts of semi hysterical laughter.

'Bloody hell, Ken!' Gracie shouted.

'You knew nothing about it, mate!'

'What d'you mean? I dived forward like a leaping Salmon, and used the pace of Danny's brilliant cross to deflect a bullet header into the net!'

Closely followed by, 'oww, bollocks!' As he rubbed his right eye.

'I wootent do dat, Kenny.' Said Marco.

'You coult scratch your eyeball, rubbing it like dat. Gedding sant in your eye is not a lot of fun.'

'You don't say?' Whined Kenny.

'No, I do say, actually.' Marco replied, missing the irony in Kenny's response.

'You need to wash it out, mate.' Volunteered Scott.

The general consensus was to advise Kenny to cross the road and go into one of the many Cafe's, Bars, or Restaurants, to use their facilities to get the sand out of his eye.

Gracie, being the good Samaritan he always was in these situations, volunteered to accompany him, and assist him in hopefully relieving his discomfort.

'Are you sure, Gracie? I don't mind looking after him.' Ash piped up, seeing an opportunity to spend time alone with Kenny.

But Gracie had already taken charge of the situation.

'No, it's fine. I'll sort it. Come on, Ken.'

As he led the sand covered Kenny away, Dino helpfully called after them.

'Hey, Ken! You've always moaned about never having a nickname, haven't you?'

As Kenny turned back to face him, his face contorted and his right eye squinted shut, Dino continued.

'Well, now we could call you Nelson? What d'you think?'

Kenny gave a predictable reply as he turned away, amidst a mixed response to Dino's suggestion from the collective.

Chapter Forty-Eight

The game went on for only a little while longer after Kenny's dramatic exit.

There were various complaints of old age, lack of fitness, wet sand on trousers, and other minor misdemeanours.

But the general mood was lifted somewhat by Bertie, when he suddenly announced, after checking his phone;

'Bloody hell, guys! We've had another winner. And that's not all. It was only twenty five to bloody one!'

'How much have we won Bertie?' Scott led the chorus of enquiries.

'Hang on a minute. I've got a Lucky 15 calculator on my phone.' Bertie answered.

After less than a minute, Bertie, having very adroitly scanned his phone for the information, came up with a response.

'Just over five grand! Works out at just over two hundred quid each, so far!'

'Wow! Nearly pays for the day then,' said a smiling Gary Chivers.

'But you said, so far, Bertie?' He continued.

'Yeah, well....we've still got the last two bets to go. But to be..' Bertie's reply was cut short by Dino.

'We weren't too sure about the last two though, were we?'

'That's what I was about to say!' Bertie concurred. 'But, either way, we've had a decent touch!'

The general excitement included enquiries about when the last two horses were due to run, and whether or not they could watch the races.

Bertie advised that both horses were running in an evening meeting, but he could get both races on his phone.

'Think this calls for a cheeky beer though boys, eh?' He said encouragingly.

They cleaned themselves up a bit, by which time Gracie and a semi recovered Kenny returned.

'How are you doing, Nelson?' Enquired Dino.

'I think I've scratched my eyeball getting that sand out.' Kenny said forlornly, after first fixing Dino with what he intended as a mean look.

'What are you winking at me for, Ken?'

'Leave him alone, you pillock!' Rob leapt to his mate's defence.

Marco, who seemed to know a lot about medical situations, suggested to Kenny that he should wear sunglasses for a while to avoid the sunlight aggravating his stricken eye.

Having then chosen a pair of black shades from one of the many souvenir and gift stands, Kenny was ready to resume his place in the group.

But Dino wasn't quite finished with him.

'Nice one Ken. They make you look like a white Ray Charles. If we find a live music pub later, perhaps you could give us a turn on the organ?'

Kenny had recovered sufficiently to muster a reply worthy of the insult.

'You keep on sunshine and the only organ getting turned'll be yours!'

Chapter Forty-Nine

Next stop for the group was a bar that had been converted from what used to be a bank. Although only mid afternoon, there was still a fair amount of drinkers and diners, both inside the establishment and also utilising the tables on the street outside.

'This'll do nicely, eh boys?' Gracie said, surveying the bar area inside.

Having seen that the bar heavily catered for cocktails as well as conventional ales, he enquired if any of the collective fancied an 'afternoon aperitif.'

There were several takers for that suggestion, as well as the hardened beer drinkers, who stuck to their preference.

But Gracie baulked a bit when it came to the bill for the round.

'Jesus!' He said to Dino and Bertie. 'I'm charging way too low for cocktails at my place. Ten quid in here for a double G and T alone!'

Having been brought up to speed with the Horse Racing news, he continued;

'I think we'll need that two hundred quid each, if we stay in here for long!'

Kenny and Rob, having been two of the takers for large Gin and Tonic's, had managed to grab one of the tables outside as people vacated to move on.

'How are you doing, Ken?' Rob gestured with his glass towards Kenny's eye.

'Keeps bloody watering and it still feels like I've got something in my eye. But we definitely got all the grit out. I'll be alright. More importantly, what are WE gonna do?'

'I dunno, mate. The way that Marco bloke was questioning you earlier, I thought he was going to arrest you or something. You stood up to that a lot better than I would've.'

Kenny leaned forward, checking no one was within earshot.

'They don't seem like coppers though, the Dutch guys, Bog. They seem alright. You know, laid back. And I'm sure the biggest one, that Rudi, fancies Speedo!'

Rob laughed.

'Yeah, I know what you mean. Do you think we could say we found that money to them, but stress that we fully intend to hand it in, but wanted to do it anonymously, as we don't want to be implicated in anything?'

Although Rob couldn't see Kenny's eyes through the lenses of the black shades he was wearing, he could easily work out his friend's reaction to his suggestion by the appearance of his eyebrows above the sunglasses and the amount of worry lines on his now furrowed brow.

'Are you joking, Bog? They might seem laid back, but whether they're coppers or not, that won't pan out too well for us. They'd only give us grief for not handing it in straightaway. And if they're not real coppers, and they're mixed up in some way with bloody Ash, then we could be in for a whole world of shit!'

'Yeah, I suppose so. I guess we should just play it cool then and wait till we get back and then leave the bag, either back where we found it, or outside the Pro shop. We could maybe back that up with a phone call to the Police, anonymously letting them know where we'd left it?'

Kenny nodded slowly.

'I think that's our only option mate. At least then we can breathe a lot easier.'

Ash had lost sight of Rob and Kenny inside the bar and started to panic, until he suddenly saw them sitting outside.

His mind was in turmoil, and he had no real clue as to what he should do or say next, other than thoughts of self preservation.

Since the appearance of the four Dutchmen he had felt rudderless and probably sold down the river by Sue.

Her attitude and demeanour was much calmer in their last phone call when she'd inadvertently mentioned the amount of cash that Ron was supposedly paying for the drugs and having pondered on that for some time now, Ash felt a nagging doubt about her part in Ron's comeuppance.

He knew he was out on a limb. Given his previous association with Ronnie Senior's activities, he had more to lose than anyone if that all came out.

He had made small talk with all of the guys who'd been in the pub last night, and replayed some of the events about the wind up and the fake money with them, in the vain hope that something new would come out.

But, deep down, he knew that none of them had any clue about the real money, and the only ones who could were sitting outside the bar at the moment.

Marco and the other Dutch guys had not thrown their weight around as he thought they would and he guessed that they had arrived at the conclusion that Rob and Kenny were the only potential suspects from this group for taking the missing cash.

That was apart from himself, of course. The more he thought about their arrival and the reason for them being there, the more it pointed to obvious danger for him, whether Sue was a part of this or not.

He decided that it was time for him to be more direct with Rob and Kenny, even if that opened him up to obvious suspicion.

Chapter Fifty

Ash wandered outside holding 3 glasses and placed 2 of them down in front of Rob and Kenny.

'There you go, guys. Gracie said you were both on large G and T's. The whip's taken a battering, so we've all put in again. I've already put in for you two, so you owe me twenty quid each.'

Before either of them could respond, he continued;

'To be honest, I wanted to have a word with both of you, and being as you were out here in the sunshine, and it's so bloody noisy in there, I thought now would be as good a time as any to join you. If that's ok?'

Kenny and Rob looked at each other, but gave none of their shared anxiety away.

'Take a seat, Ashley, and enjoy the sunshine.' Kenny replied cheerily.

'How's the eye, mate?' Ash smiled smarmily.

Kenny fought every urge inside him to say what he really wanted to say to Ash, but instead replied generously;

'It's ok, thanks. Itches like a bastard, and keeps watering. But I'm getting used to it.'

But Ash was done making small talk.

'I need to talk to you both about yesterday at the golf course.'

Rob felt the need to be involved in the conversation, as, somehow, talking felt more comfortable than trying to appear calm and saying nothing.

'What particularly about yesterday?'

Ash laid it all out. He said he'd been contacted a while ago by colleagues at work. He said they'd advised him that a witness had come forward to say they had seen a man carrying what looked like a heavy bag onto the golf course yesterday morning. They had thought the man looked suspicious, but hadn't challenged him, or reported the matter till now through fear of reprisals.

But since the local news report of the arrests made by the Crime Squad yesterday, and a later press release that Ash told them had been made by the police a couple of hours ago, this witness had come forward.

'We believe the man seen by the witness was carrying money that was removed from the house of one of the criminals that we arrested yesterday morning.' Ash advised.

As he spoke, Ash observed Rob and Kenny very closely for signs of nervousness or anxiety. But both appeared calm.

He went on.

'The witness said they saw this man from some distance, but he was walking from the road near the railway line and went towards an old shed just off the course and eventually stopped there. They believe he left the bag somewhere around there, as they saw him again a few minutes later, running back towards the road without the bag.'

Kenny decided to intervene at this point, as he was getting pretty sick of the intense stares that Ash was fixing upon him and Rob.

'All very interesting and enlightening, Ash. But what's that got to do with us?'

Ash was momentarily bemused by the confident nature of Ken's reply. But he soon recovered his composure and pressed on.

'Well I'll come to the point, Ken. From all that was said last night and from conversations I've had with Bertie again today, it would seem that your wind up scam with the fake money took place in more or less that exact same area near the old shed. Didn't it?'

Rob decided to intervene this time, and he was pleasantly surprised when he heard the timbre of his own voice, which remained calm and he sounded like his 'normal' self.

'Well, I can tell you that the plan we made for the wind up was for Bertie to hide the fake money by a large industrial mower near that old shed. But that aside, what else has that got to do with us?'

Ash again looked at them both piercingly, as he said;

'Look guys. A lot of money was removed from a criminal's house, by a person or persons unknown yesterday. And this siting by the witness of a guy who presumably left a heavy bag in a random area of the golf course, which was right next to where you guys were some time later, is something worthy of further investigation. Don't you agree?'

Ken had had enough at this point.

'No. You look, Ashley.' He said, trying to remain calm. 'We are here on a day out with mates, supposedly trying to have fun. We're ordinary blokes, who have done nothing wrong. Yet this feels like we're part of an investigation. So, I for one, can tell you that I have no fucking idea what you're asking us and I know nothing about any money, other than the wind up money that you already know about. OK!'

And before Ash could respond, Rob also weighed in.

'And I for another can also confirm that in my opinion, you are way off line and out of order if you think, just because we were in the same vicinity as where this guy was seen, that we must know more about it. How do you know that this witness didn't go and get this bag, after the other bloke had run off? Or somebody else took it? Or the original guy came back for whatever it was?'

Ash was defeated. And now he'd said what he'd said, he also felt completely vulnerable. If they were to say anything to the police about this, then Ash knew that he would be arrested.

However, although his brain was racing with countless thoughts, he retained the image in his mind of finding Rob's golf hat yesterday, at the very spot where he'd buried the sports bag in the undergrowth.

The anger he'd felt at that moment returned to him and he played his last card.

'Fair enough, guys. I know this is all very unconventional. But I was only contacted by work colleagues a little while back as I said. They've been over to the course with the witness and found a disturbed area of ground near where the witness saw the man yesterday. And they found something there.

'Tell me Bog. Did you lose something at the golf course yesterday?'

This time Ash's dart penetrated its target and Rob's expression momentarily changed. His eyes fixed on Ash for a second or two, before he suddenly looked down and tried to regain his composure.

Kenny, although inwardly panicked, was still indignant.

'What on earth are you on about? I think we've both had more than enough of this now.'

Ash returned to his usual smarmy persona. He knew he had Rob Gordon flustered, and as he now felt in freefall anyway, he decided to press a little further.

'The reason I asked if you'd lost anything yesterday Bog, was because my colleague told me they'd found something so unusual at the spot where they believed the bag had been, that he thought it worthy of sending me a photo of it. It's a hat Bog. A very distinctive hat. Not to my taste, but one that I soon realised that I'd seen before, when you was wearing it. Here's the photo, look!'

Ash held his phone towards Rob and Kenny, showing them the image of the hat he'd found yesterday and had taken a photo of this morning before he'd left home.

Although Rob was churning inside, any fear he felt was surpassed by anger at Ash having a photo of something that Sally had bought for him.

As ridiculous a gift as it was, the hat was a private joke between him and the wife he adored, and his anger gave way to a sturdy resolve and clarity of mind and more than sufficient defiance to counter Ash's inquisition.

'You are a bloody Arsehole, Ash! We spent ages looking for that hat yesterday didn't we, Ken? I fell over in the rough after tripping on some loose ground on the first hole.'

'Yeah, that's right.' Laughed Kenny. 'Got us in trouble with Bertie. He bollocked us and told us to get a move on!'

Rob and Kenny, both motivated by Rob's indifference to Ash's grandstanding ploy, laughed as one.

Rob then looked Ash squarely in the eye and said;

'Tell your mate, I'll be happy to have my hat back, if he's still got it. Was a present from the wife. And if that's what you're basing all of this on, I think you need to go back to Detective School, sunshine!'

Rob then got £40 from his wallet and threw it across the table in front of Ash.

'There's your £40. We're straight now, so fuck off and bother someone else!'

Chapter Fifty-One

After Ash had slunk off back inside the bar, Kenny gave Rob a bear hug and, still giggling, said;

'Where did all of that come from, mate? You were fantastic. I'm proper proud of you!'

Rob grinned.

'First of all I was shitting myself, to be honest. But when he showed us the photo, it was like time slowed down. I had so much going through my mind, but I seemed to have so much time to process it all. In the end I was so bloody angry that the twat had a photo of my hat and was in my face as well, that he just had to be told where to get off!'

Still chuckling, Kenny said; 'Your timing was spot on though, Bog! "Go back to Detective School," and "there's your £40. We're straight now, so fuck off and bother someone else!" Magic, mate! Absolutely magic!'

He continued. 'I think it's time for another drink, don't you?'

Rob agreed. But first they had a brief chat about how things stood. Then, having agreed their joint stance going forward, they went back inside the bar.

Ash was now in a bind. He was still convinced that his original theory about the missing money was correct. But his resolve had been shaken by the joint response he'd just received from Rob and Kenny.

Probably more so at Rob's reply, than anything Kenny had said, as he'd always had Kenny down as the craftier and more self assured of the two.

But the fictitious story he'd told them about the witness and the press release had left him wide open should any of this get back to the police and that alone was enough for him to be very careful around them.

He had at least mumbled an apology before leaving them to return inside. So he felt that he hadn't quite burnt all of his bridges with them.

For the time being, he hung on to the edge of a group including Dino, Scott, Bertie and Gracie and attempted more normal conversation.

He led off with;

'What time is our next race then, Bertie.'

'Not till half five, Ash. Plenty of time yet. But don't get too excited, as that and the last horse are less likely winners than the other two.'

After one more drink they all elected to move on to a more traditional pub and opted for one facing the sea front that also had a seating area outside.

Kenny and Rob worked their way into conversation with a group that included Marco and Danny, who both seemed to be fairly chilled and without edge.

When there was a pause in the conversational flow, Kenny interjected and casually asked; 'how long have you been in the police, Marco?'

Marco had relaxed to the point where his 'cover story' had become unfamiliar to him, and he was slow to come to terms with the question.

'Eh? Oh, I am sorry, Kenny.' He deliberated, before recovering slightly;

'Err...a few years. It's changt a lot and I don't see myself doing it for too much longer.'

'What else would you prefer, if you don't mind me asking?' Rob joined in pleasantly.

Marco smiled.

'Well, my dream is to haf my own bar. A beach bar ideally. Maybe also doing foot. Somewhere hot!'

He laughed self consciously.

Danny laughed. 'I cannot imagine you as a barman, Marco. Maybe more front of house, eh?'

'Not so much, Danny.' Marco said still smiling.

'I haf put a lot of sought into it, ant I sink in der right place and location it woult suit me just fine. Rudi ant I haf often spoken about it in the last few years, and my sister Dafne too. She is an ecsellent cook.' He continued wistfully.

'Well, I certainly don't think you'd get any bother from your punters, mate!' Kenny smiled.

'Punters?' Marco queried.

'Customers.' Rob explained. 'Two big geezers like you and Rudi.'

'I like the beach idea, fine...for a holiday.' Said Danny. 'But I prefer city life mainly.'

'Each to his own though, eh?' Rob offered, continuing;

'There's a saying in England. One man's meat is another man's poison. Have you heard that before?'

'Not so much. But I understant der meaning.' Marco answered.

The laid back tone of both Dutch guys led Kenny to venture;

'I think your mate Ash could do with some time at a beach bar.'

'Why do you say dat?' Marco queried.

'Well, he's just a bit full on with his questions. A little while ago he was practically accusing us of stealing a bag full of money, wasn't he, Bog?'

Rob nodded confirmation, adding; 'Yeah, he made a bit of a twat of himself!'

Kenny and Rob both laughed disarmingly. But Kenny felt the need to add an adjoinder;

'We don't mean to be nasty about your friend. But he was just a bit rude, that's all.'

Marco looked at Danny before answering;

'I sink I can speak for both of us, when I say dat he is not ecsactly someone who we woult call a frent?'

Danny nodded and added; 'More of an acquaintance, I woult say.'

Marco then asked what Ash had said to Kenny and Rob and was given the low down. Although the guys were careful to be respectful of the supposed position of the Dutch 'officers.'

Marco also asked Kenny; 'Why do you refer to Rob as, "Bog?"'

Kenny and Rob both felt the need to explain that and both Dutch guys laughed at the revelation.

'Most of the time, only my Missus and my Mum call me Rob, or Robert in my Mum's case.' Rob added.

A while after, when Rob and Kenny had a moment to themselves, Kenny said;

'I think that little exchange went ok, don't you, Bog?'

Rob nodded, adding;

'Yeah. It seemed they'd almost got that opinion of Ash already?'

'I got that vibe as well.' Kenny agreed.

Chapter Fifty-Two

Speedo and Rudi were deep in conversation about their respective music collections.

'We share so many similar tastes, Kevin.' Rudi said enthusiastically.

'Yeah, that's funny, isn't it?' Kevin/Speedo replied.

They were halfway through comparing notes on their joint love of Bob Dylan when Marco came over, with Danny close behind.

'I'm so sorry to interrupt you, guys,' Marco said, taking hold of Rudi's arm.

'But I just neet to haf a wort wit Rudi for a moment, OK?'

'Y..Yes. Of course.' Speedo smiled, continuing; 'Is everything alright?'

'Absolutely.' Marco said, smiling. 'Just somesing to do wit work.'

He drew Rudi away from the bar, to a less crowded corner.

'Danny ant I haf just been talking to Kenny and Rop.'

Marco then filled Rudi in on the revelations as outlined by Rob and Kenny, about the accusations made to them by Ash.

'It wasn't so much dat he was accusing dem. Dat's fair enough. But dey set he was talking about a witness der police haf, who he set saw a man wit a bag on der golf course yesterday. Ant also about a press release a liddle while ago.'

Rudi pondered this information for a few seconds, then answered;

'But, dat cannot be true, can it? He was der man on the golf course, wasn't he?...Unless he meant dat dis witness saw anudder man later on?'

'No. I'm sure he did not mean dat.' Marco replied confidently, continuing;

'Because he tolt dem dat der witness saw der same man a few minutes later, running away from der course widout der bag. So, der man must haf left der bag on der golf course.'

'So he was trying to spook dem?' Rudi replied.

Marco shrugged. 'I guess he was. But making up a story about a witness and accusing dem like dat, just makes him sount desperate.'

Rudi agreed and asked Marco what response Ash had got from Kenny and Rob.

Marco looked at Danny and they both smiled, before Marco said;

'Rop tolt him to go back to Detective School, and den tolt him to fuck off!'

Rudi laughed. 'I'm glat dat somebody finally agrees wit us dat Ash is an arsehole! I sink we neet to haf a wort wit him.'

Marco smiled with a trace of menace.

'Ecsactly wat I was sinking too! We know he put dat money on der golf course, by his own admission. So he's eeyser lying about der whole sing, including dat bit. Or it is all a smokescreen and he went back and moovt der money somewhere else and is using dese guys as cover?'

Rudi nodded. 'Well we can discuss all of dat wit him when we talk to him.'

They looked across the bar to where Ash was standing, pretending to listen to a conversation between guys he patently had no interest in.

Marco clapped Danny on the shoulder.

'Go and round up Johann and meet us outside. Rudi and I will bring Ash, ant we'll take him for a liddle walk. OK?'

Danny smiled.

'Sounts goot to me, Marco!'

Chapter Fifty-Three

Marco and Rudi were aware that Ash was trying hard to avoid their gaze, as they tried to attract his attention without making it too obvious to any bystanders.

But eventually their burrowing stares caused Ash to briefly look their way and he caught the gesture from Marco to join them.

'We neet to haf a chat. Somewhere more private, where we will not be overhert.' Marco said, as Ash drew close by.

Marco and Rudi caught the change in Ash's expression immediately.

'W..w..what about?' He replied nervously.

'Der money, obviously!' Marco said, rolling his eyes at Ash's failure to comprehend.

He continued; 'We've been speaking wit pretty much all of der guys here and we neet to compare notes wit you.'

They ushered Ash out of the nearest door and caught sight of Danny and Johann, standing across the road from the bar.

Crossing the road, they walked in silence, until they were out of sight of the bar. They then crossed back over and led Ash down a narrow side street that looked quiet, eventually stopping in an entrance to a small factory unit between the terraced houses on that side of the road.

Although the road was crammed with parked cars on both sides, there were no people about and the factory entrance was set back sufficiently from the road to afford sufficient seclusion.

Ash had false started several attempts at conversation since they'd left the bar and was now showing obvious signs of nervousness.

'W.why did we need to come up the road, guys?' He said in a wavering voice.

Marco looked at his three colleagues, and then turned to Ash.

Leaning close to him he said;

'Ash, it's time to stop fucking wit us and start telling der trut about yesterday. What haf you done wit der money you took from Ronnie Senior's house, eh?'

Ash rolled his eyes and tried to feign annoyance. But he was too scared to appear as anything other than defensive in the extreme.

He gathered himself as best he could and replied;

'Fuck me, Guys! I cannot tell you anymore than I've already told Ron's missus! Look, I don't even know where you guys come into this, but I can only assume that your boss is the guy who Senior was dealing with over yesterday's botched drug deal? Is that right?'

It was Marco's turn to roll his eyes.

'I sink you already know dat to be the case? We know you got well over half a million pounds out of der house yesterday from our sources, ant all we haf hert since, is dat you lost it on some golf course!'

'I didn't lose it. I hid it there, because I got a call from my boss to go back to Senior's house and had no time to put the money anywhere else.'

Ash could see their patience with him visibly draining away, so quickly added;

'I hid it in a spot where I could easily find it on my return. But I couldn't go back for it until late yesterday afternoon. And as you've already been told, or found out, when I went back, it wasn't there. I knew I was in the right place though, as I'd taken a photo of the location where I left the bag when I was there originally. Then I found this bloody awful golfing hat at the scene where the bag had been and I know that hadn't been there earl...Ooooof!!!'

Ash recoiled in extreme pain, as Marco punched him with full force in his lower abdomen. The impact caused him to double over in pain, and Marco swiftly grabbed him by the throat and forced him back upright.

Coughing and spluttering, and with his eyes now watering, a terrified Ash looked at Marco and the others and pleaded, in a rasping voice, between gasps;

'I know how ridiculous this all sounds...but there is no way... I would try to rip off Ronnie Senior...knowing what kind of man he is...and what... pain and aggravation... he could cause me.'

Marco shaped as if to hit him again, but Rudi held onto him and pulled him to one side, before taking his place in front of Ash.

'Ash, our job here is very simple.' Rudi said calmly. 'We haf been tolt to fint out where dis money is now. You were the last person known to haf it. But you cannot tell us where it is. Dat does not help us, does it?'

He held up his hand to stop Ash from interrupting him and continued;

'Now we haf been tolt dat you set dat you know dese guys Rop ant Kenny haf taken der money. But how do you know dat for sure, Ash? Dis hat you fount yesterday is no proof of dat, is it? And your story, frankly, sounts like a lot of horseshit!'

'I know... it does.' Ash said wearily, still gasping, as he tried to regain control of his breathing.

'But it proves... those guys were... exactly at the spot... where I buried the bag. They even admitted... that Rob fell over at that spot, and... he didn't deny it being his hat... when I showed him a picture of it.' He looked at them pleadingly.

'I am shit scared, guys. Ok? I'm scared of you... I'm scared of whoever your boss is... I'm scared of anyone associated... with Ronnie Senior. And I am scared... beyond belief that any of this might get back to the police, because... then I am screwed completely! I have more to lose... than anyone here! I haven't got that money! I wish... I had, but I haven't!'

Ash's voice had risen by about an octave by the end of his pleading speech.

Marco said. 'We've beaten confessions out of people who were holding out on us, many times you know.'

Ash shook his head.

'I can't stop you beating on me, obviously... But I cannot tell you what I do not know... If those guys didn't take that money, then... it's either been found by someone else who's kept it, or... it's been handed in to the police.'

Rudi and Marco shook their heads. Danny and Johann looked at each other and Danny thought about volunteering to further Ash's pain. But it was obvious to the four Dutchmen that any further violence towards the clearly terrified man in front of them was pointless.

Rudi looked Ash in the eye.

'Ok. Obviously, dis is gedding us nowhere. We neet to decide what action to take next. I haf to say dough Ash. You are a fucking disgrace! Any Cop who does what you do, or haf done, is worse than the majority of any so called criminals. Ant you are a fucking cowart too!'

Rudi, so often calm and smiling, had in his closing exchange with Ash, worked himself up to extreme anger and he therefore felt moved to say;

'So just one last thing, you crooket piece of shit!'

As he finished speaking, he threw a stupendous right hook, fuelled by his boxer's knowledge of how to exert maximum force from the shoulder. His punch landed squarely into Ash's Ribcage. As it thudded home, doubling Ashley Richardson up and pitching him forward, Rudi stepped aside and let him topple to the ground.

The four Dutchmen walked away, leaving the stricken Ash on all fours, vomiting, and in extreme discomfort with very sore ribs.

Chapter Fifty-Four

Ash managed to get himself into a seated position on the ground, before using a low wall as a prop as he struggled very painfully to his feet.

The sharp pain in his ribs became more acute as he'd pulled himself up and it was all he could do to avoid screaming out.

But biting on his lip, he was able to lean on the wall and then push down on it to propel himself upright.

The Nausea rose from his stomach as he strove to steady himself. He wiped the back of his hand over his face and felt the dampness of his tear stained cheeks.

He tried to take several deep breaths to clear his head, but the pressure that put on his stomach and his rib cage increased the level of pain. So he settled for tiny breaths while he leant on the top of the low wall next to him.

After a minute or two he decided to sit again as he wanted to phone Sue Senior.

Despite feeling that there was nobody he could trust, she had been his last link with semi normality in the madness of the last day and a half, and he felt the need to question her to gauge any clue of what to do next.

Sue answered on the third ring.

'Hello, Sue.' He said, through gritted teeth, as the pain was still strongly evident.

'Ash?' She replied, questioningly.

'Yeah, it's me.'

'You sound different. Are you ok?'

He couldn't help but make a small attempt at an ironic laugh from her comment.

'I'm very far from ok, Sue. Very far indeed. I've been worked over, I guess you could say. And I believe you'll know who by. Just tell me...what the hell is going on? Who are these Dutch guys?'

Sue spoke quietly, as Rinus was downstairs talking on his phone.

'I'm really sorry, Ash. They work for the guy that Ron was dealing with in that shipment yesterday. He came here. He's made it pretty clear that he wants the missing money, and it seems he knows all of what the police know, including how much they seized yesterday. So obviously, someone from your lot is in with him.'

'Was he there when I spoke to you last, Sue?' Ash said through gasps.

'Yes, he was. Are you alright, Ash? You sound terrible!' She sounded genuinely concerned.

'They only belted me a couple of times. But they knew what they were doing, so I think they could've cracked a couple of ribs. Hurts like hell.'

Although deep down he didn't trust her, Ash needed comfort right now and the relationship he'd had with Sue, intermittent as it had been, had also been warm enough for him to have shared genuine moments with her.

That was something he felt more than a little need of right now.

'He told me he was sending some guys to "help you" in getting the money back, Ash. I'm really sorry they beat you.'

Sue's voice carried more than a trace of genuine sincerity and emotion.

'Well, if "helping" me meant doing me over, then they've certainly "helped" a lot. I couldn't tell them any more than I've told you, Sue. I've also spoken to those other guys I mentioned. I came right out and accused them of being where the money was. Made up a story about work being in touch and pretended a witness had come forward and some other stuff, trying to spook them. But they flatly denied it all, laughed at me and then got annoyed, and told me to do one. So I'm no wiser as to where that money is now, than I was yesterday.'

'Oh Jesus! I am so sorry you went through that. Especially after getting out of here with so much of the cash yesterday. Do you think someone else might've found the money and handed it in to the police?'

Sue's voice was increasingly emotion filled as she spoke.

'I don't know, Sue. Maybe? But surely if the police had it they would've been round to you asking more questions, even if they had no direct proof that it was part of Ron's money? And if this other bloke you said Ron was dealing with has inside information from someone in the know in The Job, then he'd have been told too? How did you leave it with him, Sue?'

Sue heard Rinus call from downstairs. She put her hand over her phone and went out onto the landing and gestured to Rinus to be quiet.

'S..sorry Ash. I thought it was someone at the door. False alarm. He said he'd be in touch and told me to contact him if I found anything out.'

Ash had been a policeman for long enough to sense when something didn't sound quite right and he'd noticed a change in the tone of Sue's voice in her last comment. It flashed through his mind that he was still being played.

'Am I on Speaker phone, Sue?'

'No. Why?'

'Well, whether I am or not, doesn't really matter I suppose. But I know he's there now, isn't he?'

This time she sounded genuine again and tried to convey that in her next response.

'Yes, that's right. Well I guess we'll see what happens then. I'd better let you go.'

She sounded fearful and although Ash was in extreme discomfort, he felt some sympathy for her and understood she was under some pressure.

'You take care, Sue. I've no idea what I'm going to do next. But I'll be in touch if I find out any news, assuming I can? Although, I'm sure the Dutch guys will keep you both informed anyway.'

'Take care, love.' Sue said tearfully.

Ash felt rudderless. He was genuinely out of ideas. The only route open to him at present that he could perceive, was to go back to the Pub to rejoin the others, even though that also meant rejoining his recent attackers.

Although he believed that they had no further business with him, at least for a while.

Chapter Fifty-Five

'I presume dat was Ash?' Rinus asked.

'Yes it was. And he's just been beaten up by your guys! What's that going to achieve, eh?' Sue replied tearfully.

'Sooo. They hit him a couple of times. He is a prick, and he deserved it! But we are still nowhere nearer finting out where der money is, ant dat is the most important sing, surely? Why are you so upset, eh?'

Sue was at boiling point. She wasn't even sure why she felt so angry. But her conversation with Ash had been the trigger for a release of a lot of the tension that had built over the last couple of days. All of the intrigue and double dealing had taken its toll on her.

'Because I didn't want any of this violence! I've had enough of it Rinus! I've lived my bloody life around beatings and excuses for beatings and I'm fucking sick of it, alright? That's why I'm "so upset," you stupid arsehole!'

Rinus bridled at her insults. No one talked to him like that.

'I sink you haf forgotten your place in all of dis, Soo. You haf been closely involvt in senting your Husbant to Jail. Ant if you want any goot to come out of dis, I sink you hat bedder keep your mouth shut ant do as you are tolt.'

'Or what, Rinus? Eh? Or what? What are you going to do to me, then?'

'Oh Dear, Soo. I sink you haf become just a liddle bit strung out over dis whole sing. Best for you to haf a lie down ant chill out for a while.'

'I've spoken to my guys, ant dey set dat dey will haf one more try at finting out if any of dose udder men know anysing of where dis money is. But if dey cannot get any more information, den we may just haf to forget about it ant keep a close eye on Ash. Like you set, we can't just go arount killing people, can we?'

Although Rinus's tone made it clear that his last line wasn't really a question and was more of a statement of fact.

But Sue still wasn't sure if even that statement was true or not.

Chapter Fifty-Six

Back at the Pub in Cleethorpes, there was a general atmosphere of excitement as the minutes counted down to the 5.30 race at Kempton Park.

Bertie had spoken to the Pub Landlord, a very large and rotund man called Barry, who duly obliged and put the Racing Channel on one of the screens in the main bar for the guys to watch.

He'd figured that way he'd keep the free spending group in his bar for at least a while longer, as they were good fun, as well as being good for business.

'What one's ours, Bertie?' Asked Gary Chivers.

'It's number six. The Jockey's wearing a dark blue top. The horse is called Fighting Chance. It was four to one when I backed it earlier, but yet again the price has gone out to sixes.'

'What's sixes?' Queried Malcolm Tweedie, one of a trio of guys who had come for the day, but had kept a very low profile, till now.'

'Six to one, Malcolm.' Dino replied just ahead of Bertie. 'Getting excited, are you?'

'Just a bit.' Malcolm and his two mates, Ben and Trevor, all replied together, laughing.

Dino turned to Bertie and Gracie and whispered;

'I think the booze has finally loosened those three up.'

The Dutch quartet had come back into the bar a couple of minutes before and immediately noticed the heightened atmosphere.

Word had got around a few of the locals in the bar, about the bet that the guys had had earlier.

Their interest had added to the level of excitement, which had become infectious and the general hubbub in the bar grew louder as the race approached.

Despite Bertie's protestations to Barry and several of his regulars about putting any money on Fighting Chance, as he doubted its chances, it hadn't stopped them having a few quid each on it too.

'Just don't blame me if it shits the bed, guys!' He laughed.

Kenny and Rob, having felt pretty good after their earlier chat with Marco and Danny, had then noticed when the Dutch guys left the bar with Ash, and also saw how uncomfortable Ash had looked.

Since then, although caught up in the conversation about the upcoming race, they'd both kept an eye on the door to check if any of them had returned.

So, when the quartet of the four large Dutchmen re-entered the bar, they both immediately noticed their pensive demeanour.

Kenny felt a knot in his stomach, as he surmised things were not as friendly as they'd been before.

'I'll just have a quick word with them, Bog, and ask them if they want a drink. Just want to check that things still seem alright.'

Rob also felt a tinge of apprehension.

'Yeah, ok. But don't lay it on too thick. We don't want them paying any more attention to us.'

Kenny took a few steps towards Marco and Rudi, who were the closest of the group to him.

'Guy's, the race is starting in a minute. What are you drinking?'

'Oh, just four more bottles of those light beers, please Kenny.' Rudi said pleasantly.

'We neet to watch ourselves, as we're driving later.'

Kenny smiled and swallowed hard, before committing himself;

'Is everything alright, guys? Don't want to poke my nose into your business, but it all looked a bit serious when you left a little while ago.'

'All goot.' Rudi replied with his customary smile.

'We just hat to sort a work issue out. Dat's all.'

Kenny settled on a thumbs up gesture to them, and withdrew to get their drinks.

'Seems ok.' He whispered in Rob's ear, without drawing any attention.

Ash had made slow progress back to the bar and had stopped off in the toilet of the previous bar they'd all been in to clean himself up a bit, before going back to join the throng.

He came into the main bar to a wall of noise. The crowd inside were all glued to the large TV screen watching the start of a horse race, which Ash remembered was significant.

He avoided the crush at the bar, as his ribs were very sore and still throbbing.

As the race progressed, Fighting Chance didn't, and his lack of progress began to draw a few derisory comments around the bar.

But, just as the collective dream began to die, Fighting Chance's Jockey suddenly began to get the horse to respond, and it made a stirring run to close on the leaders.

'Come on number six! Come on number six!' The collective were duly engaged now.

'Come on my Son! Come on Fighting Chance!' Chorused around the bar.

And for some reason, known only to Kevin 'Speedo' Morris, his individual, confused encouragement was;

'Come on Farting Chance!'

But there was no time for any dissing of Speedo, because, as the finish line approached, Fighting Chance got its head in front and claimed the race.

The noise in the pub was a cacophony.

All of those at the bar were shouting and cheering and either clapping each other on the back, or hugging each other.

Kenny broke free of the bear hugs and took the bottles of beer to the Dutch contingent, who he was pleased to see were all grinning broadly.

'Nice one, eh guys? Cheers!'

'Fantastic race, Kenny!' Marco grinned, taking the bottles from him.

'Thanks!' The four of them echoed.

Johann added; 'Kenny. How much haf I won, so far?'

His three companions all fixed him with glares that needed no explanation.

Johann laughed loudly.

'Look at dere faces, Kenny! I was only joking, guys!'

Kenny laughed and said; 'I'll get Bertie to work out how much we're up in a minute. But, we're all on for a few quid now!'

As he turned back towards the bar, Kenny saw Ash over in the corner near one of the entrance doors.

As much as he disliked the guy and as much as that had been compounded by his questioning of him and Rob earlier, he cut such a forlorn figure standing alone, that Kenny felt moved to walk over to him.

'Great result, eh Ash? We're all set for a decent win now!'

Ash smiled wryly.

'Yeah, nice one!' His voice sounded muffled and very subdued.

'You alright, Ash? You look a bit rough.'

'I'm ok, Ken. Just had a tumble outside on something slippery. Banged my side. Bloody ribs are sore. Stupid thing to do, I know.'

'Accidents happen, Ash! I keep getting asked why I'm winking at people. But I had to take the shades off in here, because I kept on kicking tables and treading on people's toes!'

Ash smiled.

'How is your eye?'

'Still feels like I've got something in it, and it's still a bit watery. But I'm getting used to it and trying to drink it into submission now. Do you want a drink?'

'Thanks Ken. I'll stay on G and T, please. Can't face any more beer at the moment.'

As Kenny turned to go, Ash continued;

'I'm sorry about earlier, with you and Bog. Work is a bit manic at the moment and I didn't mean to come on so strong.'

Kenny's conversation with Mo earlier had cleared his mind of so much worry.

As a result, fuelled by a steady intake of alcohol, a large plate of Haddock and chips at lunchtime and now the feelgood factor of the horse racing win, he had moved on from the stresses of Mo's perceived ailments and the additional hassles that the bag of money had brought him and now felt benevolent enough to let his earlier anger towards Ash go.

'It's ok. No harm done. I'll get your drink. Why don't you come to the bar?'

'To be honest, I'm a bit worried about getting bumped into, mate. My bloody ribs hurt!'

'Sit over there in the corner by the bar. No one's sitting there 'cos you can't see the telly.'

'Ok, I'll follow you over. Cheers, Ken.'

As Kenny walked to the bar, he saw the expressions of the Dutch guys change as they noticed Ash behind him. They certainly didn't seem like the type of looks that a friend or even an acquaintance would give.

'Jesus! They fucking hate him!' He said under his breath.

Chapter Fifty-Seven

'So, how much are we up then, Bertie?' Gary Chivers shouted at him from about three feet away.

'Sorry, Gaz. Couldn't quite hear you mate.' Bertie said ironically, as he finished checking some figures on his phone.

Gary was too merry to catch the irony, so replied, more loudly;

'HOW MUCH AR...'

'Whoa, whoa, whoa!' Bertie interrupted.

'I heard you first time, you dick! Right, according to my Lucky 15 Calculator, we are now guaranteed at least £1,726.64 back each. And that includes your £10 stake too, Gaz. As I know you particularly needed to know that, too!'

Gracie was pretty good with figures, and after a brief calculation, he said;

'So what's that in total so far? About forty three grand odd?'

Bertie looked suitably impressed.

Smiling, he said; 'Wow! Check out the big brain on Gracie! Spot on mate. £43,166.06 divided twenty five ways. Biggest win I've ever been a part of chaps!'

'Biggest win any of us have been a part of I'd say!' Gracie smiled.

Dino laughed. 'Nah, Gaz here picks up three times that much every month in his salary, don't ya?'

Gary had sobered sufficiently from the talk of money and figures to reply;

'Nearly that much Dino. Just a few pence short!'

'Well I think we all owe Bertie and Dino a drink for suggesting we do a bet, and also of course, for coming up with three great winners too!' Scott said.

That brought a chorus of general assent from the collective.

Dino was definitely in piss taking heaven now and couldn't help picking on the quiet trio of Malcolm, Ben and Trevor.

'What? Even from you guys, Malcolm? Blimey! That'll be a first. You know they don't take white fivers anymore, don't ya?'

The response was a considered and measured; 'Bollocks, Dino!'

'Well, we've had a great day, so far boys, eh?' Bertie offered, to another approving chorus of assents.

He continued; 'Just over an hour to the last race. But I can't see our luck holding for that one. It's been an incredible run of coincidences so far, though. Every one of those horses was way shorter in the betting first thing. But they all drifted. Even that last one was only four to one earlier. But the other two, blimey, a seven to two that ended up ten to one, and an eight to one that ended up twenty five to one! I've never seen that before!'

Rob smiled and interjected; 'Well, given the type of day it's been, you never know Bertie? It could just be one of those, "once in a lifetime days?" '

Dino wasn't finished with his selected targets.

Seeing Kenny standing next to Rob, he fired off another barb;

'So, Nelson.' He said, turning to Kenny; 'Do you fancy spending some more of your hundred grand tonight, eh?'

Kenny, never too good on the receiving end of banter, countered with; 'Oh, ha, ha! Ancient history that is now, Dino. Although nowhere near as long as you've gone without a shag, eh? Still going for "private dances" at that place in town?'

Dino laughed as loud as anyone, as he thrived on the cut and thrust of pub banter.

But privately, he so wanted to share the fact that he really fancied his chances of making a go of it with Kirstie Walker,

Ash's current, but soon to be ex partner, whom Dino had been getting really good vibes from recently and who he genuinely liked and had feelings for.

He winked at Scott, sitting next to him, who was the only person he'd confided in about Kirstie, knowing that his best mate wouldn't divulge that snippet of information.

The next hour was spent reminiscing about old times, rehashing embarrassing moments from the past misdemeanours of several of the usual suspects and treating themselves to one or two top shelf tipples from Barry's well stocked bar, to celebrate their success on the horses.

The Dutch guys were all fed up with Rinus, who had again upset Marco on the phone, just after the incident with Ash.

They had all seriously considered getting out of their connections with him. Especially as Rudi had heard from Bruno, who tended to be tasked with ferrying Rinus around and 'protecting' him, that he believed this latest deal had been all about making a large amount of money for Rinus and not so much for anybody else.

Bruno had told Rudi that Rinus had business opportunities that the money from this job would fund, and he doubted that their services would be needed long term, apart from maybe doing 'door work' at one of the clubs Rinus was involved with.

The camaraderie amongst the group had also struck a chord with the Dutch men, as they had been accepted without any major inquisitions and had enjoyed the banter across the day.

Therefore, unless there were any developments to change things, Marco and Company had discussed maybe staying overnight in Cleethorpes, and then heading to Hull tomorrow to catch the ferry to Rotterdam and home. Although, for the sake of appearances, they wouldn't divulge that to any of their present company.

Ash sat at the far corner of the bar, occasionally listening to the banter, but the rest of the time still trying to fathom what he would do on his return home. If there was someone within the police who was in cahoots with the guy who'd arranged Ron's fall from grace, then there was more than a chance that he would be exposed, dependant on anything that may or may not have been said by Sue Senior.

She had sounded genuinely upset at the news of his beating. Ash remembered a similar reaction from her on one of the first occasions he'd met her, when Ron had arranged for a rival gang member to be 'seen to.' He remembered Sue and Ron having more than a few choice words about it. Indeed, he had been asked by Ron to take Sue home that night, to get her out of the way.

That was also a night he certainly wouldn't want Ronnie Senior to know anything else about, given what had happened afterwards.

Bertie announced that he'd give everyone his mobile number, so that he could arrange to pay them all their winnings once their bet had been settled.

'Yeah, no running off on one of those old people's hedonist holidays and blowing it all, Bertie. Even if you have got the shirt for it,' Dino jibed, referring again to the Hawaiian style garment that had been attracting ridicule all day.

Bertie blew him a mock kiss and replied;

'Well I guess yours will be at least one call that I'll be dodging from now on Dean. Or would you prefer it if I used your middle name, Dorian?'

Dino's horrified expression was all the confirmation that those within earshot needed to know that Bertie had said his name correctly and hit the comedy bullseye.

Gracie, who'd been in mid gulp of his pint, nearly spat it out as he struggled to contain his convulsion of laughter.

'Dean Dorian Willis! Bloody hell! What were your parents trying to do to you, pal?'

Dino smiled ruefully at Bertie, before replying;

'How did you bloody know that, Bassett?'

'Saw it on your passport once, when we were taking the piss out of your old photo with the dodgy hairstyle. What was it, a mullet?'

Dino nodded shamefaced.

'I'd forgotten all about that. Jesus, that was years ago!'

But he recovered some kudos back with a quick riposte;

'Still, they do say that Elephants never forget!'

Bertie laughed. 'Touché, Dorian.'

Dino Dorian then turned his gaze back to Rob.

'Mind you, getting on to dodgy hairstyles, talk us through your latest "do," Bog!'

Rob gave a middle finger salute in reply, with the addition of;

'I think you're confusing me with someone who gives a shit! Such a lot to say, for a bloke called Dorian Willis. Perhaps you should be a hairdresser yourself, love?'

Chapter Fifty-Eight

Spirits remained high as the Mickey taking and general banter continued. This kept the guys going, as the minutes ticked down to the time of the race that included their last bet.

More regular customers had swelled the ranks in the bar by this time. Several of them wore Grimsby Town shirts or scarves and had returned from the match.

Their expressions gave away the sad news that Grimsby had lost.

However, after a few pints and the news about the ongoing situation of the group's betting success, as divulged by Barry the Landlord, several of them were soon quizzing the guys for the name of their last horse.

Bertie, as before, was not confident that their luck would hold for the horse to win. But having looked at the betting, he was happy to announce that the price of their horse, Laughing Jackal, had increased to sixteen to one.

Barry, a man as large as any of the Dutch contingent, whose girth made him almost as wide as he was tall, had 'encouraged' any of his regulars who fancied an each way 'punt' on Laughing Jackal to give him their money, so that he could put the bet on for them before the race via his phone account, rather than lose custom via a migration to any nearby betting shops.

So, as the horses came out to parade before the race, pretty much the whole pub was invested financially in the fortunes of Laughing Jackal.

Rob turned to Bertie and asked; 'Do you regret not backing it each way, mate?'

Bertie shook his head.

'Look Bog, we've had a fabulous day, and we've all won more than any of us have ever won before. And we've got that from a ten quid stake each. If we'd have known earlier that the prices were all going to go crazy and had halved our bets to a fiver each way, then we wouldn't have won as much as we have. So let's just enjoy it whatever happens, because we can't lose what we've already got.'

'Well said, Bertie!' Gracie said, raising his glass.

'Yeah, fair enough.' Rob agreed.

Dino and Scott nodded and similarly raised their glasses.

Kenny, who by now was feeling due south of mellow and slurring proficiently, also raised his glass, and shouted;

'Allforrrone annoneforrall!' Slightly spoiling his stirring, slurring cry by overbalancing forward, but was fortunately saved by the bar in front of him from falling over completely.

Laughter convulsed the group at the bar.

They ordered another round as the horses prepared themselves for the start.

'Cheers boys! Happy Days!' Bertie said, raising his glass to his surrounding mates.

There was a general round of 'cheers' from the collective.

But Speedo, delving into his misty memory banks from a previous good night, finished the salutations with a raucous, 'UP YOUR ANORAKS!'

Which seemed a fitting enough way for the race to start.

The noise in the bar had risen to a new height and the atmosphere was electric. Complete strangers were shouting their encouragement to Laughing Jackal in unison, and Barry the Barman felt the need to turn the volume on his TV up to the max.

At the halfway mark Laughing Jackal was about five lengths off the pace, behind a blanket of four horses in a group.

As Bertie looked at the screen, he said to no one in particular; 'He's going to struggle to get through them. He's got nowhere to go.'

The shouting and hollering at both horse and jockey from the pub crowd wasn't making any difference either and although Laughing Jackal looked full of running, his jockey just couldn't make headway past the screen of horses in front of him.

Then, in the last furlong, the tiniest gap appeared in the centre of the group of the four ahead, as two horses veered slightly to the right and the other two slightly left and Laughing Jackal's jockey steered into and through the gap.

The noise in the pub at this point became even louder, and the TV's volume was drowned out.

You would've thought that people had bet fortunes on the horse, such was the level of excitement. But the news of the guy's successful day, which had spread around the pub in the lead up to the race, had enthused everyone outside the group, and re-enthused the guys themselves.

But as Laughing Jackal made his bold bid for the finishing line, the two horses to his immediate left suddenly swerved again to the right and the encroaching horses forced his jockey to steer him on a slight diagonal line, which checked his progress.

Although he continued to press, he was just touched off at the line by the nearest horse to his left and finished second.

The noise at the finish was as if a home crowd at a football match had witnessed their team miss a last minute penalty.

Despite the fact that the majority of the regulars had still won money, as they had placed their bet each way, there was still genuine disappointment that 'the guys' as everyone was calling them, hadn't quite pulled it off.

Bertie was genuinely angry though.

'That's bollocks! There has to be a Stewards Enquiry, surely? Those two horses ran across ours and it still nearly got up! I can't believe there isn't an enquiry!'

The rancour from Bertie and several of the others went on for a minute or two and then, as the noise in the pub reduced and the TV commentary became audible again, they suddenly heard, 'there will now be a belated Stewards Enquiry following complaints from the Trainer of Laughing Jackal.'

The noise in the pub then completely stopped.

Suddenly you literally could've heard a pin drop.

Everyone stared at the screen open mouthed.

Some of the guys were holding each other's arms.

Then the tannoy at Kempton Park announced;

As a result of the Stewards Enquiry, the result of the 7 o'clock race has been reversed. First, Number Nine, Laughing Jackal...

Any further TV sound was obliterated as the pub erupted into a cacophony of shouting, cheering and screaming.

There were a lot of man hugs and claps on the back going on all around.

Ash felt mixed emotions, due to the overall worry about his immediate future. But at least there would be some money coming his way now.

He cringed every time a nearby mini celebration got within a few inches of him and as he continually tensed himself for any potential impact, it put more strain on his very tender ribs.

But all around the pub, a general celebration had started.

Dino led the collective choir in a rousing rendition of;

'We won the cash, we won the cash, ey, aye, addio, we won the cash!'

Bertie had already got his phone out and was checking his bet calculator, buoyed further by the sight of the TV screen in front of him, which not only confirmed the first place for Laughing Jackal, but also showed its starting price had increased to eighteen to one.

As the figures on his phone screen finally began to compute in his brain, Bertie shouted;

'Jesus Christ! Guys! We've only won Nine Hundred and Fifty fucking grand!'

'How much?' Came from all sides.

There was another round of claps on the back, from both mates as well as total strangers.

Several of the guys were a little tearful, with the outpouring of emotion and adrenalin.

But, as the noise and the dust settled and things returned to a little more normality, Bertie was able to confirm that they had each won £38,000.

'Well, thirty eight thousand pounds and six pence, to be exact.' He said.

Chapter Fifty-Nine

Barry the Barman, the Licensee of the pub, was holding his phone out to no one in particular.

'Who's your spokesman, guys? The Telegraph wants to speak to you. The word's got out already! Probably from someone who's been in here. Sorry.'

After a brief interlude, Bertie was nominated and took the phone.

A short conversation ensued, while Bertie revealed brief details of the successful bet.

When the call ended, he advised that the Grimsby Telegraph were sending a Reporter down to the pub, to interview a few of them about their famous win.

Although everyone in the group was obviously pleased at the outcome, the reality had still to sink in and the majority of them were a little shell shocked.

Another round was ordered, although Barry insisted on treating everyone to a drink, 'on the house.'

But there was almost an air of anti-climax afterwards, as the guys struggled to make initial sense of the aftermath of their euphoria.

'I feel knackered!' Bertie said.

'Me too.' Agreed Gracie.

Speedo, surprisingly, summed up the general feeling of the group with;

'It hasn't sunk in yet!'

Rob put an arm around Speedo's shoulder and said;

'You've had quite a day mate, haven't you? Met your Dad for the first time, and won yourself and him, 38 bloody grand each!'

Speedo looked slightly mystified.

'Oh yeah, I'd forgotten all about Maurice being involved!' Said Dino.

Speedo suddenly came to from his bewilderment.

'I need to ring my Dad!'

So while he stepped outside to make the call, most of the others re-congratulated each other.

But in the main it was a slightly subdued group.

Gary Chivers had sobered up considerably.

'Do you know something?' He said quietly, to no one in particular.

'There's a guy at work whose little boy needs an operation to potentially change his life, that he can't get on the NHS. This poor guy and his Wife have looked all over for help and it turns out that there's a Surgeon in The States that could do the op they need for their boy, but the cost is nearly two hundred grand. Sobering thought, eh?'

'Oh Jesus! That's awful.' Dino exclaimed.

The other guys within earshot made similar comments.

Gary continued, almost as if he were talking to himself;

'When something like this happens, it makes you think how lucky you are. But in reality, as long as your family, your loved ones, are ok health wise, then you're already lucky. That poor sod and his Missus must be going through so much shit right now. I'm going to try and do something for them. Maybe Crowd Funding, or a Just Giving page.'

Bertie agreed and added;

'There must be so many deserving causes out there. But it would be nice to do something good with some of this, maybe?'

Gracie asked Gary; 'Is this family local then, Gaz?'

'Yeah, He's been in the pub with me a couple of times, but not for a while. Nice guy. Phil Norman. He's got three kids, two girls and a boy, and it's the little boy, Callum, who's ill. Six years old, bless him. Bertie knows them.'

Bertie nodded. 'Yeah, I didn't want to say anything, as I know it's hit them hard. But I'd definitely be up for contributing. Especially now!'

Gracie shook his head, sorrowfully and replied;

'I'm sure that if we get the word out locally, we can get some sponsorship for him.'

Rob and Kenny took the next lull in conversation as a cue for stepping outside for some air.

Dino and Scott looked at each other, both feeling a little uncomfortable at the downturn in mood and took the opportunity to go to the Gents.

Scott looked at his mate and rolled his eyes; 'I hate anything like that, same as anybody, Dino. But, I'm not being funny, I hope they're not going to suggest that we give up a lot of what we've just won, 'cos I really can't afford to do that right now, mate.'

'Neither can I Scott. I'm living hand to mouth at the moment and trying to get my business up and running. It's been hard since I got Divorced. But I feel for any family with a sick kid.'

Scott nodded; 'So do I. Course I do. But it's just a bit tough at work at the moment.'

Dino reflected and said;

'Well, we'll see what happens. They were only talking about maybe getting some sponsorship. And I'd be up for helping with anything like that.'

'Yeah, me too.' Scott agreed.

Marco and Rudi, not being a party to the conversation at the bar, and having taken in that they had seventy six thousand pounds to come between them, now began to seriously talk of putting their dream venture of a beach bar into reality.

Ash still sat on his stool at the corner of the bar, contemplating his situation.

He owed over half of his potential winnings to several money lenders, who had already begun initial debt recovery procedures against him. But, at least he now had enough to pay them off.

But he still needed more than that would leave him to put back the money he'd withdrawn from the investment that his Grandad had left for his kids.

He sat alone feeling more miserable than he could ever remember, as he ruminated every bad decision he'd made and the money he'd wasted in the last few years.

He was suddenly fully aware of his desperation, having kept it all in the back of his mind for so long.

Kenny and Rob couldn't believe the turn of events over the course of the last twenty four hours.

They stood outside the pub, and checked that nobody was within earshot, before speaking.

'Do you think if we'd have decided to keep that money, that any of this would've happened, Bog?' Kenny led off.

'I was just going to ask you much the same thing.' Rob smiled.

'You seem a lot more sober than you did before that last race, Ken!'

Kenny had put his shades back on as the sunshine was still quite bright in the late evening of this late summer's day, so Rob couldn't see him rolling his eyes as he pondered over recent events. But eventually, he broke into a smile and said;

'Yeah, I feel a bit more normal now. I think it was as much the excitement and adrenalin, as it was the booze! But it would be the biggest understatement ever to say that the last twenty four hours or so have been a bit of a rollercoaster, eh?'

Rob laughed.

'Well, like I've said several times now, you said you wanted an adventure, mate!'

Kenny smiled ruefully.

'And we've certainly had one! But it's not over yet, is it? We've still got to decide how and where to dispose of that bag and its contents. And on that subject..'

The two of them looked at each other.

'I know what you're thinking, Ken. It was pretty awkward just now hearing about that poor kid, wasn't it?'

'Yes, of course it was. But like it or not, we do have the means to sort that family's problems right away, don't we?

All we've got to do is get the money they need to them without anyone knowing. And then get rid of the rest.'

Rob looked around nervously.

But before he could speak, Kenny continued;

'I think that something went on between Ash and the Dutch guys when they went outside earlier. Apart from the fact that they came back separately, Ash was complaining about supposedly falling over and hurting his ribs and then, as he followed me to the bar, I saw the four of them giving him the filthiest of looks. I think they've had a major fallout.'

Rob shrugged and then nodded, before replying; 'But to be honest Ken that doesn't surprise me. They've not exactly been acting like mates, or even like work colleagues since they turned up, have they?'

This time it was Kenny's turn to nod before speaking;

'No they haven't. And as much as they seem like genuine blokes most of the time, I wouldn't want to get on the wrong side of them. When that Marco was speaking to me earlier in that first pub, I felt really uneasy. I've never met any Dutch people before, Bog, but those blokes don't strike me as being anything like Coppers. I know I said that earlier, but I'm pretty sure of it now.'

Rob shrugged and nodded.

'I've thought that too, though. All that crap Ash came out with earlier about witnesses and press releases, I think it was all made up. I said to you last night that I felt sure he knew we'd had that money away and we both said yesterday that it must have been left there by someone dodgy. Well, I reckon Ash left that bag and maybe the Dutch blokes are mixed up in that too. I mean, why would they just turn up on a jolly with blokes they don't know, if they're supposed to be working a case here?'

Kenny kept up the nodding, before replying;

'Yeah, they're obviously not friends of Ash's. They said as much earlier before they disappeared with him. Their questions earlier about the windup we were all a part of yesterday were odd. I mean, that information would be of no interest to anyone, unless it was to do with how close that had all been to where the real money was?'

Rob looked around again to make sure they couldn't be overheard.

'That's right, and also, do you remember how worried Ash looked when he stayed on the coach, after we stopped earlier? We definitely need to be getting rid of that cash as soon as we can mate. I feel desperately sorry for that family, and I know we can make that operation a reality for them. But we have to be careful.

They considered their options for a while longer and formulated a few ideas for what to do after they got back home, before going back inside the bar.

Chapter Sixty

While Bertie, with a little help from Dino and Scott, fielded the questions from the Grimsby Telegraph Reporter, Gracie did the rounds of the group to gauge the current mood regarding their plans for the rest of the day.

Having gathered a few of them together, he was of the opinion that, with the time now after eight, they had two choices. They could either stay in Cleethorpes for a bit longer, or get some booze and maybe a takeaway for the coach trip back and then, dependant on how people were feeling once they were home, they could cap the day off with a late drink in The Feathers.

It was an overwhelming vote for the latter, as most of the guys preferred to be back home tonight, regardless of how late in the day they eventually wrapped things up.

In truth, the prolonged excitement they'd all experienced, particularly in the last couple of hours, had rendered them all in need of some time to chill out.

Marco had again spoken to Rinus as he'd been requested to do earlier.

He made no mention of the events culminating in the joint Horse Racing win, but advised that they had no further clues concerning the whereabouts of the missing cash. Marco advised that it was their opinion that Ash was probably telling the truth about leaving the money on the golf course, but they couldn't be sure if the money had then been taken by persons unknown, or people in league with Ash, or had been handed in to the police.

He told Rinus that he believed the guys would soon be returning back on the coach, and therefore suggested that he, Rudi, Danny and Johann return to Holland tomorrow via the North Sea Ferry from Hull.

However Rinus' mood was not good, and he wanted them to stay with the group and return to their village. He said that if they were still unable to determine what had happened to the money, they would at least be close by and could assist him and Bruno if necessary before they returned home.

Marco and Rudi were now determined to end their association with Rinus. But they knew they had to extricate themselves carefully and without bad blood between them and their 'boss.'

Marco conveyed the news to his three countrymen, who, like him, were annoyed at what, they thought, was largely a waste of time.

Danny and Johann, so full of bravado earlier in the day, were now disinterested in Rinus' whims, and couldn't care less what had happened to the money.

And all four of them, by now, had nothing but good feelings for the majority of the guys they had spent the day with, and of course, the little matter of them each winning £38,000 hadn't done anything to sour that view.

Once the Reporter had gained sufficient information for his story, including a plug for Barry's Pub where the drama had largely unfolded and also a mention for The Feathers as being the establishment where the winning 'syndicate' had set off from earlier, he wished them well and departed.

Gracie then gathered the guys together and they decided to buy sufficient 'refreshment' for the journey back from a more than grateful Barry, who also gave them a recommendation for what he considered was 'the best' local Pizza, Burger and Kebab shop, to enable them to place a large takeaway order to sustain them on the way home. Mick the coach driver having given his seal of approval to allow this on his coach.

Ash was pleased to hear that things were being wrapped up as he was keen to get back. The money remained a constant thorn in his side, but he also needed to try and find out how things stood for him at work and whether or not he was under any suspicion.

He had tried to contact Kirstie a couple of times in the last few hours, but had only reached her voicemail and none of his text messages to her had been responded to.

However, his mood was not helped when he heard Gracie, Bertie and a few of the others invite the Dutch contingent to join the guys back at The Feathers.

'Oh, sanks guys!' Said Marco; 'Dat's very kint of you. If you don't mynt, we will meet you guys back at your Pup. As we prefer to take the car back ant not leaf it here overnight. I will be ok to drife, as I haf only hat a few light beers, ant a burger will be all I neet to set me up for der drife back.'

Although Marco was as imposing a figure now as he'd been hours before when they'd all first met him, Dino felt brave enough to 'initiate him' into the fraternity with a little ribbing.

'Marco, What did you mean mate when you said, you'll meet us back at our "Pup?" None of us have got a dog.'

Marco was familiar with piss taking, and he smiled warmly at Dino.

'Oh, you're der guy wit der gay sounding name, aren't you? What is it, Dora Ann? You see, Dora Ann, I am a Dutch person, ant when I speak your language, Dora Ann, I pronounce certain worts a liddle different to the way you may say dem. So, Dora Ann, when I set der wort "Pup," I was not meaning a liddle Dog. What I meant Dora Ann, was a bar, where people buy drinks. You see, Dora Ann?'

Dino felt somewhat diminished as his mates convulsed in gales of laughter all around him, including his best bud, Scott.

But Marco wasn't quite finished.

Still generating a genial smile, his gaze fell on Scott, sniggering away at his mate's discomfort.

'Ant you are Scott, is dat right?'

Scott felt the immediate need to respectfully nod and reply;

'Yes, that's right, sir.'

Marco surveyed him for a second.

'Hmmm. Ok. So I see dat you fount your frent Dora Ann's liddle joke amusing, eh? You are der one dat your frents call "Starfish." Is dat also right?'

Scott nodded again, feeling suitably chastened. He attempted to explain the circumstances of how that nickname had been bestowed on him, but Marco talked over him.

'Yes, it's ok, I alretty haf der mental image, sank you! So, it is as I sought. Ok, Dora Ann ant Starfish. See you back at der Pup!'

Marco laughed and clapped them both on the shoulder, which although meant in a friendly manner, still served to knock them both sideways. This was the cue for more laughter at their expense.

Forty five minutes later, with the requisite booze and takeaway food ensconced on the coach and in the black people carrier containing the four Dutchmen, the journey home began.

Chapter Sixty-One

Speedo finally got off the phone after another long call to Maurice.

'Jesus, that was an epic, mate!' Gary Chivers exclaimed, continuing;

'Was everything alright?'

Speedo smiled; 'Yeah. Everything's fine. I spoke to Dad again and then to two of my Sisters and my Brother. They weren't in earlier when I spoke to Dad. It was really great to finally speak to them! And they were so happy about the horse money. We're going to all meet up properly next week.'

'Did you give him my number, Kev?' Asked Bertie from a couple of rows back.

'No, I forgot. But I'll be speaking to him again tomorrow. I can sort out getting his money to him though.'

'You've had a bit of a red letter day, mate, haven't you? Bertie smiled.

Speedo beamed and looked a bit choked up.

'Fantastic day!' He said quietly.

The noise level on the coach had been initially muted due to the serious business of chowing down to everyone's chosen takeaway choice.

Mick's choice of music from the Coach's radio had come in for a bit of criticism from Dino and Scott. But was soon quelled when Gracie reminded them of their recent chastening experience at the hands of Marko.

He also added; 'Mick wants the local station on, so he can catch the news in a minute, so shut your faces!'

Dino's, 'Dora Ann' rebuke had now morphed into 'Dora the Explorer' jibes from a few of his 'friends,' who felt it suitably lifted it to an even higher level of insult.

As the local news came on a cheer greeted the last of the initial headlines read out in the opening announcement; 'And a syndicate of day trippers to Cleethorpes scoop a near million pound jackpot on the horses this afternoon!'

'Blimey! Didn't take long to get our story out, did it?' Said a smiling Gracie.

'That reporter told me that he thought the Nationals might pick up on our story, depending on how much other news there is today?' Bertie added.

'Fame at last, boys, eh?' Dino chipped in.

Despite the excitement of the last few hours, it was a subdued atmosphere on the return journey, as quite a few of the guys relaxed, snoozed, or drank a couple of beers and reflected quietly on the events of the day.

The effects of steady drinking, a fair amount of food, and an adrenalin filled rollercoaster over the latter part of the day had taken its toll.

Ash had retreated to the back of the coach and nursed his sore ribs. He still experienced sharp pain if he breathed in quickly, or shifted his position in his seat.

He stared out of the window after trying Kirstie's phone again without success, not bothering to leave another voicemail message. He was disgusted that he felt so sorry for himself and resolved that, whatever happened from here, he would meet it head on and 'man up.'

The lull in the noise and excitement of the last few hours also gave quite a few of the guys the opportunity to catch up with their partners on the phone and share their good news.

Both Kenny and Rob made simultaneous calls to Mo and Sally respectively.

Although there was a fair amount of background noise when Mo answered Kenny's call, she made her way outside the restaurant that she and the other girls were in to better hear her Husband.

'How are you, Ken?' Mo said, sounding happy to be hearing from him.

'I'm ok, love. Really good, actually. We've had a pretty fantastic result!'

He told her the news about the big win and everyone's share and Mo made a predictably enthusiastic response.

'Oh wow! That's amazing! Well done darling. That's just fantastic!'

'To be honest, it was more down to Bertie and Dino I think. They picked the four horses. But we got amazingly lucky with the prices and the excitement in the pub when the last one won was unbelievable!'

'Are you having fun, Mo?' He continued.

'Yes I am. We've had a good day too. But I'm really looking forward to coming home to see you tomorrow, love.'

Rob's conversation with Sally and those of the other guys who phoned their Wives and girlfriends all went along the same happy theme.

Sally sounded more than a bit merry and Rob teased her accordingly;

'You sound like you're having a good time, Sal!'

'I am thank you! But that's what we're here for, Rob. What a fantastic result you've had though!'

'Yeah, we'll do something nice with some of that money, eh?' He smiled, happy as always to be speaking to his wife, who always made him feel more at ease.

'Oh, I can think of quite a few things already that we could do with that sort of cash, love!' Sally replied, giggling.

'Fun things though, Sal, eh? I think we deserve that.'

'Absolutely! ...' He could hear squealing and cheering in the background, drowning her reply out, as news was spreading among Sally and Mo's friends from the other calls being made to them.

The feelgood factor afterwards was immediately apparent amongst each of the guys who'd made similar calls.

In the SUV following the coach the four Dutch men were fairly ambivalent about the way things had gone. They were all obviously pleased to know they'd be in receipt of a far bigger payday than they usually experienced from their working association with Rinus.

But they'd all now lost interest in the affairs of their boss. They'd been given a task that, in the circumstances, had been highly unlikely to bring any positive conclusion. So as far as they were concerned, there was little else they could've done.

Sue Senior though had had a completely different change of heart.

Her disagreement with Rinus had escalated over the last couple of hours, since her conversation with Ash.

She had reached a point where the use of violence and the whole criminal lifestyle had finally worn her down and she'd had enough.

Although she had been supported by Ron for a number of years and had enjoyed a very good existence, she figured that she'd paid her way by running and maintaining her own business throughout.

Rinus had not long received a call from one of his associates in Holland which had left him both worried and angry.

It seemed that the suppliers of the drugs were unhappy that full payment had not yet been made, and threats of retribution had been issued if they were not paid in full, plus an extra amount for late payment.

Rinus had, until now, kept all of this to himself and had painted a picture of his all powerful position in the Dutch underworld, which now seemed to be a complete fabrication.

The reality was that he now desperately needed to sell the consignment of drugs that he had replaced with fake substances in the shipment Ronnie Senior had been expecting.

The realisation that there may not now be any further money available to him from what Ash had managed to remove from Senior's house had been a catalyst for expediency.

In truth he now seemed to Sue to be a shallow, desperate man who appeared to be running out of time.

Rinus had left with Bruno a few minutes ago; after she'd heard him set up a meeting which he said was with a potential buyer for the drugs.

But his almost pleading tone during the phone conversation had more than amplified his desperation and Sue had told him as much afterwards.

She had been mulling things over since the conversation with Ash earlier and her subsequent row with Rinus. But by the time he'd left, Sue had finally calculated how she felt about her personal situation.

She figured that, if she avoided any implication of conspiracy in Ron's demise, she was solvent and was more than set up financially, even if the police withheld a chunk of the money they had seized in the search of the house.

As much as she'd initially wanted the money that Ash had removed from the house yesterday, it now represented all that she now realised she'd come to despise from years of being around violence and criminal behaviour.

The lifestyle that Rinus had described only a few hours ago, now appeared completely unlikely and not without danger going forward and that was the last thing she wanted or needed.

So she decided to take matters into her own hands.

She made calls to Clive Russell, Ron's long time Lawyer and then to Mike Phelan.

Both of which she knew would bring about some pretty dramatic changes.

Chapter Sixty-Two

Mick pulled the coach into The Feather's car park after a largely uneventful and reasonably quiet journey back and was closely followed by the car containing the Dutch contingent.

Both groups disembarked and the majority followed Gracie into the pub, apart from a few dissenters who stated that tiredness had defeated them and said their goodbyes.

Having made sure that Ash had gone inside with the others, Kenny set off for home to follow a plan he and Rob had made outside the pub in Cleethorpes earlier.

There were a few late night revellers in the bar as the guys entered and their appearance caused an instant lift in mood for the vast majority.

Gracie immediately adopted his familiar position behind the bar and started taking orders and serving drinks.

'This one's on me, guys!' He smiled.

Being back on familiar ground for the pub regulars, induced a feeling of contentment in them and it felt good to be drinking in their local again, after what had been a long, but highly enjoyable and momentous day.

As was their usual practice on previous occasions like this, an immediate replay of the day's highlights began. The guys laughed as they swapped stories and reran reactions, silly comments and embarrassing moments.

The people in the bar on their return had prior knowledge of their big win as Gracie had called the pub on the way back to make sure everything was alright.

As Gracie pulled pints and ensured everyone was being attended to, he called to Rob; 'Bog, is Kenny having a beer? I presume he's having a slash?'

Rob, anxious not to raise any alarm or suspicion from either Ash or the Dutch guys, answered in a matter of fact manner;

'Yeah, I'm sure he'll be on beer for now. He won't be a minute, he's just sorting something out over the road.'

Gracie knew that 'over the road' meant at his house, as Kenny lived less than 100 yards from the pub.

He laughed and replied; 'He's got all day tomorrow to tidy up the mess he's probably made of the place before Mo comes home!'

Rob smiled back and surveyed where everyone was, before joining Bertie, Dino, Scott and a few others along the bar.

About ten minutes later, Kenny reappeared and joined his mates.

'What was that, another dump mate?' Enquired Bertie.

Kenny feigned high dudgeon.

'You're very nosy, Mr Bassett! I just had to sort a couple of things out, that's all.'

'Yeah, a dump!' Dino offered, before continuing;

'How's the eye now, Nelson?'

Kenny hid his hand inside his jacket, shut his stricken eye and replied, smiling;

'I see no ships, Dora Ann.' Then added; 'It's a lot easier now, thanks.'

Rob made a questioning face to him and Kenny nodded to confirm that he'd completed a successful mission.

The night then progressed into the early hours, via drinking games and general silliness. Dino and Scott unwisely took on the four Dutch men, whom, they soon found out, could all more than hold their own in regard to alcohol consumption and quickly came to regret their error.

Gracie, who rarely indulged in a major way anymore, had rekindled a lost love with a decent bottle of dark Rum and had settled in for the duration. But, he was receiving able support from three of the Dutch contingent, who seemed keen to sample any concoction.

Rudi though, was in deep conversation with Speedo about their many shared musical interests and also to chat generally for the first time. They had been pretty much left to their discussion by those remaining at or near the bar.

Gary Chivers had again mentioned his workmate's dilemma regarding his stricken child.

'It's awful.' Said Kenny, standing next to Gary at the bar. He continued;

'I'm still trying to place the boy's Dad. You said earlier that he's been in here with you?'

'Yeah, he's a lovely guy. Ian Norman. You'd know him if you saw him. Lives next door to Bertie.'

'Oh right! Bertie said earlier that he knew the family, but I didn't know he lived next door to them.' Kenny replied nodding.

Gary shrugged and continued;

'I'm sorry to go on about it. I suppose it's because of our good fortune? No, strike that. Obviously it IS because of our good fortune! But that makes their horrible situation resonate even more strongly.'

Kenny gulped, before replying;

'Gaz, it'll be alright mate. I'm sure it'll all work out ok.' He patted Gary on the shoulder.

'How can you be so sure, Ken? They need such a lot of money.'

'Well, we've all said we'd help with trying to get local sponsorship, and there's a lot of big firms around here. We'll sort something out.'

Gary smiled thinly.

'I know people will try. But time is so important to them. Their little lad is really not well.'

The thought of any small child suffering was an awful concept to try to come to terms with.

Kenny and Mo had lost a baby years ago, the memory of which was the catalyst for Kenny to want to try even harder to put his mate's mind at rest by outlining a guaranteed solution. But he also saw this as a possible solution to his and Rob's remaining worry about the money.

A half formed idea that sort of dovetailed with what he'd done when he went home earlier spurred him on.

'Look Gaz, Bog and me, well...we can help. PROPERLY help!

Kenny's head was spinning more than a bit from the effects of the few Jack Daniels chasers that had accompanied his beer over the last hour and maybe he should have discussed his plan with Rob first before saying what he was currently saying.

That thought was triple underlined by the look of horror on Rob's face as he stared open mouthed at him.

'How can you "PROPERLY help," Ken? You sound so sure!' Gary replied, puzzled.

Ash's radar had tweaked and from along the bar, looking pointedly at Kenny, he said;

'Yeah Ken. Just how CAN you "PROPERLY help" eh? You make it sound so definite and easy. Don't forget, it is an awful lot of money.'

Ken was in a flap. Losing his nerve to press on, he looked at Rob for support.

Rob's mind was racing as he tried to remain calm in the face of crisis.

Ash was looking at both of them now, and appeared to have sharpened his gaze to burrow deep into Rob's skull.

'Well'.....Rob heard the word, but failed to compute who had said it, as he was stuck in a time warp in which he'd been deprived of both speech and a functioning brain.

'You were saying, Bog?' Ash enquired, more than a little quizzically.

The sound of Ash's voice propelled Rob back to the present and as the fog lifted, he realised that the 'well' had come from his own lips.

He composed himself as best he could.

'Well, what I'm sure he meant was, our Chief Exec Jakob is always on board with stuff like this. You know, sponsoring good causes and getting the staff at work to support and raise the profile of things. Isn't that right, KEN?

Rob had added slightly more vehemence to his mate's name than he intended in his reply and he supported it with a death stare to match.

Kenny rapidly backtracked.

'Y..YES! That's EXACTLY what I meant!' His voice ascended the scales as he continued. ' Jakob's a great guy, and he's got a little boy too! They're Swedish! He's bound to be on board for such a worthy cause as this!'

Gary smiled gratefully.

'Any help would be greatly appreciated, guys, thank you so much!'

Ash continued staring at Kenny and Rob, before adding;

'Yeah, guys. Thank you, SO much! That's really good of you. A real eye opener!'

Kenny smiled awkwardly and felt the need to sit on a bar stool to ease his quivering legs.

Just before the party broke up Rudi took a call from Bruno.

After a short conversation he ended the call and relayed the information to his Dutch compatriots.

'Bruno just callt me. He set dat Rinus has been arrestet!'

Marco and the others looked surprised, but not exactly concerned.

'What happent?' Danny enquired.

Rudi calmly relayed the story he had just heard;

'Bruno set dat der police turnt up after dey arrived at where dey was due to meet some guys who Rinus was going to sell drugs to. He set dat der boot of der car was full of dem. Bruno set he was able to get away in der confusion as der police closed in, but Rinus was too slow. He set Rinus was definitely arrestet ant so were der udder guys. He set the police came out of nowhere. Dey must haf been tippt off.'

'Fuck! What does dat mean for us, eh?' Marco said quietly.

Rudi smiled.

'Funny, Bruno just set der same sing. Ant I set, it means we get to go home! I dit not tell Bruno dat we haf all hat a nice pay day, as I dit not want to upset him!'

The four giants laughed.

Rudi, still smiling, continued; 'Guys, Kevin has been so kint to offer to let us stay at his house nearby. We can pick up der car in der morning.'

One by one, the guys gave way to tiredness and the need to be able to fight another day. Plans were made to reconvene at Lunchtime on Sunday for a final flourish, before the return of the better halves of several of the group.

The evening wrapped up shortly after two and goodbyes were said all round.

They confirmed they'd meet back at the pub about one ish. There was also football on TV, so they could make an afternoon of it.

Ash, as always, had been on the periphery of the handshakes and salutations. But as the guys went their separate ways in a couple of mini cabs and the rest on foot, he surveyed the scene.

He had been out of earshot of the Dutch guys' conversation about the arrest of their boss and was therefore oblivious of that news.

But Kenny's little faux pas a while back had again raised Ash's expectations and focussed his attention. He was sure that Rob and Kenny had 'his money' and despite the nagging pain in his ribs, he was determined to get his hands on it.

Chapter Sixty-Three

Mike Phelan had had self preservation firmly on his mind ever since receiving a call from Sue Senior earlier.

After she'd explained the change in circumstances in regard to Rinus's position, it was clear that the opportunity for Phelan to benefit financially, from either a share of the missing money from Ron Senior's house, or the cache of drugs still to be sold by Rinus, had gone.

Sue had given him the location for the meeting that she'd heard Rinus arrange to potentially sell the drugs and her take on the situation was the same as his.

The best thing now was to ensure that he acted as a police officer and make sure that arrests were made, thereby hopefully removing any further threats to his status.

But, in order to preserve his own skin, he obviously needed to stay out of the actual arrest of either Rinus, or his associates.

So, he contacted a mate of his who was a Detective Inspector in the Drugs Squad, to advise him of a tip off he'd received from 'a reliable source' about the imminent meeting and the location for it.

That call then sealed Rinus's fate.

Phelan knew that Rinus would be interviewed and charged by Drugs Squad officers and therefore hoped that he wouldn't be implicated in helping to bring Rinus down.

He'd even advised his mate in the Drugs Squad that he wanted no credit for the tip off as it may compromise another operation that the Regional Crime Squad were involved with.

In the time since making that call Phelan had played and replayed all of his conversations with Rinus Rensenbrinck and was pretty certain that he'd covered his tracks.

As far as he was concerned, Phelan believed that if anything was said by Rinus about his part in Ronnie Senior's arrest, he would just say that he had acted on the information of an unknown informant about a planned drug deal by a known criminal.

The arrests made subsequently would only underline his credibility as a diligent police officer.

Although the financial gains he had hoped to make from the aftermath of the raid on Senior's gang and their arrest had not come about, Phelan figured that the operation would do no harm to his potential for promotion to Detective Inspector.

He sat back in his armchair and sipped at a large glass of his favourite single malt whisky, savouring the aged, peaty flavour.

His enjoyment was interrupted by the sound of his mobile phone.

The call was from Ray Edwards, his mate in the Drugs Squad who he'd phoned earlier.

'Hello, Ray.' He said.

'Surprised to hear from you, mate. Did everything go ok?'

Edwards hesitated before replying, which gave Phelan a few seconds of sudden recall about something he might have forgotten.

'Yes, Mike. Everything went smoothly. We arrested the Dutch guy and the blokes he was supposedly meeting and as you advised, a car load of Heroin and Cocaine worth about a million quid.'

'Oh, that's gr...' Phelan's reply was interrupted, as Edwards continued;

'Just a couple of things though, Mike. You said earlier that it was a tip from a reliable source, didn't you?'

'Y.yes, that's right, Ray.' Phelan's voice faltered slightly.

'So, you don't know this Dutch guy, or the blokes he was meeting, then?'

Something was now nagging at Phelan's brain. What had he forgotten?

'I don't think so, Ray. It was just some information about a drugs deal. So I wanted to make sure it was passed on ASAP.'

'You see, Mike, we've looked at the Dutch guy's phone and there's several calls on it to your mobile number.'

Phelan's head was starting to buzz. Hold firm, he told himself.

'Look, Ray, I get a bit of information from criminal types from time to time. I don't know how you guys work, but in the Squad we don't care if we get decent info from one crim about another, just as long as it ends up in taking scumbags off the streets! Maybe this guy has phoned me before, unbeknown to me. Bu....'

Edwards interrupted him again. But as he did so, Phelan made the connection to what he'd forgotten.

'Yes, I get that Mike. But there's also quite a few texts from him to you, and quite a few replies too..'

Phelan's brain was in overdrive as he replayed in his mind the content of texts he'd received from Rinus and also replied to. He'd obviously deleted all such texts, but evidently Rinus hadn't.

This time Phelan interrupted Edwards;

'Ray, if there's anything that sounds iffy, I'll be able to explain it, mate. I sometimes play along with these guys to gain their trust, in order to get more information from them an....'

Edwards interrupted for the final time;

'Well, I did say at the beginning that there were a couple of things, Mike.

You see, I got a call from your guv'nor a little while back. He'd had a call from a Lawyer who represents a bloke you guys nicked yesterday. A guy named Senior. Seems like this Dutch guy and the bloke you nicked had some sort of deal going.

Anyway, your Guv' nor asked me to ring you and keep you talking for a bit while they came over to yours. Should be there by now. Is that someone at your door I can hear, Mike?'

Phelan froze. The sound of his door bell ringing was accompanied by loud banging and raised voices.

Chapter Sixty-Four

Ash meanwhile, slowly made his way along the road from the pub to the place that he called home.

As he approached it, a random thought occurred to him.

'It's not actually my house at all this, is it?' He smiled wryly.

The truth was that he'd moved in with Kirstie a couple of years ago, but nothing had ever changed to make their relationship 'official.' Although he had contributed randomly towards the bills, it remained Kirstie's property and hers was the sole name on the mortgage.

The realisation of that rendered his sombre mood to turn even more morose and further heightened his wish to get away from the area he'd been born and brought up in.

In addition, he reflected that his ex wife was a great Mother to his two children and had remarried to a decent guy, who was an ideal Stepfather. While Ash had been a lousy Dad to his kids and had no real relationship with them at all.

Although that was a sad fact, he had always thought that there was still time for him to change things. But he had never done anything to bring that change about.

'It's true what they say.' He whispered to himself.

'You reap what you sow.'

The house was in darkness when he went in, as you might expect at gone two in the morning. But there was a stillness about the place that suggested no one had been in or around for a while.

As he stepped forward in the dark, his leg banged into something heavy and he almost fell over. But he managed to reach forward and hold onto the edge of the table in the passage that housed the house phone and several knick knacks.

The sudden wrench forward sent a burning pain through his ribcage and side, that almost brought tears to his eyes. But he managed to avoid crying out.

When he eventually found the light switch, he discovered that the heavy object he'd just banged into was one of two suitcases that belonged to him.

The same two suitcases that had contained his clothes when he moved in two years before.

On top of the cases was a piece of paper, which he immediately recognised to be a note in Kirstie's handwriting.

He picked up the note and took it into the lounge, turned on the light and sat down carefully to read it, already knowing what it would say.

He opened it and read the short message.

She had packed his bags. She had gone to stay with a friend. She wanted him to leave. No recriminations. Blah, blah, blah.

But to be honest, he couldn't blame her. They were going nowhere and it was right that he should leave and a clean break was probably best.

He actually admired her for the way she'd gone about it.

'So, here we are, Ashley.' He laughed quietly.

'Well at least I'm allowed to get away with calling me that!'

But as the reality of his situation fully dawned on him, Ash felt that he now had no option.

As far as he was concerned he needed to get away and start a new life.

All he needed to bring that about was a sports bag full of cash.

Chapter Sixty-Five

Kenny and Rob had talked about nothing else since they'd got back from the pub.

Rob threw his hands up in disgust and glared at his mate, as he'd done several times since then.

'We bloody agreed not to do anything to draw attention to ourselves and to be careful, you dick!'

Kenny looked suitably shamefaced.

'It just came out, Bog. I heard myself saying it and I couldn't believe it. But I couldn't stop myself. When Gary mentioned that poor boy again, I just thought it would be a way to lead Ash in. I lost my nerve a bit, but I still reckon it might work out better for us. I know I should've spoken to you first and I'm sorry!'

'Well, it's done now. But now he DEFINITELY knows we've got it.' Rob sighed.

'I guess so, mate. But, one way or another, we're getting rid of that bag in the morning!' Kenny pointed to 'that bag' as he said the words.

The sports bag stuffed with cash had been retrieved a little earlier by Kenny from his compost heap and now sat in the corner of his living room by the French doors leading to his garden.

'To be honest though Bog, when I came over earlier I thought that this might work out better if he does take the bait, you know? That's why I repacked the bag as I did to cover us either way. If we end up taking it to the course we'll obviously only leave the real cash, minus our 'donation.'

Rob shrugged before replying;

'We spoke about that before, though, didn't we? It would be a huge gamble that could easily backfire on us if we're wrong.'

But Kenny saw things differently.

'Yeah, but we're not wrong, though, are we? And I've primed the bag just in case now anyway. Ash definitely put that money on the course. Probably because he couldn't hide it anywhere else? The fact that he came out with all that old bollocks about your hat earlier, almost certainly proves that he went back for the bag and found your hat where the bag had been. I can't see how else it could've been. He's at the end of his tether.

He looked done in earlier and after all the crap he said to us, I'm sure he'll make some sort of a move, or be watching us in the morning. So we'll have to be careful, even though he's been pretty banged up and won't be able to be too active in getting about.'

Rob shook his head and replied;

'Yeah, but he's still a bloody copper, and he's such a dodgy bastard that he could still try and twist things.'

They sat in silence for a couple of minutes contemplating the empty coffee cups in front of them.

Rob fidgeted in his seat, and then finally stood up.

'I keep thinking about that poor kid and his family. I mean, god forbid that was us. But trying to help them has made it more awkward for us, hasn't it?'

'I don't know mate. I just think it's the right thing to do. Its dodgy money in the first place, isn't it? By the looks of it Ash is acting alone. If he wasn't, there would've been more shit coming down on us if he'd told anybody he was in league with that he thought we had their money.

Like I said, we've set it up now anyway, with the bag and the cash. If he makes a move or not, we know what we're going to do.'

'Maybe?' Rob said. 'We can't fret about this anymore now. We'll do as we said in the morning and play it by ear. We'll have to be up early, though.'

'You might as well stay here mate. It'll be light enough by six, and that's only three hours awa....'

The guys looked at each other in a panic, as they both heard a soft tap on the front door.

The colour had drained from Kenny's face as he slowly made his way to the door.

Rob was just as scared, but felt the need to accompany his mate.

But Kenny stopped in his tracks and he turned and whispered;

'Better put that bag out of the way, mate. Stick it in the utility room by the washing machine.'

He gave Rob a few seconds before approaching the front door.

As he nervously opened it, he wasn't altogether surprised to see Ash standing a few feet away, looking sorry for himself.

Kenny suddenly felt in control of his emotions. Aided by the sobering effect of the coffee consumed since coming back from the pub, his nervousness disappeared and was replaced by calmness and clarity.

'Ash?' He said, quizzically.

'Sorry to bother you, Ken. I know it's an imposition, but I saw your lights were on. Can I come in, please? Kirstie's kicked me out.'

Kenny wasn't totally surprised at the last piece of information, as he knew that Ash's relationship was more than a bit rocky, from things he'd heard Mo say.

'Alright, Ash. Come in. It's a hell of a time to kick someone out!'

Ash stepped inside and accepted Kenny's immediate offer of a coffee.

'I wasn't exactly expecting this to happen tonight, but it's been sort of coming for a while, I suppose.' Ash said, in an unusually flat tone.

Kenny shrugged, before replying; 'Don't quite know what to say Ash, other than sorry to hear that.'

'I could've probably kipped on the sofa. But in that atmosphere it was best I got out. I was going to sleep in the car, but I went for a short walk to take it all in and clear my head, and then I saw your lights on.

Like I said, I know it's late and a big imposition. But if you don't mind me crashing on your sofa for a couple of hours until it's light and I'm sober enough to drive, then I'll get out of your way.'

At that point Rob walked into the kitchen, which took Ash by surprise.

'Hello, Ash. We was just putting the lid on the day and trying to take it all in.'

'Yeah, it's been very eventful, hasn't it?' Ash smiled wryly.

Kenny made three coffees.

'Do you mind if I sit down, please mate? My side is still pretty sore.'

'No, go through, Ash.'

Kenny raised his eyebrows at Rob from behind Ash, and mouthed; 'Somehow, I was expecting this!'

As Ash sat carefully down on one of the two sofas, Kenny and Rob sat opposite him on the other one.

'Yeah, quite an eventful day for so many reasons.' Ash repeated.

'Have you two got any plans for what you're going to do with the money?' He smiled.

Chapter Sixty-Six

Kenny didn't take the bait, if indeed bait was being offered. He answered;

'Well, once we've got it, I guess my missus will have something to say about what we need to do with it. But to be honest, the reality of the win still hasn't fully registered yet.'

Rob felt the need to fully agree with his mate.

Kenny kept the small talk going by asking Ash what he intended to do.

'Well, obviously I need a new start!' He laughed, but immediately regretted it, as it caused a sharp stabbing pain in his ribs which was accompanied by a couple of wheezing coughs that caused his face to contort in pain.

'Jesus, Ash! Are you ok?' Kenny asked, sincerely.

'Yeah, I'll be alright. Probably need a few days for it to settle down. I could go round my Brother's, as he's got a spare room I could use for the time being. But I'd really like to get away. You know, far away.'

'Bit of a line in the sand moment, I expect, eh?' Rob asked.

'Yeah, I guess so. But it really does feel like a good moment for me to move on, if I'm being honest. Not much around here that I haven't seen or done over the years, and a change of scenery would be a good thing. Just need the wherewithal to make that happen.'

Ash was reflecting, but it seemed he just wanted, or needed, to keep talking;

'Terrible thing, about that poor family with the sick kid, isn't it? Things like that stop you short. Thank god my kids are ok. Not that I've been anything like a proper Dad to them. But you still want the very best for them, don't you?'

Although they were not comparing notes, both Kenny and Rob were independently of the same thoughts; Ash was unravelling before their very eyes.

'Guys, I'm glad you're both here. I want to talk truthfully to you. I know I'm not a popular bloke around here...around anywhere, so it seems and I guess that's no one's fault but mine. I've done some really stupid things and some really awful things, without ever really thinking about the consequences of what I've said or done.

But I know you two are good blokes. Proper good family men. Popular and well thought of and both really kind and decent.

So I wish neither of you any ill will. But, please be truthful with me. I know you don't owe me anything. But, I'm just asking you to please be truthful with me.'

Although this was all like some dream sequence unfolding, Kenny was amazed that it all seemed so 'normal' to him. Like he had been expecting it, and was more than ready to deal with it.

Rob though, was struggling to handle the intensity of Ash's outpourings.

Ash continued; 'I know that when something completely out of the ordinary happens to basically good, normal, everyday people, they would struggle to come to terms with it in a hurry. But, I know what I know. So, please tell me, what did happen yesterday on the golf course?'

Rob wasn't ready or able to confess all, even to a man appearing to be baring his soul and who was clearly incapacitated.

He started to reply; 'Oh, not this again, I.....'

But Kenny was more than ready.

After all of his about turns and soul searching over his mistaken belief about Mo's 'illness' and his subsequent total and utter relief that she was fine, it was like a salvation to him. The euphoria he felt about Mo being without any health scares was the single most important thing in his life, apart from the similar well being of his kids, who were equally fine, as far as he was aware.

He had not been able to fully comprehend his thoughts over the course of the day since he'd spoken to Mo, due to the rollercoaster of events. But now, he had total clarity and wanted to unburden himself and his best mate sitting next to him, from any further stigma or worry.

So he interrupted Rob's reply to Ash;

'It's alright Bog. Let's straighten this out.'

Kenny proceeded to explain the course of events of Friday afternoon to Ash, who sat facing him, without expressing emotion, and without interrupting him.

He explained his and Rob's initial surprise at finding a bag full of money, Rob's part in a planned wind up of Kenny, and his own conflicting emotions fuelled by his mistaken belief that his wife was seriously ill. Then, the subsequent discovery of the fake cash and all that went on afterwards.

He confessed the fear they'd felt and the doubts they both had about keeping the money. And then, Rob's adamant stance that he wanted nothing more to do with it and his own subsequent revelation that his wife was perfectly well, thereby removing any thought that the money was something they wanted or needed. From then, late Saturday morning, their only thought was to put the money back, or hand it in.

Ash listened intently until Kenny had finished.

He watched Rob Gordon's facial expressions during Kenny's revelations and knew that what he'd heard was the truth. His years as a police officer had at least provided him with the skill of knowing whether or not a statement of some detail was a faithful relaying of the facts, or a concoction of lies.

'Well, you two have certainly had an eventful couple of days, haven't you?'

Ash again smiled wryly.

'So, where does that leave us? Obviously, you are well aware that most of what I've said about the money up till now is total bullshit and should we all be questioned by my colleagues, it would only end badly for me. You've said you both want nothing more to do with this money and apart from me, nobody knows that you've had anything to do with it in the first place.

I know you can't possibly agree with any crooked schemes of mine. Especially given my total disregard for the laws that I'm supposed to uphold, and you have no reason to believe anything I say, given my track record.

But, if you let me take the money when I leave here, it would be your last association with it. I'd take full responsibility for whatever happened afterwards. If things don't go to plan for me, then, as far as I'm concerned, that would be my misfortune and nothing for you to worry about.

You found some money and you handed it to a police officer in good faith.

So, what do you say, guys?'

Chapter Sixty-Seven (Sunday)

Although Dawn broke before six and light streamed into the Lounge of Kenny's house through the gaps in the blinds, the three of them remained asleep until just after Seven.

Kenny was awake first. He'd had a fitful couple of hours sleep in his Armchair and was immediately aware that he had a stiff neck and his back ached from the uncomfortable sleeping position he'd evidently chosen.

Rob and Ash were asleep on each of the two sofas. But, as Kenny stood and stretched, it was apparent that neither of them had been sound asleep as both stirred and sat up.

Kenny made tea and the three of them barely spoke as they contemplated the day ahead.

Decisions made a few hours before, after the soul bearing revelations that preceded, had rendered anything but basic communication redundant.

Ash asked if he could freshen up and shortly afterwards, said his goodbyes and left.

He took with him a sports bag.

He only had to make a short walk to his car, as he'd parked it just along the road from Kenny's after driving the short distance from Kirstie's a few hours before.

He'd figured then, that if things went as he'd hoped, he wouldn't have to walk too far with the heavy bag.

Having managed to lift the bag into his boot without causing himself undue discomfort, he set off to his first destination.

After a short drive, he stopped and wrote a brief note. Then he got out of the car and went to the boot and retrieved several bundles of cash from the bag, which he counted as he took them out.

The 'withdrawal' totalled £100,000.

He placed the money in an evidence bag that was one of a pile he had in his boot and then also put the note inside.

Then he walked up the driveway of one of the smart detached properties he'd parked outside and left the package by the front porch behind a green recycling bin.

Once back in his car he sent a text message to his ex wife and told her that he was going away, but had left something in a package for their children's future outside the house. He said there was a note which would explain both that money and some additional funds she would be receiving on their behalf.

As he'd written the note, and again when he composed the text, he'd welled up and had to fight back tears.

But then he composed himself as he looked at his reflection in the rear view mirror.

'What might've been, eh?' He said.

But after only a moment's thought, he smiled and caught sight of that all too familiar image of his own swagger and it was if a reset button had been pressed.

'Not your style though, old son, is it? Onwards and upwards, Ash!'

He turned the ignition key and drove away.

Chapter Sixty-Eight

After Ash had left the house, Kenny and Rob sat opposite each other. Both were lost in thought for a few minutes, until Rob felt the need to ask his mate a few questions to ease his personal doubts;

'Do you think he'll get away with it?'

Kenny shook his head.

'No and I don't think he really believes he will either. From what he said last night, or should I say this morning, he mainly wants to try and right a couple of wrongs. But he must know he hasn't got much chance of staying free and clear.'

'Do you think he'll still keep his promise to us to say nothing, when he finds he hasn't got as much cash as he thought he had?' Rob asked.

Kenny nodded; 'Yeah, I do. He's still got nearly four hundred and fifty grand! He knows we won't dob him in, as we don't want to be connected with that money. So he doesn't really have any further quarrel with us, apart from that ''donation'' we've taken from the cash. He's hardly likely to come back and have it out with us afterwards mate, considering the trouble he'll be in once the cops and those other guys know he's gone.'

Kenny sounded a lot more certain that he was. But he rationalised;

'I don't think things would have gone much better for him, even if we hadn't found that bag, you know. He's a troubled soul, but I think he's probably more at peace with himself now, than he was yesterday morning.'

'I hope so.' Rob said earnestly. Continuing;

'But if I'm honest, more so for our sakes than his.'

They both laughed at that.

As an afterthought, Kenny said; 'Hopefully though, he won't suss that there's any money missing until he's well away from here. Like I said earlier, I repacked the bag to weigh pretty much the same as it did originally by putting paper in the bottom and the fake notes on top, with the real cash on top of everything else.

The way things have turned out is a lot more straightforward for us than it might've been if we'd had to leave it at the shop on the golf course. But it's certainly been an adventure though mate, hasn't it?'

'I'll say! But we're not finished yet, Ken, are we?' Rob reminded his friend.

Kenny looked at his watch and got to his feet; 'Best get cracking then. It's gone eight.'

The two of them briefly washed and tidied themselves up, before leaving.

They took with them a plastic bag, containing their 'surprise.'

Kenny and Rob had also written a note prior to leaving the house, which they put inside the plastic bag containing £200,000.

When they reached the row of houses where their friend Alan 'Bertie' Bassett lived, they sat in Kenny's car for a few moments, until they were certain which house the Norman family lived at.

'Bertie's is number thirty seven isn't it, Bog?' Kenny queried.

'I thought you said you were sure?' Rob replied.

'We've both been there before, you dick! I was just confirming... No, I'm sure, its number thirty seven. And I know number thirty nine is that geeky lot we see out cycling sometimes. I think the guy's a Scoutmaster, or something.'

'Ok.' Said Rob. 'So the Norman's must be at number thirty five then?'

'Right. You go then, Bog.'

'What if someone sees me?'

'There's no one about, yet. Go on. Look, they've got a porch. If the door opens, just leave the bag inside. Otherwise, leave it by the bins.'

'That's a bit chancy, isn't it? Surely we need to put it somewhere a bit more secure than that?'

'Look, we're wasting time. Just try the porch door. People often leave them unlocked, as long as they lock their front door. Go on!'

Rob nervously got out of the car and walked along to the driveway of number thirty five.

He could see through the window at the front of the house into the Lounge. There was no sign of anyone, so he walked quickly up the path towards the front porch.

He felt his heart hammering in his chest as he tried the handle on the porch and attempted to pull the door towards him. But it took a few seconds for him to comprehend that the door actually opened inwards, and the transference of his pulling to pushing motion caused the door to open more quickly than Rob had anticipated and he half stumbled into the porch and onto the mat, banging his knee on the doorstep.

He ignored the throbbing in his knee and quickly placed the bag inside the porch next to two newspapers, that had presumably been left by the paper boy.

Getting quickly to his feet, he closed the door and walked back out of the drive way, but heard a tapping sound on a window behind him.

He looked around to the Lounge window, but then caught sight of movement at the upstairs window above it.

A small angel faced blonde haired boy was at the window waving to him and smiling.

Rob stopped in his tracks and felt a lump in his throat. Forcing his face into a smile he waved back, before going back to the car.

As he got in, Kenny said; 'Are you alright, mate?'

'I saw him, Ken. That little lad. He waved at me and smiled. Bless him.'

'Perhaps he thought you was the paper boy, mate!'

Wiping his face as his mate drove away, Rob scowled at him.

'You are a twat sometimes!'

Chapter Sixty-Nine

Ash stopped at a Diner and treated himself to a full Breakfast.

He read the free newspapers and ate at a leisurely pace, ordering a second pot of tea to kill a bit of time.

Apart from the nagging pain in his ribs every now and again, he felt relaxed. He was setting out on a new life.

He had no real plan at this stage, but he figured that the best initial move was to leave the country via a car ferry to Europe.

He thought that an Airport departure would be problematic with a bagful of cash, unless he transferred the money into one or both of his suitcases.

But he figured that he could maybe move on by plane at a later stage if need be.

For now, in his still incapacitated state, it would be easier for him to travel by car and have his luggage in the boot.

Although Customs checks were made on some vehicles at sea ports, he thought it less likely that he'd be stopped via this mode of travel.

But before he departed the UK, he had his heart set on a present for himself.

There was a nearby car dealership that he sometimes passed, that stocked just the sort of vehicles he'd always dreamt of driving.

So he stalled for time at the diner until the dealership opened.

He fielded a phone call from his ex wife Marie about the 'package' that he'd left. He briefly explained that he needed to get away, but there were no traceability issues with the money and he would leave it to her and her Husband to decide where they wanted to invest the money for the children. But he hoped it would provide them both with a decent start in life.

Although she had been freaked out to discover £100,000 in cash outside her house and also read in his note that another £38,000 would follow, she eventually agreed to comply with his wishes.

He then texted Bertie with Marie's account details, to enable him to transfer Ash's share of their horse racing winnings to her for his children, as he'd already explained to her in the note he'd left with the cash.

Then he phoned Sue Senior.

When he heard her voice, he almost had a change of heart.

But the memory of her duplicity yesterday and the feeling that she had been playing him steeled his resolve.

'Hello, Sue. It's Ash.'

'How are you, babe.' She sounded sincere.

'My ribs are pretty sore. Probably be ok in a few days. But I'm going to lie low for a bit.'

'Where are you, Ash?'

'Going to stay with family, Sue. Why?'

'I was just concerned about you. There's been some developments.'

'Oh yeah. What sort of developments.'

'Well, Ron's Lawyer, Clive has been on the phone. He said that the Dutch guy, who Ron was supposed to have been dealing with in that disaster on Friday, has been arrested. And he also said, that one of your lot has been nicked too.'

'Do you know who?'

'He said it was someone from the Crime Squad called Phelan. He was supposed to have been getting info from the Dutch guy about Ron, and they were going to share some of the money from the sale of the drugs.'

'Really?' Ash replied. He smiled to think how flash Phelan had been on the couple of occasions he'd met him and hoped that his arrest might deflect attention away from him and the money he now had.

'Have you found out anything else about what happened to that money, Ash?'

'No, Sue. I don't think those guys I suspected had anything to do with it after all. Maybe someone else found it, or handed it in. Although you'd think it would get some publicity if that happened? Did my name get mentioned when you spoke to Ron's Lawyer, babe?'

'No, not yet, she lied. Like I said yesterday, Ron knows that we managed to get some money out of the house, but he doesn't know it's gone missing. But he'd sooner it go missing than the police being able to seize it under the proceeds of crime.'

Ash decided against bringing up any further details of his conversation with Ron, prior to the raid on Friday morning.

Sue seemed calmer and he saw no reason to discuss it further.

'Well, it's probably best I keep my head down for now, Sue. I need to rest up anyway.'

'Ok, Ash. Keep in touch though, eh?'

'Of course I will, babe.'

He was pretty sure she was being genuine with him. But he was still set on getting away on his own. He figured that the revelation about Phelan's arrest would keep the investigating officers busy and would hopefully buy him enough time to get out of the country and far away, even if the missing money then became a factor in the investigation.

He left the diner and drove over to the Classic Cars dealership as it opened.

Being their first customer of the day Ash was smoozed by the Sales Consultant Keiron, who wore a garish, shiny suit and was identified by a large silver name badge on his lapel.

Ash spun Keiron a story about how he'd sold his business for a considerable sum and now wanted to travel for a while. He said he'd closed his UK accounts and was taking a large amount of cash abroad with him. But he said that he was going to treat himself to a couple of gifts along the way.

Keiron saw the opportunity of some decent commission, which had been a rarity lately, especially on a Sunday.

When Ash was shown a black 2017 three litre Porsche 911 his mind was blown. It was a dream car for him, and although he could've spent far more than the £85,000 this car would cost, he was also conscious of not wanting to commit too much of the half a million or so that he still had in the bag.

He negotiated a part exchange on his old beat up Ford Mondeo for £5,000 and agreed a small premium to get immediate insurance cover in place for the Porsche.

Ash then went out to retrieve the sports bag from his car.

As he reached into the boot to pick it up, he attempted to swing the bag up and out of the boot, but only succeeded in twisting awkwardly, causing a sharp stabbing pain in his side which caused him to drop the bag onto the forecourt in front of him. The bag turned upside down as it hit the ground.

Wincing in pain and quickly looking round to make sure nobody had witnessed his discomfort, Ash was at least pleased to see that he was all alone.

He composed himself and picked up the bag, took it into the showroom and proceeded to count out £80,000 from the mass of bundles onto Kieron's desk.

The young salesman had never seen that much money before and was completely dumbstruck.

The dealership had a policy in regard to potential money laundering and the acceptance of large cash sums. But Kieron was the senior sales consultant on duty today and he was desperate to be of service to this cash rich client, rather than potentially losing the deal.

They completed the paperwork and within an hour of walking into the dealership Ash was driving out in his pristine used Porsche, with less than 8,000 miles on the clock.

Ash took the car for a proper road test and was thrilled at the response and handling the vehicle provided.

He felt that he finally had the right car to suit his image of himself.

He had checked ferry departure times and planned on taking the ferry that evening from Hull to Rotterdam. Although he knew he had plenty of time, he couldn't resist the thrill of speeding in his new purchase.

Keiron was feeling extra pleased with himself, until he boasted about his early morning sale to his two junior colleagues.

When they asked if he would show them the paperwork he'd completed for money laundering regulations, as neither of them had gone through the forms before and also mentioned the Dealership's £10,000 maximum limit for cash transactions, Kieron started to feel more than a bit panicky.

One of them called the Dealership Manager to verify the rules, as Kieron had shut himself in his office to read the company regulations book.

The manager then told them to phone and advise the police of the large cash sum paid and also to check the cash for signs of it being counterfeit.

Half an hour later the same member of staff phoned the manager back to advise that some of the notes were without a watermark and were definitely counterfeit.

The police were alerted and the index number of Ash's vehicle and his old vehicle index were passed on. This cross reference check confirmed the identity details he gave were correct. But given the large amount of cash he'd paid for the car and the presence of some counterfeit notes within it, they were obviously keen to speak to him.

When Keiron also advised that Ash had said he was planning on going abroad in the car, an alert was issued to all sea and airports, and a description of the vehicle was issued county wide in all port areas.

Ash though was oblivious to any further hassles, as he enjoyed his drive in the late morning sunshine towards Hull in his shiny black Porsche.

Chapter Seventy

After dropping Rob at home and then going back to his own house to eat, shower and freshen up, Kenny had a cursory tidy up to prepare the house for Mo's return.

Then he made his way along the road to The Feathers, arriving a few minutes after One o'clock.

The sunny day was a natural mood lifter and he felt more relaxed than he had for ages as he entered the pub garden.

The place was fairly full and all but a few seats in the garden were taken by a variety of groups of mixed ages, ranging from families with young children, who ran joyfully about and played on the swings, slide and climbing frames, to older aged groups and couples. Quite a few of whom were either waiting for, or had already partaken in their Sunday Lunch.

Kenny showed out to one or two people he recognised, before going inside to the half empty bar.

Bertie and Gracie were exchanging pleasantries across the bar as he came into view.

'Oi, Oi!' He exclaimed, smiling.

Both of them beamed back at him.

'Still wearing your "Rock Star" shades then, Ken. How's the eye?' Enquired Bertie.

Kenny smiled as he removed his sunglasses; 'It's barely noticeable now, mate. Just had them on for the sunshine. It's lovely out.'

'How you doing, Ken?' Gracie smiled at him, extending his hand across the bar.

Kenny shook his hand and gave Bertie a brief hug, before replying;

'Feeling surprisingly good, thanks Gracie. Looking forward to the return of my better half later. Just been speaking to her actually. She's already got a list of things that she wants to spend "our money" on!'

Gracie laughed, but Bertie smiled wryly and replied;

'Yeah, so's Barbara, mate. They're on the train home now, aren't they?'

'Yeah. Should be back by about five, Mo said.'

'You heard about Ash?' Bertie enquired.

Kenny hesitated briefly, before replying;

'Well I know he's looking for alternative accommodation.'

Both Gracie and Bertie grinned, before Bertie offered;

'Yeah, Gracie was just saying that Dino's been on the phone this morning, telling him about the revolving door situation along the road. One out and one in!'

Gracie added; 'Yeah, Dino said he was moving in with Kirstie, as she kicked Ash out last night. Evidently they've liked each other for ages, but held off until now.'

They all agreed that it was a good result for Dino and Kirstie, who were two nice people who would hopefully be good for each other.

'How did YOU know Ash was out then, Ken?' Bertie asked.

'Oh, he turned up at mine about three this morning. Said he saw my light on. Me and Bog were having a c..'

'Shag?' Interrupted Bertie, smiling.

'No. Close though.' Kenny smiled ironically. 'We were actually having a coffee, pre shag, when he knocked. He was really unAsh like though. Very upfront about it. Said it was for the best. He mentioned this morning that he might go to his Brother's?'

Gracie looked puzzled.

'Well, his Brother's been in. Still here, I think? He didn't say anything though and he's not the type to not want to talk about anything and everything that goes on with that family.'

Bertie then mentioned that Ash had texted him a while ago about his winnings and told him that he'd wanted the money paid to his ex, for his kids.

The three of them said they didn't quite know what to make of that, although Kenny was bluffing, as he had some idea about Ash's mood a few hours ago.

However, he couldn't fathom why Ash couldn't have just done something with the money himself, rather than delegate it to his ex wife.

Shortly afterwards, Rob, Scott and a few others from yesterday's trip wandered in and the warm greetings were all repeated.

Then Dino, fresh from moving some essentials into his new abode, also turned up, full of smiles.

He received a few well meant congratulatory remarks from his mates, and he seemed genuinely happy.

'Nice one, mate.' Kenny offered. 'She's a nice girl. Far too good for the other twat!'

Dino was almost shy and contrite in his response. But it was obvious that he had genuine feelings for Kirstie.

'I hoped it would happen, but it surprised me how quickly it came about in the end. We'd spoken about my crappy flat coming up for renewal of the lease and how I wanted to move, but I hadn't expected things to move quite so fast. We've liked each other for ages though and after we spoke on Friday, I think we both knew we were serious.

Kirstie phoned me this morning. She knew I'd be on the lash all day yesterday. But she said she'd stayed at her mate's last night and left Ash a note. When she got back a while ago, he'd left a note in return to say, "no hard feelings" and he'd gone. So we both said how we felt and...well, we didn't see any point in being coy.'

Kenny couldn't resist a tiny dig at his love struck friend.

'I'm really pleased for you, mate. Christ knows what she sees in you, but I'm pleased none the less!'

Dino laughed.

'You can ask her yourself, Nelson. She'll be in a bit later.'

Kenny didn't say anything about Ash turning up at his place to Dino, but made a mental note to remember to ask Kirstie later if she knew Dino's very flattering middle name.

Chapter Seventy-One

Sue Senior felt more settled than she'd done for some time.

The call earlier from Clive Russell, Ron's Lawyer, advising her of the arrests of Rinus Krul and Mike Phelan late the previous evening, had been a weight off her mind.

When she'd phoned Clive yesterday evening, Sue had told him that Rinus had showed up at the house and made veiled threats in regard to money he was due for a deal he'd done with Ronnie.

After embellishing the story to paint Rinus in the worst possible light, she had gone on to mention a conversation she'd heard him having with someone who she'd guessed was a police officer, from the parts of the conversation she heard. She then went on to say that it was obvious from what was said, that Rinus and this police officer, who she'd heard Rinus mention by name as 'Phelan' and then again afterwards as 'Mike,' had been in cahoots to stitch up Ronnie and share a large chunk of his cash in so doing.

Sue also told Clive about Ash having removed money from the house during the police search with her full awareness, in order to avoid it being seized, although this had now supposedly gone missing.

But she'd advised Clive that Rinus was somehow fully aware of that and wanted to get his hands on the money.

Sue said that she had denied all knowledge of 'any other money' to Rinus, other than what the police had seized during the search.

Clive told her that the details of both Rinus and the police officer Phelan had been passed on to the police as 'a gesture of goodwill' by Ron, following the receipt of that information from 'an associate.'

He'd also said that Ron was attempting to fully comply with the police in a bid to be co-operative and hopefully bring about a reduction in his inevitable sentence following trial.

He told her that Ron was concerned about her and had passed on his love, which, despite their differences, Sue had found quite touching.

'That was more like the old Ron,' she thought to herself and smiled.

She hadn't passed on any details of the meeting she'd heard Rinus arrange to Clive, but had saved that information till she called Mike Phelan straight afterwards, telling him what she had overheard Rinus say about the time and place.

Phelan had been so keen to save his own skin that he was glad to be able to arrange Rinus's arrest.

He told Sue that he was confident that Rinus had nothing on him and if he tried to implicate him, he would use the protection his status as a police officer provided and say that he was just getting information from a criminal to bring about quality arrests.

But the news of both subsequent arrests from Clive had brought a wave of relief to Sue.

She was contemplating phoning her friend and Business Manager Chloe to chat and also discuss ideas for increasing revenue, when she heard the doorbell ring.

When Sue opened the door she was completely taken aback by the sight of a man she hadn't seen for some time.

'Hello Frankie! How are you, darling?'

Sue threw her arms around Frank Senior, her Brother in Law.

'Hello babe. I'm good thanks and I can see you are looking pretty great too.'

Sue smiled sweetly at the compliment.

'Come in Frankie. It's great to see you, babe.'

Frank stepped inside and they went into the kitchen, where Sue made them both coffee.

They made small talk for a while and caught up on a few memories from the past.

But throughout, Sue's mind was ablaze with wonder at the reason for Frank's sudden appearance after so long.

Eventually, for the sake of her peace of mind, she asked him;

'So Frank, not that I'm complaining, but to what do I have the pleasure of a social visit from you after all this time?'

Frank had always been a smooth operator. He'd always had a reputation for being ruthless in business and sometimes being as cold and unemotional one minute, as he could be warm and tender the next.

So, when he looked at Sue without any trace of emotion, she began to worry.

'I've had a call from Ronnie, Sue. I'm up to speed on all that's happened over the last few days. Let's just say that Ronnie is fully in the picture and knows what happened to him and why.'

Sue gulped, but tried to smile and pass off any apprehensions.

'Ron asked me to take care of you, Sue.'

The words were delivered dispassionately and seemingly without any trace of feeling and their impact chilled Sue to the bone.

She had heard both her husband and his brother use that phrase several times before over the years. Sometimes, it had very unpleasant connotations for the recipient of the message.

Frank's tone of voice and his accompanying look gave absolutely no clue to Sue what the true meaning of his remark held for her.

Despite her misgivings, she smiled her most radiant smile, before replying;

'Well, that's nice to know, love. What girl could fail to feel secure with you in her life, eh? It's been a shock, what happened to Ron. But I'd tried to warn him that he was taking risks that he really didn't need to take.'

Frank nodded and said;

'Like I said, Sue, Ron knows exactly what happened now, which is why he wanted me to come and see you.'

Sue was determined to remain in control of her misgivings and managed to at least sound calm as she spoke;

'It's lovely that you're here, Frankie. It's been far too long since either of us have seen you and I've certainly missed having you around. But I'm ok, I've got my business and I'll keep busy. But it would be nice to see more of you.'

She and Frank had always been close through the years she'd known him, until he'd legitimised his business dealings several years ago.

Since then, he and Ron had parted ways and any contact with him after that had been rare.

But Sue had always felt that Frank held a torch for her though.

'Another coffee, Frankie?' Sue said demurely, as she gazed into his eyes.

His stern look finally broke into a smile, as he replied;

'Why not Suzie. I'm in no hurry.'

With her back to Frank as the kettle boiled, Sue undid two more buttons of her shirt and prepared herself for whatever fate had in store for her.

Chapter Seventy-Two

Ash pulled into a service area to get some travel essentials and also make his Ferry booking.

It only took a few minutes to arrange a standard deal for a cabin on the night crossing to Rotterdam via his phone. He had plenty of time to kill as the sailing time wasn't until 8.30 and boarding didn't start till 4pm.

He felt calmly detached. The events of the last couple of days had been emotionally draining. But he'd made the break without any real regrets.

He figured that, if he successfully got away without detection at work, he would phone and tell them he was giving his notice.

But everything still seemed a bit dreamlike for now. Maybe this was his new normal he mused.

He collected his planned purchases and resumed his journey, before stopping at a retail park mid afternoon to kill a bit more time and browse for some new clothes to further stroke his ego.

As he neared Hull in the late afternoon sunshine, Ash became a little apprehensive at the thought of passing through any checks at the ferry terminal.

But he passed this off as a reflex action and prepared himself for natural responses to any questions, should they occur.

At the port he joined the small queue of vehicles ahead of the ferry terminal entry gates. He noticed a couple of police vehicles parked near the entry point, but thought that this was nothing unusual.

As he got closer to the entry point Ash had his passport ready, as well as the confirmation of booking email on his phone.

He noticed the car behind him was full of people who were enjoying the music emanating from their vehicle at what sounded like maximum decibels and hoped that he wouldn't be in a cabin anywhere near them once onboard.

When the vehicle in front of him passed through the entry point he began to move off, but was directed to a parking bay to the left of the entrance to the ferry.

Given the demeanour of the official who had directed him to where he was requested to park he assumed it was a routine check of some sort.

But then he saw two police officers come out of the building in front of him and then noticed two more get out of one of the police cars to the side of him.

Ash felt his stomach muscles clench as the first police officer asked him to step out of his vehicle.

For a brief moment he thought about making a break for it, but he knew that would be pointless.

He slowly got out of his dream car and caught the admiring glances at the vehicle from the police officers.

He smiled at them.

'Nice car, sir.' Said the older of the four policemen, who Ash noticed from his epaulettes was a Sergeant.

'Thanks,' Ash replied, still hoping that this might just be a routine stop and check.

'Must've cost a few quid, Mr Richardson?' The Sergeant enquired.

Ash smiled wryly as the full reality of his situation now became abundantly clear to him and he resigned himself to his fate.

Chapter Seventy-Three

As the afternoon session in The Feathers warmed up, Bertie announced that he'd had a call from a reporter from one of the National Newspapers earlier, asking for some further details of yesterday's win. He said the story would feature in Monday's paper.

He also said that the local BBC Television News Team would be sending a crew tomorrow, to do a piece for Monday's news show.

'Fame at last, eh boys?' He laughed.

Dino swiftly reminded him that he'd said that last night, but got the response he expected.

Speedo then arrived, accompanied by his four Dutch minders.

The noise levels went up a bit at this point, as the reunion was almost complete, with the added surprise of the Dutch guys returning.

'Well, we dit not want to just go witout saying a proper goodbye.' Marco explained.

'Sorry we're a bit late.' Speedo said, smiling; 'But Rudi and me were making an early Lunch for the five of us.'

'Get you, Kevlar!' Scott said, continuing; 'What was it, Beans on Toast?'

'No, we had Chicken Parmigiana.' Speedo said, very off the cuff.

'I was Kevin's Sous Chef.' Rudi said, smiling; 'Kevin is an ecsellent cook!'

'It's wasted on this lot, Rudi.' Speedo said, shaking his head. He continued;

'If it's more difficult than a sandwich, then they're all lost.' He said to his Dutch friends, indicating the throng of his English mates at the bar.

'Rudi's offered me a holiday job, once his and Marco's beach bar opens.' He said smiling.

'Is that a definite then for you guys, now?' Kenny asked Rudi and Marco.

'Yes, for sure. Once we haf der money from Bertie, we will look at locations.' Marco replied.

'So, are you giving up the police work, then?' Rob asked.

There was a slightly awkward silence for a few seconds, till Marco answered;

'Yes. I sink der time is right for us to quit.'

A few minutes later, amidst the general hubbub of replaying and rehashing of some of yesterday's events, Gary Chivers came in, accompanied by a companion.

After a few pleasantries had been exchanged, Gary introduced his friend as Ian Norman and then announced Ian's good news.

'Something unbelievably brilliant has happened, guys! This morning, a mystery benefactor left a bag outside Ian's house with a note and £200,000 for Ian's boy Callum's operation fund!'

There was a cheer and many congratulatory comments to Ian, who was treated to a free pint from Gracie.

When the initial excitement had died down, Ian expanded the story of the discovery a few hours ago. He said that Callum told him that he'd seen a man come up to the house earlier on and he'd waved to him and the bloke waved back.

'We can only assume that he was the one who left the money? But my wife and I can't believe it! The note said it was a gesture to hopefully give Callum the chance he deserves. But it's just so kind and obviously, fantastic news!'

Ian was understandably emotional.

'I just wish we could thank whoever was responsible.'

Rob felt slightly uncomfortable. But Kenny was more Gung Ho and said;

'I wouldn't worry about it mate. Whoever it was, obviously wanted to remain anonymous and the most important thing is that your boy will get the operation he needs now. That's truly great news, eh?'

There was a general consensus of agreement and more than a few of the guys exclaimed comments to the effect of;

'What a weekend this has been!'

Kenny smiled and looked across at Rob, who smiled back.

'Well, you certainly got your adventure, mate. I think we all did. Just a thought though, Ken. As we're both off till Tuesday, let's take the girls out for a curry later, as a welcome home. Be a nice way to finish off the weekend, eh?'

Kenny smiled a contented smile, although he did still resemble a man with trapped wind. He replied;

'That sounds good, mate. It's certainly been some weekend. One to remember.'

Printed in Great Britain
by Amazon